HOTSHOT AND HOSPITALITY

GREEN VALLEY LIBRARY BOOK #8

NORA EVERLY

WWW.SMARTYPANTSROMANCE.COM

COPYRIGHT

This book is a work of fiction. Names, characters, places, rants, facts, contrivances, and incidents are either the product of the author's questionable imagination or are used factitiously. Any resemblance to actual persons, living or dead or undead, events, locales is entirely coincidental if not somewhat disturbing/concerning.

Made in the United States of America

Print Edition
ISBN: 978-1-949202-71-7

DEDICATION

For my dad.
Love you.

AUTHOR'S NOTE

Molly Cooper is a fictional character who is directly inspired by a person I have known and lived with for over twenty years.

Her hearing loss, the way she handles it, talks about it, and its cause are specifically based on this person. Therefore, it is not possible for her to entirely encompass, represent, or express everyone's experience.

Thank you PJC for letting me borrow a little bit of your life, I love you.

CHAPTER 1

MOLLY

*T*onight had been a big mistake. The hugest ever. I should have never swiped right. Swept right? Sweeped right? *Fricking tequila!* Sticking to my man moratorium would have been the better decision because MEN! *UGH!*

"Your sister is on my list," I slurred before sucking the juice out of a wedge of lime with a pinch-faced scowl. Tequila flowed through my system, fueling my bad mood as I sat in everyone's favorite corner booth in Genie's Country Western Bar. With clumsy hands, I slammed the shot glass to the table and slid it across.

Green Valley, Tennessee, had been my home since birth. Located smack-dab in the middle of Small Town, USA, where everybody knew every-body and gossip was its own currency. The fact that I was drunk off my ass and all alone at Genie's would not go unnoticed. Plus, the Tinder-date thing was a tasty nugget of information that would probably be passed all around town by morning since eyes and ears were everywhere and a few of them had managed to put two and two together when they spotted my pathetic party of one. My eyes dropped to the table and I tried to disap-pear into my booth. I was all dressed up with nowhere to go but back home. Instead of chatting with a date over Genie's famous fried chicken and a beer, I had skipped dinner and gone straight to shooting tequila. I couldn't drive home like this.

How sad was I?

"Uh-oh, the shit list?" my smirky blond waitress asked as she set a glass of water in front of me. One eyebrow rose as she fished my hearing aid out of one of the empty shot glasses lining the side of the table.

"Yep. Thank you, Willa. And don't ask." I swiped it from her hand and shoved it in the front pocket of my jeans. It was toast; tequila did not mix as well with tiny battery-powered devices as it did with salt and lime.

Most people in town knew about my hearing and graciously made accommodations, like making sure to keep their head up and not mumble or sitting on my right side so I could better hear them speak. But there were always a few jerks who dismissed me if I said "What?" one too many times. Or got annoyed if I couldn't differentiate between their voice calling out to me versus the ambient sounds in a room. Occasionally I would run into a real asshole who would mock sign language at me or point at my hearing aid and tell me to "turn it up." But it didn't happen often anymore, at least not here in Green Valley, because my three older brothers had spent the latter part of my childhood "educating" the town jerks who now knew better. I was in a car accident when I was eight and the concussion damaged the hair cells in my cochlea and the ossicles in my middle ear. The end result was profound hearing loss on my left side, and moderate loss on the right. I could still hear some in my right ear, but without my hearing aid I had a hard time understanding what was said to me without reading lips.

Willa shrugged. "I won't ask. But I'm here all night if you want to talk. Are you okay?"

I nodded as my eyes darted around the bar for one last search for my date. Since he was now over an hour late, it was, of course, fruitless. I had previously given up on dating but stupidly let my friends push me into one more try. Being alone was hunky-freaking-dory, and who needed men anyway? I could have just as much fun in bed all by myself

2

as I could with any man. And bonus, I didn't complain when I fell asleep right after.

"Yeeaaah." I let out a huge sigh before continuing, "She said I needed to go out with someone random to get me out of my Chris phase." I added air quotes around *Chris phase*—date one too many guys named Chris and it became a talking point among your friends. I waved a hand in front of my face before letting it flop to the table. "I wasted perfectly good makeup for this, and I'm not happy about it. MAC is expensive, dammit." I pointed a finger at a trying-not-to-laugh Willa. "Your sister is lucky she lives in Knoxville or I'd be texting her to pick me up. She put me on Tinder against my will. No more dates. No more men. No more drama. I'm done for good this time," I huffed. My drunken mood swung from a slightly disgruntled melancholy to a burst of righteous fury spiked with a healthy dose of humiliated indignation. I was pissed off and embarrassed and I wanted to go home, dang it.

"She forced you to swipe right, huh? Some kind of BFF," Willa gently teased.

"Force *is* a bit strong," I conceded as the wind flew out of my rage sails. "And I guess it's not her fault the dumbass stood me up…"

"Don't let her off the hook, Molly. She deserves to haul her butt out of bed and come get you. Clara is bossy. You should teach her a lesson." My head tipped back with a thump against the wooden booth as I contemplated my crappy night. Letting my eyes drift across the crowded bar full of people dancing, laughing, throwing darts, and singing along to the live music, I wished I could be as carefree as they seemed to be.

I spied my first school friend, Jackie, who was now an ex-friend and also one of the current town gossip queens, across the dance floor and let my head crash forward to land on my arm on the table. The weight of my future embarrassment made it too heavy to hold up. She'd had it out for me since we were fourteen and took every opportunity to rub whatever was going wrong in my life right in my face. Now that she'd spotted me here alone, everyone in town would *absolutely* know about my lack of a date along with whatever other stuff she was likely to make up to make me look even more pathetic. *Damn.* "Nah, it's okay, I already texted Becky Lee to come get me," I mumbled into my arm. Becky Lee Monroe used to babysit me when I was a kid. My older brothers and I used to spend every day at her house from toddlerhood until junior high. She used to be friends with my mother, but now she was *my* friend and sort of like the mother I'd always wished I had. Becky Lee was also Willa's mother-in-law.

Willa nudged me and pointed. I lifted my eyes and squinted down the length of her finger. Just like Jack popping out of the box, my head shot off my arm as I noticed it was Becky Lee's youngest son, Garrett, she was pointing to. "Coop!" I saw him shout to me from across the dance floor with that same slightly crooked smile he'd always had lighting up his face.

Willa grinned knowingly at me. "Looks like Becky Lee recruited Garrett to come get you. Holler if you need anything else." She waved to him before heading back to the bar with my empty shot glasses on her tray.

"Hey, Garrett," I returned with haphazard enthusiasm after he made it to the circle booth and nudged me over with his hip. Garrett and I used to be close. We were the same age and had been the best of friends until hormones, other friends, and teenage angst—mostly mine—caused us to drift apart somewhere around age fifteen. We'd remained cordial to each other during our high school years, often running with the same crowd and sometimes even hanging out, but we'd no longer been *best* friends. I hadn't spent a lot of time alone with Garrett over the last decade and a half; he'd blown out of Green Valley after graduation to go to college, then enlisted in the Marines right after. He'd been back for about four years and the laws of small-town living dictated that I saw him all the time. Small talk was our thing now—chitchat, a gathering of mutual friends here at Genie's, the occasional family barbeque, that kind of stuff. "I got stood up, there are too many assholes named Chris in Green Valley, and now I'm totally freaking drunk and alone." I felt like I could admit it to him. Garrett had always kept my secrets, and he'd know everything soon enough anyway.

His gaze warmed on me as his easy smile slid to the side. "Well, whoever he is, he's a fool. And, weirdly, I've only met one Chris who was worth a damn. The rest? All pricks. So, it seems like you're better off." He was decisive as he stole my water and took a sip with his eyes twinkling at me over the rim of the glass. I watched him set the glass down and my own eyes narrowed as his grin broadened and his dimples deepened within the dark whiskers that covered his square jaw. He was close to having a full beard. He was also pretty dang close to being the finest man in the whole stinking bar too. He leaned in, right into my space. "You should have stayed married to me," he murmured into my ear, then his eyes met and held mine as he pulled away.

My eyebrows hit my hairline and I barely managed to prevent my jaw from dropping before I shot back a response that I hoped conveyed the proper amount of flippant wit and *not* the fact that he had completely flabbergasted me. He hadn't flirted with me like this when I saw him at the Piggly Wiggly last Saturday. No, he surely did not. "We were six years old, Garrett. I don't think it was legally binding, since your dog performed the ceremony. Plus, you never even gave me a ring. Ring Pops don't count." I mean, two could play at whatever strange game this was clearly becoming.

Instead of answering me right away, he winked and studied my face with a grin. That wink hit me right between my eyes like a Nerf dart from our days of yore—I didn't just see it, I felt it. *Bam!* Tingles shot from my head to my toes. My brain scrambled inside my head and my mouth opened to say something smart, but nothing came out. Freaking tequila! I shook my metaphorical fist at the liquor that had stunted my normal standard of witty banter.

"But we pinky swore it, Coop." His comically exaggerated pout was adorable. I felt my cheeks heat as I found myself staring avidly at his mouth in lusty contemplation, rather than just merely reading his lips. Why had I never noticed how full and bitable his lower lip was? I bet it was tasty too. "Remember how we spit into our palms to seal the deal?" he asked. I shook my head while my eyes roamed all over every inch of him I could see above the table.

5

"How soon they forget." His chest rose and fell as he let out a huge sigh, and to my shame, my eyes bugged out at the sight. All my thoughts fluttered around in my brain like drunk, demented butterflies. Why was winky-flirt Garrett messing me up? I decided to place the blame on the tequila instead of the fact that he was looking ten different kinds of hot tonight. I finally managed to haul my gaze from his broad chest, which was currently testing the strength of his black T-shirt, and back up to his whiskey brown eyes that were still freaking twinkling at me.

Ugh! There was nowhere to look on him that wasn't sexy, damn it.

And was he flirting with me?

Me?

We'd known each other since babyhood, for crap's sake. We used to take baths together—me, him, and Mr. Bubble. We'd never flirted before. Ever.

Had we?

I tried to recall our last talk at the Piggly Wiggly, but all I could remember was that I'd been almost out of toilet paper and Dr. Pepper.

I silently took a vow to never drink again. This was not good. It felt like he was flirting with me, but I was just too damn drunk to be sure. I had been accused of being blind to flirting in the past. Was I blind to the opposite now? Was he not flirting with me? Was something in his eye? Or had he winked at me? Was any of this making any sense? NO! Being drunk is hard.

But before I could figure out what was up with Garrett, Jackie planted herself at the edge of my booth, full of false sympathy and smiles. "I heard you got stood up." And there it was—the passive-aggressive biotch. She'd had it out for me ever since Duane Winston asked me to the eighth-grade dance and not her. I hadn't even said yes; I'd been positive he'd only asked me to make Jessica James jealous, and duh—they're married now. But she had hated me ever since.

"You're mistaken. Obviously." Garrett gestured to himself with a bemused expression as he scooted closer to me to wrap an arm around my shoulders. "No one in their right mind would stand this vision up. Her date is right here." I listed into his side and gazed up at him with big eyes. Just what in the name of Jose Cuervo was going on here? I said a quick prayer to St. Patron—the patron saint of tequila, of course—but no divine intervention intervened on my behalf and my brain remained a liquor-soaked mess of confusion.

He winked at me again and then he kissed me. Right on the mouth. He flipping kissed me. Which turned me at least fifty percent sober—which wasn't saying all that much—and also one hundred percent confused. I tried to ignore the zing tingles that went through my body at the feel of his lips on mine and the delicious tickle of his almost-full beard against my cheek as he pulled away.

What is he playing at?

I snatched up the water and took a huge gulp, choking and sputtering on an ice cube in the process.

Her face scrunched up in feigned confusion. "Y'all two are dating now? How cute! I can't wait to tell everybody." She snickered.

"Watch it, Jackie," Garrett warned. My head bounced between the two of them as I tried to concentrate on what they were saying. I sat forward in the booth to pay closer attention to their lips. I huffed out a frustrated sigh and flopped back in the booth. Drunk lipreading was impossible, dammit.

"Just go away," I sighed, not in the mood for more of her drama. I'd been over her crap since we were kids and I wished she would just get a new hobby. Unfortunately, torturing me seemed to be her reason for living. I was more than sick of it.

"Sure, I'll let you get back to your *date*. Bye, y'all."

I sighed. "Later..."

"I never liked her," Garrett declared. "She always was a shitty friend to you. Especially after—"

Not wanting to get into it, I cut him off. "Yeah, well—are you playing games with me, Garrett?" My eyes narrowed on his mouth. I wanted to be sure I understood his answer. But I didn't need to. Garrett already knew how to talk to me, and he had always made sure I could hear him without making it awkward. He leaned in and spoke directly in my ear.

"I wouldn't play with you, Molly. You know me better than that. Plus, you know my mother would kill me if I messed with you." He pulled back and his ever-present grin shifted sideways as he placed his arm across the back of the booth. My skin prickled with awareness; he wasn't touching me, but I was alarmed to find myself wanting him to let his big sexy arm fall to my shoulders and pull me close again. I was even more alarmed at my sudden urge to take off my shirt and climb into his lap. Tinder date, who?

I laughed to cover the naughty directions my thoughts had drifted into. I couldn't figure out how to talk to him. We had ventured into uncharted waters tonight. "I love it that you're scared of your mother," I teased, forcing myself to ignore the effect he was having on my body and attempting to shift back to our old friendly dynamic.

He chuckled. "Don't try to tell me you're not scared of her too." His fingertip rounded the rim of the glass of water as he talked. Why was that so sexy? I found myself wanting him to do other, more interesting stuff with that finger. With an awkward lurch, I raised my head, wrenching my eyes from his hand on my glass and back up to his face.

"Okay, I admit it. I wouldn't cross her. She looks sweet and she *is* sweet. But she's a tough one, like a Steel Magnolia or something," I finally managed to answer.

He bit his lip to hold back laughter. "That would be her ultimate life goal. Are you ready to go home? Or do you require more tequila?" I shook my head side to side as I studied that full lower lip pouting over his darkly shadowed chin. Visions of yanking him to me by his T-shirt and tasting that luscious mouth popped into my head. *Knock that shit off.*

I forced out a laugh. "God no. I'm headed for hangover city as it is. I'll be useless at work tomorrow."

You're drunk. That's all this is. Drunk Molly is always a horndog.

He slid out of the booth and held out a hand. I took it and hauled myself up to stand at his side. Again, with the dang zing tingles. My hand in his seemed to be a conductor of sorts, causing horny sparks to shoot throughout my body. I blushed at the way it felt grasped in his warm palm. It was getting harder and harder not to stare at him or flirt back. Flirting was one of my top ten favorite things to do; *not* flirting was hard for me. And holy moly, had his hands always been this much bigger than mine?

He leaned over to grab my purse from the booth. "Don't forget this."

"Oh, jeez. Thanks, Garrett." I stumbled into his side as I hooked the strap over my shoulder.

He smiled as he held my arms to steady me. "You okay there, Princess Tipsy McPeesHerPants?"

I swayed as I pointed a finger up in his grinning face—way, way up, because Garrett was well over six feet, and I was a shrimpy five foot one. "Hey, man! That was one time, okay? Senior skip day was hard for me, and you know it. There are no bathrooms up at Sky Lake. And you're a fine one to talk. I know all about you and your ladies, Man-ho Monroe, Mr. Slick, Flirty McHotStuff."

His lips quirked into a wry grin as he bent low to speak into my ear. "My reputation is seventy-five percent undeserved, and you know it."

"I know no such thing. Okay, fine. Shut up. Whatever. I know it. I really am sorry. I say stupid shit when I'm drunk." I pursed my lips and tried to roll my eyes as I backed away from him. But it made me dizzy and I stepped on his foot, stumbled, and almost went down. How many tequila shots had I drunk tonight?

"Then I twenty-five percent forgive you. Hey now, steady, Molly. Let me help you." Bending low to wrap an arm around my waist, he guided me through the crowd toward the exit.

I stopped near the edge of the dance floor to pull his face closer to mine. "People are going to think we were really on a date if you keep your arm around me like this," I warned in his ear.

With a shrug and a half grin, he answered, "Let them." Then he resumed leading me through the crowded bar and out to his truck.

CHAPTER 2

MOLLY

"Shut up, shut up, shut up. You're not the boss of me..." Talking smack to alarm clocks was useless, yet it didn't stop me from doing it every morning without fail. Waking up was not one of my strengths. Sleeping, however? I was great at that. There was nothing better than a cozy bed and a dark room. Or a sofa and a sunlit room—who cares? I could sleep anywhere, and I did. Naps were my favorite, but I required multiple loud alarms if I wanted to be up at specific times—my hearing required it. I shut off the bedside clock alarms, then my phone alarm, then did a double take at my phone. At some point during my festival of drunken bumbling the night before, I had changed the background picture from the pic of my family's inn to one of myself grinning dopily with my cheek pressed up against Garrett's chest.

Oh my god. What else did I do? Did I have sex with Garrett?

I looked around the room before frantically throwing the covers back. I was still wearing my clothes from the night before. My chest rose and fell with a sigh of relief as I studied my bed, bod, and surroundings. There was no trace of condom wrappers, or any of the other telltale signs that I'd had entirely too much fun last night anywhere to be seen. *Thank goodness.* Not that it happened often, but who cared if it did? I was a grown-up woman, and sometimes I had needs of the non-battery-powered kind, thank you very much. I didn't *need* a boyfriend, but sometimes I required the "D" and a set of fingers that weren't my own.

Once I came down from my freak-out and regained my senses, I felt foolish. Garrett would not take advantage of me or anyone else that way. I had been more than drunk; I had been mortifyingly and unprecedentedly wasted last night. In fact, I still felt a little bit off. But even if I had been sober, I could not go there and wreck what remained of our childhood best-friendship no matter how fine Garrett was looking lately. I was a disaster at relationships. What would Becky Lee think if I dated him and somehow messed everything up, like I was so prone to doing? I shuddered at the contemplation. She would be horrified, and then I'd lose Garrett *and* Becky Lee—not to mention the rest of the Monroes.

My head pounded as I got up to shower and get ready for work. Stupid hangover. I needed a cup or five of coffee, STAT. Something carby and loaded with sugar to soak up what was left of the alcohol couldn't hurt either. I rushed through my shower, blew my hair dry and slapped on some makeup to cover up the dark circles from the night before. I was halfway out the door before I remembered that I would see Garrett today.

And every day for the next several weeks.

My family owned a bed-and-breakfast called The Smoky Mountain Inn. I ran the front desk, supervised the housekeepers, and made sure the guests stayed happy; basically, I was the hospitality guru. My oldest brother, Landon, acted as the final decision maker, but day to day, he handled the gardens and maintenance. His husband, Leo, was our chef. We also had a hostess and a front desk helper, a few part-time housekeepers and landscapers. Without the extra help we'd never get a day off. My other two brothers, Jordan and Cameron, weren't in the family business, but we all lived together on the family land and owned the property equally since we'd inherited it from our father.

Landon and Leo had dreams of expanding the inn and someday creating a restaurant within it. But they'd decided to start with the kitchen, transforming it from a basic home kitchen to a fully furnished, tricked-out, top-of-the-line chef's kitchen. Demo work was on the schedule for today.

And in Green Valley, everybody went to Monroe & Sons—Garrett being one of the sons—for any and all construction needs. Their reputation was impeccable and had been for over sixty years. Garrett was one of his daddy's crew leaders, and of course, his crew would be the one working the inn's kitchen renovation. *Of course.*

After hesitating at my front door, I decided I had enough makeup on, my jeans and baby blue Smoky Mountain Inn polo were just fine, and gussying up for Garrett would be foolish. If he had indeed been flirting with me last night, repeating whatever I had done to encourage it would definitely be stupid. And these weirdo feelings—the zing tingles, the fixation my naughty mind's eye had on his gorgeous face, body, big hands, and the curiosity about whatever he was packing in his pants—would go away eventually, they had to. I probably had leftover horny tequila still coursing through my system.

Despite my attempt to reason with myself, I still dashed back through my tiny cottage to the bathroom for more lip gloss.

Dammit.

I could feel it coming on. *The crush.* My brain was already gooing out while my heart pitter-pattered like a parade of fluffy freaking bunnies in my chest. Don't even get me started on my stomach. It fluttered with anticipatory glee every time I so much as thought about Garrett. I couldn't blame it on the tequila forever. At some point, I would have to acknowledge these feelings. But not right now; now was for denial and the impossible hope that this was all a fluke caused by too much alcohol and not the sexy fantasies that had sprouted in my brain the second I felt his lips touch mine. I wasn't even one hundred percent sure we kissed, but I had a stirring impression of it in my liquor-filled memory banks, so I was eighty percent certain we had.

With a rough swipe, I removed the lip gloss. I took down my cute pony-tail and redid my hair, fashioning an old lady bun at the back of my neck and adding plenty of hairspray so absolutely no curly tendrils could escape. This bun had to be severe. I gave myself an encouraging, deter-mined nod. I had this. I was cool, like a cucumber or maybe a whole entire bag of ice—the good kind from Sonic. Sonic ice always made everything better.

After one last glance in the mirror, I buttoned the three tiny buttons on my polo shirt and spun on my heel. Whether or not Garrett was a boob man was a fact unknown. But there would be no cleavage on display today, just in case. Which was hard for me and my big boobs; I usually had cleavage everywhere, even when I wasn't trying to show it off.

"Ha!" I said to no one as I crossed the tiny living room of my little carriage house to leave again. With a firm slam, I shut the door and locked it. Since I lived on-site with my three brothers, I only had to walk across the meandering trails distributed over the sprawling lawn to get to work.

Landon and Leo lived on the top floor of the inn while the rest of us lived at the back of the property. Jordan, my second oldest brother, and his six-year-old daughter, Abbie, lived in a house right next to me, while Cameron, big brother number three, lived closer to the forest in an Airstream trailer. My mother and stepfather took another Airstream on the road for an early retirement the second I turned eighteen. We heard from them on holidays and our birthdays and sometimes they popped in for visits.

The inn was situated up front, close to the road and surrounded by white picket fencing, lushly landscaped gardens, and various sitting areas meant for the guests to sit a spell and relax. Our land backed up to the Great Smoky Mountains National Park—the perfect location to attract tourists. And we attracted a lot. Business was booming. Green Valley's two big industries were tourism and lumber. My family made its living from both, as Jordan and Cameron worked at the Payton Mill.

I crossed over a small hill and smiled when I caught sight of the sprawling Victorian mansion, painted pale blue with white trim. The constant mist filtering down the mountains from up above shimmered in the sunrays that had managed to break through the surrounding trees, dappling the inn with bright spots and giving it a magical glow. A few years back, we'd hired Everett Monroe—Garrett's carpenter big bro—to create custom railings and whitewashed wooden furniture for the wrap-around porch, along with a massive attached gazebo. Everett had a gift. What he'd done was add a feeling of serenity to the house with his whimsical floral details and the soft sweeping lines of the furniture. I loved it here, and I adored seeing our guests relaxed and smiling. Happy families, newlyweds, girls' getaway trips and even the occasional wedding—all of it represented the best days of our guests' lives, and I loved being part of their stories in some small way. Making sure our guests had the best time possible was my mission and I never, ever wanted to leave this place.

Leo was a stickler for schedules and, as such, breakfast was served every morning at seven sharp. I supported that since I was the type who never ever knew what day it was. One last breakfast would be prepared here before the Monroe crew tore it apart for the remodel. A sudden wave of nostalgia washed over me as I pushed the kitchen door open and recalled early mornings before school with my dad in this kitchen.

"Hey, Little Miss Molly! Try this." Leo greeted me with a huge smile, arm outstretched and brandishing a plate full of scones. Strawberry—my favorite.

"You're awesome, Leo. Marrying you was the best thing Landon ever did for this family, even though he stole you from me. Where is he?" I snatched the plate while his blue eyes twinkled, and he chuckled at my enthusiasm. His dark blond hair was short and spiky, his white chef uniform was immaculately crisp, and his imposing physique hinted at his gym-rat habits. He'd come a long way from the scrawny kid who used to cut school to drink beer in the woods behind the library with me and our friend Clara, and sometimes her older sister, Sadie. Leo was now a regulation hottie and a brilliant chef. He was one of the best friends I'd ever had, and I loved him to pieces. Landon and Leo were a "best friend's older brother" romance novel come to life, starring me as the best friend.

"Jordan got called into work last night, so Landon's over at his place babysitting Abbie. And hey, I added a little somethin' extra to your dad's famous scone recipe. Let me know how you like it." I sat on the stool at the side of the counter and shoved half of one in my mouth with a groan.

15

"Almonds and chocolate chips. Yum." I glanced up as he slid a cup of coffee in front of me in my favorite mug, followed by a plate filled with bacon and eggs, sunny-side up. Another one of my favorites.

He knew about last night.

"Who told you?"

His eyes darted to the window, then quickly to the floor. That's how I knew he was about to tell a fib. "I don't know what you're talking about. Can't I make your favorites, just because?" His puppy dog eyes landed on me, brimming with false sincerity.

"Uh, yeah, and you should do it every day. But who freaking told you, Leo? Was it Jackie? I can't believe she's your sister, let alone your twin. How could the two of you come from the same womb? It's like the devil-and-angel-on-my-shoulder thing come to life. *Ugh*!"

"The mystery is everlasting, and we may never know the answer. Kind of like we may never know the reason why you keep blowing off Friday night dinners with me and your brothers." Like usual, I ignored that pointed barb. "And yes, she couldn't wait to text me all about it. In fact, she woke me up last night. I told her to move on—again."

"I do not get her. It's not like we told her she couldn't hang out with us back then. One of these days, I'm gonna forget she's your sister and punch her right—"

I almost fell off my stool and Leo jumped a foot as the outside door swung open to bounce off the springy doorstop thing with a huge *boing*. "Y'all, did I miss it?"

"Give us a coronary, why don't you, Clara? Miss what?" Leo shouted, hand to his chest, from the other side of the kitchen, where he had dashed off to.

"The hard hats, the muscles, the sweaty construction crew man-candy! I'm ready for bulging biceps, heavy lifting, and the grunting sounds of exertion." She stopped when she caught sight of my plate. "Oooh, scones. Am I early?"

16

"Yeah, Clara, you nut. You're about an hour early," I said with a laugh.

"The man-candy is scheduled for eight," Leo confirmed.

Clara sidled up to my side to hug me. "I'm sorry about last night, Molls," she whispered in my ear.

"Dang it! Who told you?"

"Willa, of course. You should have called me. I was at the farm with Momma and Sadie last night." Clara's mother owned a lavender farm called Lavender Hills, located in the foothills above town. Clara sometimes stayed there to help at their farm stand.

"Oh, *ugh*. How did that go?" Leo asked. Clara's mother was a difficult woman. They did not get along. A fact we'd been discussing ad nauseum since our delinquent beer-drinking days of yesteryear.

"It went exactly like you said—*ugh*. But I don't want to talk about that. What's with the hair, Molly? A bun?" She let out a dramatic gasp. "Oh my god, did you have sex with Garrett last night? Finally?" Her eyes got big, then she scrunched her face and shook her head. "That isn't it. If y'all two banged, you'd be off hiding somewhere freaking out . . ." I sat back and let my raised eyebrows do the talking. Clara was good at one-sided conversation. "I know! You kissed him and now you're all swirly-whirly inside your girlie parts. Did she finally get a clue?" She addressed Leo, who only chuckled in response to her question. *Rude.* I let out a huff and looked away. "Ha! You're so predictable, Molls. Buttoned-up shirt, strapped-down boobs, bad hair, no lip gloss. You want him real bad. We all know it." She snatched a scone from the plate with a self-satisfied expression. "Well?"

I let out another huff. "Shut up."

"I knew it. Another Monroe is about to bite the proverbial dust."

"We're friends. Like we always have been. Just like usual," I insisted.

Leo snorted. "*Just* friends. Okay. Nothing about the two of y'all is ever *usual*."

17

"Et tu, Leo?"

He laughed at me. "Yeah, et me. We'll see what happens when they get here. The truth will come out and that's all I'm saying."

"It sure will." Clara leaned in. "Listen, if you finally have a chance with him, Molly, take it. I stayed with Willa and Everett at their place last weekend to help decorate the new nursery. He is an entire husband, that one is. Miz Becky Lee raised those boys right. He makes her green smoothies every morning now that she's pregnant. He won't let her lift a finger around the house, and—" She turned, bouncing her head from Leo to me with big eyes. "This is classified information." He nodded and zipped his lip while I shrugged and bobbed my head in agreement. "I heard things, y'all. Those Monroe boys have stamina. Like, hours of it. If you don't marry Garrett, at least, please screw him and tell me how it was. There's no hope for me anymore. All the good men have been taken. No more available Winston brothers—my chance at Beau and/or Duane is gone forever. That hottie Tucker Haywood was single for about five minutes before getting snatched right the frick up by that new girl, and there are no more Monroes now that you've finally scented Garrett. I could use a vicarious thrill; my well has run dry. The last man I dated said he was thirty, but I swear, y'all, if you told me he was really two fifteen-year-old boys stacked up inside of a trench coat, I would believe you."

Leo smirked and shook his head at her. "What about one of those Erickson boys, the fighters?"

"They're superhot, but too overtly athletic for me. I get the feeling they're the type to run five K's on holidays, or you know, like, 'Hey, let's go out and toss this football or whatever ball around after dinner.' That's against my religious beliefs. I like to undo my top button and eat my weight in dessert on holidays, thank you very much. Hard pass."

He chuckled. "You know, the Monroes have cousins, right? And what about Barrett? He's divorced."

"No, sir, I did not know that. Tell me of these cousins of which you speak. And Barrett is taken. He doesn't know it yet, but he is. Sadie claimed that boy way back in middle school, you know that. Always following him around like a sneaky little puppy. She was so stealthy I thought for sure she'd end up joining the FBI or something but no . . ." She shook her head. "Anywho—cousins? I need some names and I need them right the-ever-loving-heck now. Tell me they're hot and where I can find one. I'm getting desperate." She batted her eyes beseechingly at Leo. She had gone full Blanche-Deveraux-southern-belle dramatic. It was known far and wide that Sadie'd had a hopeless crush for years on Barrett Monroe, the oldest of the Monroe brothers. We used to tease her about it years ago every time we drove past the Monroe house in town for her to catch a glimpse of him in the yard, where he was usually shooting hoops in the driveway or tossing a ball around with his brothers. Some would call that stalking, we called it . . . okay, there really was no other word for it. We stalked him.

"Becky Lee has six brothers and all of them have at least two kids each. One even has eight. I can't believe you didn't know this—everyone does." I informed her as I sipped my coffee.

Clara rolled her eyes. "Y'all know how I am. I pay little attention to things outside of my immediate orbit. They aren't from around here, obviously."

"No, Becky Lee is from Knoxville. I guess some of them might be there. I know one of her brothers is in Oregon, and one is in Texas? I think? I don't keep track of her entire family, Clara."

"That's right. You just keep track of Garrett. You were lookin' to get a peek at him just as much as Sadie was lookin' for Barrett back then. Don't bother trying to deny it," she shot back.

Leo barked out a laugh. "It's almost man-candy time, Clara. Let Molly be—for now."

"Fine, you're off the hook, sugar plum—for now, anyway. Just know, the time for denial is over." She winked at me and crossed the kitchen to pour herself a cup of coffee.

I decided to go back to eating my breakfast and ignored them. "Whatever, y'all," I mumbled.

"The time is nigh, and you know it. Change is afoot. The era of dickhead Chrises is finally over. You don't just kiss the love of your life at Genie's and then let him slip away." She held out her hand and Leo smacked it as he walked by to go out to the porch.

The *pfft* of air that escaped me would have blown my curls back if my hair had been down. "Again, I say *whatever*, and I would also like to add that y'all have lost your dang minds. I'm not even a hundred percent sure we kissed anyway."

Clara's eyebrows shot up as she sipped her coffee. "Well, we'll see about that, won't we?" she finally asked.

CHAPTER 3

GARRETT

*H*alfway out to my truck I realized I was smiling, and I quickly wiped it off my face. Molly probably didn't remember any of what had happened between us last night. If one of the two people involved in a situation didn't know it occurred, then it had to be like that tree-falling-in-the-woods thing, meaning *nothing* happened and I had no reason to smile this morning. With a heave, I tossed my tool bag into the back of my old Chevy truck, then climbed inside the cab. But that didn't mean something *couldn't* happen in the future. I'd be lying if I said I hadn't thought of her over the years. I thought of her a lot, even when I shouldn't have, even when I was engaged to someone else. Molly had been an integral part of my life growing up—until she wasn't.

My family owned Monroe & Sons, a construction company located in Green Valley, passed from father to son and serving this community for over sixty years. My brother, Barrett, the oldest, was our architect. Everett, our carpenter, had switched to part time to open a gamer shop in town, and Wyatt wasn't part of the business at all; he was a Green Valley deputy sheriff. Currently, I was a foreman with my own crew, but after my father retired, I would take over—we'd signed papers on Friday to make it all official. I had always expected to share the responsibility with my brothers, but I was the only one of us interested in running the business. The thought of handling it by myself was daunting, but I enjoyed learning the ropes from my father. I also knew, no matter what my mother said, he would never retire until he was good and ready. I figured I had at least a decade left to learn from him.

When I turned eighteen my immediate goal had been to get away from Green Valley. I wanted to be and see and do something else. My brothers had grown up with clear ambitions, some of which were outside of joining the family business. Not me. I had always wanted to end up working for my father, I had no doubts about that. But before I joined the company, I needed to be more than just the youngest Monroe boy, more than my family's reputation. After college I enlisted in the Marines with the goal of becoming a combat engineer, and I did it. Returning to Green Valley was like slipping into a warm bath: comforting, familiar, safe, but boring. I think I forgot how to live when I came back here.

This morning was one of those rare times since leaving the Marines that it felt like something different was on the horizon. This felt so much better than the steady monotony I had allowed myself to sink into when I returned to town almost four years ago. I had been one of the lucky ones, managing to get through my service relatively unscathed and unencumbered by the harsh memories that plagued so many others.

Gravel crunched under my tires as I turned my old truck around to head for the highway, wincing as the sun hit my windshield to momentarily blind me. When my vision cleared, it was met by the majesty of Green Valley in the fall. Colorful trees rose in the mist as the elevation dropped and the road wound down toward town. It was peaceful and familiar; it was home. Despite the boredom, I never wanted to leave again.

I stopped at Daisy's Nut House for coffee on my way to the inn. I needed something to keep me awake. I'd suffered from insomnia off and on since I was a kid, but lately it was nonstop. If it kept up, I would be forced to take a sick day just to get some sleep. I was exhausted and already struggling to keep my eyes open.

Once I was out of the hills, the drive to the inn went quick. Traffic was sparse since it was so early.

Briefly, I wondered how Molly was feeling. An involuntary grin crossed my face as I recalled her words when I dropped her off, *"I love your almost-beard. When did you get so sexy, Garrett?"* She had hugged me and mumbled loudly into my chest, then snapped a selfie before she went inside her house. There was no way she'd remember what she said; she'd been too drunk. But I couldn't get her words out of my mind.

Maybe this change in outlook was due to Molly?

Or maybe it was because being around her last night had evoked memories of a time in my life that existed before I had strayed so far away from what I had wanted to be. I had wanted to see the world and then settle down with a family, to have a wife and kids of my own. I wanted a life like my parents had. But here I was, thirty years old with none of those things. Maybe my ex had left me gun-shy. Or maybe I just needed to relearn how to love the simple things in life and appreciate the fact that I was lucky enough to still have one.

I rolled my window down to let the soft breeze fill the cab of my truck. Along with the whiff of fresh mountain air, I caught the scent of Molly's perfume still lingering on my jacket, warm and sweet, like night-blooming jasmine and tequila or a summer breeze. She was an irresistible cocktail I wanted to drink all the way down. I never knew she smelled so good. I never knew her skin was so soft and that her lips tasted so sweet. I had never allowed myself to fully imagine a lot of things when it came to her.

The last time I'd actually touched her was to give her a hug at her dad's funeral. The girl I grew up with had been a tiny bag of bones, full of planes and angles, and always willing to throw an elbow whenever I pissed her off. This Molly had curves for days, was warm and soft pressed against me when I held her, and made me ache to feel even more.

After pulling into the inn's parking lot, I stopped alongside my oldest brother Barrett's truck and spotted my father's cargo van next to it. My crew would be here within the hour. I always arrived on-site early, especially on the first day of a job. We didn't usually work on weekends but would sometimes make exceptions to keep our scheduling on track or for special clients like Molly's family.

"Hey there, Garrett!" My eyes shot to the porch and widened when I saw Clara Hill sitting on a rocking chair sipping coffee and grinning at me like she knew all my secrets. Between Molly, Leo, and Willa, she probably did.

"Mornin', Clara," I greeted as I made my way to the porch.

"It's been awhile." She tilted her head and grinned at me. "I think we last saw each other at Genie's when you asked me to dance and paid for my drinks all night so you could grill me all about our mutual friend, little miss Molly. Was that it?"

I felt my cheeks heat. Had I been that obvious? "I suppose it was," I hedged. Clara was a person who would have the upper hand in whatever situation she found herself in, and I envied that about her. We weren't quite friends back in school, but I liked how good she always was to Molly. Clara was loyal and I respected that. But it didn't mean I was above pumping her for information. "How's Molly doing?"

"Currently, she's stuffing her face with scones and mainlining coffee in the kitchen with your dad and Barrett. She's hungover, but she'll live. Her date stood her up last night. Pity, isn't it?" Her eyes darted to the side as she set her mug on the table next to the swing.

I narrowed my eyes as I took the seat across from her on a bench. "Yeah, she was pretty mad about it. And drunk."

"She'll get over it. She didn't want to go out with him in the first place, you know."

"Really?"

A small smile crossed her face. "Yep, really." She stood up and grabbed her purse from the seat. "I had wanted to stay and watch y'all rip up the kitchen, but I just remembered I have a previous engagement. Be gentle with our girl—she hasn't had a hangover since way back in high school. Oh, and tell your momma hi for me."

"Okay . . ." This entire conversation felt like she was trying to tell me something without saying it outright, but I couldn't figure out what. The thought left my mind when Molly stepped onto the porch. "Molly, hey." I stood, while Clara laughed softly to herself and Molly lifted her chin in my direction.

"Molls, I just remembered I have somewhere I need to be. I'll text you later."

"You can't leave!" Molly protested. "What about your man-candy? Barrett just told me they hired one of their cousins from Knoxville. He should be here any minute. And guess what! His name is Chris."

"Damn, seriously?" She looked pained but determined. "Next time! I gotta run. Bye, y'all." She darted down the steps, got into her car, and left.

Molly finally met my eyes, then quickly looked down. "So . . ."

I took a step closer. "How are you today?" I raised my voice slightly so she would be sure to hear me.

Her eyes popped up to mine as her lips quirked in a smile. "I'm fine. Uh, Barrett and your dad are inside with Landon and Leo going over the kitchen plans—" She gestured behind herself to the door and stepped aside to let me pass.

"I wanted to talk to you."

"Oh, okay. About what?"

My brain blanked out as I stood there looking at her. She was so pretty in the early morning sunlight. The hints of gold in her brown eyes sparkled, distracting me. Flirting was usually second nature to me; I could do it without thinking. I supposed that was the problem. I thought about Molly entirely too much for my own good, and I always had. "Well, would you like to—"

The door swung open and bounced off Molly's butt. "Oh, excuse me, honey!" My dad's rumbling laugh filled the porch as he patted Molly on the head. "I didn't hurt ya, did I?" My dad considered himself an old-fashioned southern hard-ass, but on the inside, he was mush. He'd always had a soft spot for Molly, especially after her dad died. Our fathers had grown up together as best friends and remained that way as adults. Most of our childhood weekends were spent grilling out in one of our backyards while our parents chatted and us kids ran crazy.

"I'm okay." She laughed and patted her behind. "I have plenty of padding back there." God yes, she had plenty of padding *back there.* I would like to put her in my truck, drive her home and get a handful of that padding right now. Two handfuls in fact, one of each sexy cheek. Last night had flipped a switch in me. The fact that the switch even existed at all should have been the first clue that my feelings for her were stronger than I had ever been willing to admit. Maybe I hadn't been just playing around when I proposed to her when we turned six.

Dad smiled and gripped my shoulder as he passed me to step off the porch to go to his truck. "I'm headed to the Bandit Lake site. I'll try to swing back here after lunch. Bye, you two."

"Later, Dad."

My head swung to the door as Leo's smiling face appeared. "Yo, Garrett! I just tried out a new scone recipe. You want?" A smile crossed my face as he joined Molly and me.

"Sure, man, and the chocolate soufflé turned out great. I dusted the sides of the pan with cocoa powder just like you said."

"Told you. I have all the tricks. I'll be the go-to food-nerd for all your stress-baking inquiries."

"You bake?" Molly looked surprised.

I nodded in response as Leo answered for me. "He's full of insomnia and hot-guy angst. It's getting pretty serious."

"You can't sleep? Still?" At her look of concern, my chest started to feel warm. Shit, I couldn't have feelings like this so fast. It had to be the coffee I just pounded on the drive down here.

"Yeah, still. Some things will never change. We should catch up."

"Yes, y'all should have dinner together. Garrett, make her the five-cheese soufflé. Molly is in love with cheese, as I'm sure you remember."

"Hey! I'm not *in love* with cheese. Do I love it? Yes, but we're not in a relationship or anything—I can see other foods whenever I want."

I chuckled. "You dust the pan with butter and grated parm for this one. You'll love it. I'll make it tomorrow night at my place. You can ride home with me after work."

"What? I . . . wait, what—?"

Molly's head whipped to Leo as he chimed in. "Perfect! She'll bring the veg. I'll make my spinach salad. Molls is not a cook."

"Hey—"

"Sounds good. Is this all okay with you, Molly?" It occurred to me I should actually ask *her*, and not let Leo speak for her. Molly wasn't like other women. And I didn't mean that in the sexist way that would make my mother slap me upside my head if she heard me utter those words, either. I knew Molly as a kid. We used to be close, and that made her different. I was torn between the desire to flirt with her and wanting to run off with her to play Mario Kart. It was confusing and exhilarating all at the same time. I wanted to make out with her just as much as I wanted to bust out the Uno cards and kick her ass in a game.

"Y'all are going too fast for me to keep up!" she complained.

"Molly, would you like to have dinner at my place tomorrow?" I grinned at her.

She puffed out a sigh. "I can't. I'm babysitting Abbie tomorrow night. And maybe having dinner together isn't such a good idea after—" She turned to Leo. "Go inside for a minute, please?"

The sigh that came out of Leo was almost as disappointed as I was beginning to feel. "Molly, don't—" he started.

"Please?" she murmured.

"Okay, sure thing." He stepped behind her toward the door and she turned back to face me, but before he went inside, Leo mouthed *flirt with her* to me and batted his eyelashes. I stifled a laugh and studied her face, which had that same stubborn look she used to get when we used to play video games together in my parents' basement. Something was bothering her. I doubted she remembered much about last night; that's probably what it was.

"It doesn't have to be tomorrow," I said.

"I . . . think we should steer clear of each other for a while. I don't exactly remember last night. But I have feelings. I have impressions, Garrett, and I think we need to stay away from each other so we can still be friends."

"You realize that makes no sense."

"It doesn't have to make sense when it's how I think I feel."

"How you *think* you feel? But you don't know for sure?"

"I have a picture of us on my cell phone. I hugged you, I feel like maybe we kissed, and I don't want to wreck the friendship we have left—"

"You worry too much," I argued.

Her hands hit her hips as she scowled at me. "You don't worry enough! You never did."

"I have to go to my truck. My crew will be here any minute. We can talk about dinner later."

"We aren't having dinner. Unless our families are there, just like we used to do. We shouldn't be alone."

"Maybe we need to be alone. I remember last night, and clearly. I did kiss you, briefly. Just a peck. You were drunk, and I probably shouldn't have done it, but Jackie was at the table getting in your face about being stood up. I wanted to shut her up. I kissed you without thinking and I'm sorry. You hugged me goodbye on your porch. You told me you liked my beard and you called me sexy before you went inside. Nothing else happened between us. You made me feel good, Molly, and I want to have dinner with you. I want to know you again—what's wrong with that?" All my cards, just thrown all over the fucking table.

Shit.

I turned away from her and stalked down the porch steps, stopping at the bed of my truck to get ready to start work. I grabbed my tool belt and strapped it on while I waited to hear whatever she was about to say. She had me flustered and feeling like I did when we were teenagers and she'd avoided me.

"Okay, maybe we should talk," she shouted as she stomped down the stairs toward me. "We're friends. Garrett and Molly are friends—that's who we are." She waved her hand between us as she yelled. "So, yes, we can get together, but no flirting and no date sorta situation. We can talk like friends do over lunch at Daisy's or something like that. We can order cheeseburgers with lots of onions. No-kissing food, because there will be no more kissing. Okay?"

"I don't kiss anyone who doesn't want it. You don't need onions to keep me away from you. But I'm just saying, if we were together and you *wanted* my kisses, onion breath wouldn't stop me—nothing would. I would make sure you had everything you needed from me. *Everything.*"

I saw her sharp inhale; I watched her cheeks flush and her lips part. Her half-mast eyes and the fact that her hand had drifted up her chest to stop at her neck told me all I needed to know. I let my eyes wander down her curvy little form and back up again as a slow smile crossed my face. "I like your hair. The bun is cute." She resembled a Hershey's Kiss with her chocolate brown hair pulled into a knot at the top of her head. Completely adorable and probably sweet as hell.

She gasped like I had called her a troll or something equally terrible. "It is not! This bun is non-flirty and definitely the polar opposite of cute. My

29

great-aunt Belle sometimes wears her hair like this and she's at least ninety! Take it back."

"You're using Annabell Cooper as your defense?" I scoffed. "Everyone knows she's the biggest flirt in Green Valley! And I will not take it back. By the way, your attitude is only making you cuter. Something told me that warning you of this fact would be interesting." Crossing my arms, I leaned back against the bed of my truck to watch her. I had no doubt her reaction to my statement would be memorable.

"You're impossible! Just like always!" She flung her arms to the sides, huffed out a breath and whirled away from me to storm off toward the inn.

"And you're adorable, cutie!" I shouted to her back, making sure I was loud enough for her to hear me. I smiled as I flashed to when she used to call me a buttface and stomp into the house whenever I beat her playing basketball in my parents' driveway, almost twenty years ago. *Damn.*

"Ugh! No flirting allowed! And don't call me cutie, buttface!" she shouted before turning to stomp up the porch steps.

I chuckled as she spun around to face me once more, flinging her hand up and down, then pointing at me. "You think you're some big hotshot because you used to be a badass Marine and now you're a big, buff construction guy in a tight, sexy T-shirt with a super cool tool belt. Well, you're hot. I mean, you're *not.* You're still a buttface, Garrett."

Getting to know her again was absolutely going to be the most fun I'd had in years.

CHAPTER 4

MOLLY

I couldn't figure out how to handle him. Combine that with my new and screwy feelings for him, and I'd reverted all the way back to my childhood methods of communication—pouting and mild drama. *Not a good look, dumbass.*

"That was so smooth, Molls," Leo drawled, hip against the corner of the counter as he sipped his coffee. Barrett and Landon were at the table in the bay window, studiously perusing the plans spread out in front of them and I'd like to think they had ignored my outburst, but I knew better.

"I don't even remember what I said, Leo. I need more scones. Where are the scones?"

"The word *buttface* was uttered, or rather, shouted," he informed me with a smirk.

Barrett raised his head from his blueprints. "Don't listen to him, honey. Garrett is a pushy little buttface sometimes. You do whatever you need to do." His eyes were sympathetic and only a tiny bit laughing at me. He'd always been big-brothery and sweet. He resembled Garrett, and Everett, and Wyatt too. All the Monroe brothers looked alike and they all took after their dad. They also looked kind of like Henry Cavill—totally tall, dark, and handsome. Why had I said no again? Oh yeah, the friend thing and the Becky Lee thing and other things I didn't want to think about. With a shake of my head, I poured a second cup of coffee. I needed more caffeine in order to truly examine my life choices. And more scones. Definitely more scones.

"Maybe give the kid a chance though," Landon chimed in. My actual big brother coming in with the push. "He grew out of most of his buttface behavior. In fact, I bet he'd even let you win at basketball," he teased.

"Ha ha ha." I pulled a chair out and plopped into it.

Garrett entered the kitchen followed by his crew, and I'm sorry to poor Clara, but she was absolutely missing out. There were way too many muscles in this kitchen. Dusty work boots, hard hats, and huge sledge-hammers completed each of their jeans-and-a-T-shirt ensemble. Do not even get me started on their low-slung tool belts and the literal acres of broad, sculpted man chest spread out before my eyes. I tried not to ogle but it was impossible. I wanted to feel Garrett's muscles, for quality assurance, or science, or my own perverted curiosity. *Ugh!*

"I'm sorry I called you a buttface," I announced to the room, because why not go all the way down the embarrassment spiral. Also, it was the right thing to do and acting like a grown-up was always a good idea. *Maturity for the win!*

He chuckled. "I forgive you."

I exchanged a glance with an equally bug-eyed Leo as I stood up to get the heck out of this kitchen. It was pulsating with testosterone in here, and it was dangerous to my girlie parts. They were already swirling with barely suppressed lust over Garrett.

"Take a last look around, y'all. Make sure you have everything you want to keep," Garrett instructed.

Landon slid up next to me to put his arm around my shoulders. "Don't worry, Leo and I got all of Dad's stuff out of here," he whispered into my ear.

I nodded and glanced around the kitchen, suddenly flooded with child-hood memories. The fact that Garrett was here today emphasized how much this place was going to change. The last time he was in this kitchen with me, we had been kids and my dad had been at the stove making us pancakes. My dad had loved to cook breakfast for dinner—pancakes and bacon, biscuits and gravy, strawberry scones for his favorite girl in the world . . .

My nose tingled. The tears were imminent but I didn't want to cry, so I fought it like I always did, managing to beat back most of the emotions and only letting a huge sigh escape instead of an avalanche of sad feels. "Okay! So, I have to go check on stuff. I'm going to take a break. Listen for the phone for me, Landon?" My voice was falsely bright, a high squeak choking its way out of my throat.

"I got you, sweetie." No sweetie, no kindness, definitely no no *no* to sympathy, empathy, and soft eyes that understood—and Landon *under-stood*. He took care of me after our father died. He was there for all of us. He was twenty-three years old when our dad died. He came back here and took over the inn, took over our family. His big-brother/surrogate-father sweetness caused tears instead of preventing them. I inhaled a huge breath and held it as he continued. "Take the rest of the day off if you need to. Hear?" With a nod, I turned tail and all but ran through the dining room, across the lobby and out the front door of the inn. I stopped on the porch and looked side to side trying to decide where to hide out.

I couldn't go home; either he or Leo would be on their way to check on me and I didn't feel like talking to anyone. For moments like this, I preferred to be alone so I could miss my father in peace for a minute before I reburied my feelings and built my walls back up. When people were around, they always wanted to talk about it, or reminisce with me, or try to make me feel better when I knew I would never *be better* when it came to missing my dad. It would just be different, always different. Bursts of grief like this would always hit at random. We all got them. We all expected it, even though it was impossible to predict a trigger. It was the entire rest of my life that I could never seem to get a handle on—he was gone and never coming back. There was no way to put that into an acceptable perspective, no matter how hard I tried, so I preferred to avoid thinking about him entirely.

Behind me, I felt pounding footsteps echo beneath my feet from the other side of the door. I darted aimlessly off the porch, through the rose garden at the side of the inn and across the lawn toward the tree line near the state park. Part of the forested area belonged to us, but once the land began to ascend into the mountains, it was no longer ours.

I swung open the gate in the picket fence and stepped through the trellis onto the brush-covered dirt that led into the woods. The forest was sparse right here, but it grew denser as it moved up the foothills until there was nothing but colorful treetops as far as the eye could see. From yellow to russet to brown, the trees unfurled up the mountain like an earthbound autumnal rainbow. The ever-present mountain mist swirled between my feet as I walked to my treehouse destination. My father and Bill Monroe, Garrett's dad, had built it years ago for us kids to play in. Bill's involvement meant this was no ordinary treehouse. Its twin turrets and faux stone facade gave it a magical feel, like a castle in the trees. I could live in it if necessary; it had electricity, running water, and a small bathroom and kitchen. Everything you would ever need was inside. Bill came out to inspect it every so often, to make sure it was safe for Abbie and any future Cooper offspring to play in.

"Aunt Molly, wait for me! My legs are too short!" I whirled around with a smile and braced for impact as Abbie took a flying leap into my arms. Lucky for her, I too was short, so the leap was not a big one. "Daddy said to give you emergency hugs and here I am!" she yelled in my ear. We were still working on decibel levels when it came to her and my hearing. I glanced over her shoulder to see Jordan, still in his work clothes, heading out of the rose garden toward me. Jordan was divorced. His wife left him when Abbie was a baby to make it big in Nashville. So far, she had managed to make it medium. She was currently employed as a studio backup singer and waitress. They shared custody of Abbie and occasionally shared a night together, if you know what I mean.

"You okay, Molls?" he asked. He must have arrived right after I ran off.

I nodded while Abbie answered. "My hugs are helping her already! Look at her smile, Daddy!"

I kissed the top of her head. "Your hugs are the best, Abbie. I feel better already." And I did. Over the years, I had perfected the art of shoving my sorrow out of my head. It usually required a few minutes alone to regroup, or a distraction—and Abbie was my favorite distraction. The loss hit hard sometimes, but I'd grown adept at compartmentalizing it. Ninety-nine percent of the time I could nip it in the bud before it took over my day.

"You sure you're alright?" he questioned. Jordan was a sweetheart and his ex-wife was an idiot for leaving him.

"Yeah, it's just the usual. I had a moment in the kitchen. Memories, you know?"

"Gotcha. Yeah, it's going to be weird when it's different in there. It's bringing up a lot of memories for me too." He smiled. "Remember when—"

"I don't want to think about it anymore, Jordan. I'm sorry. But I'll hang out with Abbie if you want to go get something to eat and take a nap?" I offered.

His smile was knowing and sympathetic. I had to look away from him. "Okay, Molls. Thanks, I'll take you up on that. I'm beat."

Abbie yelled her enthusiasm in my ear again. "Yay! Can I brush your hair? Daddy, will you bring us cookies and milk in the treehouse?"

"Yep, I sure will. Then I'll crash for a couple hours, okay, Molly?" Jordan leaned over to smack a kiss on Abbie's cheek, then mine, before turning away to the inn.

"Fine with me," I agreed, glad that he dropped the Dad subject. I felt bad that I never talked about him with my brothers, but it was just too much for me to handle and I was afraid it probably always would be. Luckily, they understood me.

I set Abbie down and held her hand as we crossed the rest of the distance to the spiral staircase that led up into the treehouse. I pushed up the hinged door, we climbed through, and I sat at the small table-and-chair set on the deck that surrounded the interior space. Abbie went behind me to search through my hair for the pins holding my bun in place.

"Your hair feels weird. It's all crispy when the pins come out of it," she mused.

"I sprayed it with hairspray so it would stay in the bun."

"Don't do that anymore. I like it when your hair is pretty and soft," she murmured as she ran her fingers into my hair, removing the last pin.

"I don't know. I kind of liked the bun. It was cute." I spun in my chair to find Garrett, not Jordan, poking his head through the hinged door with a smirky smile on his face. "Take these, sugar pie, so I can climb up," he instructed Abbie.

"Uncle Garrett!" Abbie cried as she grabbed a Tupperware container from Garrett's outstretched arm. I knew Garrett and Jordan were still close, but I hadn't realized it had extended to Abbie too.

"Uncle?" I questioned.

He climbed the rest of the way up and stepped closer to set a half gallon of milk and a stack of red Solo cups onto the tiny table. He sat next to me in the small chair and I smiled when his knees hit his chest. "Jordan and I still play basketball together almost every weekend, only now we have Abbie and Mel join us. Not quite as competitive, but we have fun, right, Abbie?" Mel is Wyatt's six-year-old daughter, Garrett's niece. Mel and Abbie are in the same class at school and thick as thieves.

"Mel is my best friend forever. Daddy said you two used to be best friends forever." She glanced briefly at Garrett before returning her focus back to my hair.

"We were, Abbie." Garrett caught my eye and continued. "Jordan and I don't need to *catch up* like you and I do. In fact, out of all you Cooper people, you're the only one who has ever drifted away from me." I could only manage a light shrug in response.

"Isn't her hair prettier like this? It looks like shiny chocolate syrup." Abbie finished finger combing my hair and pushed it to flow over my shoulder. I had let my hair grow to the middle of my back with long layers cut in since it was so thick. "I'm done with your hair and now it's cookie time! I'll get the little plates from the treehouse," she declared before darting inside and slamming the door behind herself.

"You're beautiful, Molly," Garrett answered, his eyes hot on my face. He reached out, gathering the strands at my shoulder, letting it sift through his fingers as he pulled his hand away. I exhaled as my hair drifted softly against my neck. We'd always had a certain way we had acted around each other and *this* was not that way. Never before had his voice been this deep and gravelly when he addressed me. Never had his gaze drifted from my eyes to my mouth and back up like it did just now. But most of all—never had I *wanted* his eyes on me like this. Not only want it, but like it, crave it, contemplate ways to seek it out.

I was in trouble.

Last night had changed everything. And what I couldn't figure out was the cause of it. Had it started with that fake kiss? But worse, even though I couldn't completely remember it, I felt it too. I wanted to let my hair down, unbutton some buttons, make the effort to be pretty and have him notice it. I wanted his eyes on me, his hands on me, I wanted more than I should, and I had to stop these reckless thoughts before I ruined everything.

"Why do you keep pushing me away, Molly?" he murmured. Because he had spoken so softly, I wondered if he had intended for me to hear him. In fact, I hadn't heard his voice; I had read his lips.

My mouth opened slightly but no words formed to answer him. Instead of talking, we were caught up in each other's gaze. Except this was an experience vastly different from the staring contests from our olden days. This time, neither one of us stuck out our tongue or attempted to tickle the other. He ran a hand through his lush, nearly black hair. It wasn't

37

long, but it wasn't short either. It flipped behind his ears, dipped over his forehead and curled down to touch the back of his neck. His hair needed *my* hands in it, not his, dammit.

"Daddy said I could have seven cookies." Startled, I jumped in my seat as Abbie broke our moment, stepping out of the door carrying a stack of tiny pink plates.

Garrett came out of our lusty eye lock first and took the plates from Abbie. "Oh really? Then you'd better go back inside and grab a very big bowl." A confused *V* dropped between her eyes and her nose wrinkled adorably in question. "So you can throw up in it after you eat seven of these huge chocolate chip cookies," he added.

"You're crazy, Uncle Garrett. I will never throw up cookies. They will stay in my tummy 'till I poop them out." She was all little-girl attitude as she glared at him with her hands on her hips.

"He usually gives you two," Garrett argued.

With an eye roll good enough to compete with any teenager, she huffed. "Fine. He did say only two. But you're not a dad yet, so I think you should give me three and we'll keep it a secret."

"What happens in the treehouse, stays in the treehouse?" I interrupted their staredown and grinned at Abbie.

She smiled back at me. "Yeah! A secret cookie pact."

"Okay, three it is. She's just like you, Molly. And we both know I never could tell you no." Garrett held out his fist and Abbie bumped it.

I exhaled a huge breath because, what the fudge? "I want three too," I said with a nervous deflecting chuckle. Statements like the one he just made went beyond the friend zone. The way he said it made it feel like a flirt. "Leo is a cookie genius."

"He really is," Garrett agreed as he stuffed an entire cookie into his mouth. "He gave me this recipe. It's my favorite."

"What is up with the stress baking?" I asked.

"Grown-ups are so boring. Who cares about baking and stress? Eating cookies is the important part. I'm going in there to watch *Trolls*. Tell me if you get sad again, Aunt Molly, and I'll come back out." Abbie got up and went inside the treehouse. It wasn't long before the theme song blasted from the television.

Garrett chuckled and shook his head. "If I answer you, does it stay in the treehouse?"

"Of course," I agreed.

"I still get insomnia—it's a little worse since I've been home."

"From the Marines?" He nodded but said nothing more. "Do you have PTSD?"

With a noncommittal shrug, he grabbed another cookie from the container and took a bite.

"Do you ever talk about it?" I prodded.

He swallowed and pinned me still with his eyes as he studied my face. His lips quirked up in a smile, but his eyes were sad. "I don't have PTSD, Molly. I just can't sleep sometimes, like always. Do you ever talk about your dad?"

I drew back in my chair. "No, I deal with it through denial and bad jokes. I eat pie to cope, and occasionally I make dramatic exits to brood in this treehouse."

He wasn't amused by my flippant yet truthful response. "I thought not." He looked past me toward the forest. "I remember being here with you that day." I watched him as he stared passively at the trees behind me.

My mouth opened to say something, but whatever it was, it wouldn't come out. Ever since that day, I had lost all the words I'd ever had about my father. My chair screeched, then tipped over as I stood up to get away. "I—"

"I'm sorry, Molly," he called to my back before I could leave.

That stopped me in my tracks. I spun to face him. He had also stood up. His tall form towered over me and blocked out the early morning sunlight. "What for?" I demanded.

His eyes swept over me before settling back on mine. "For not being able to help you back then—that day. You broke right in front of me and I didn't know what to do." For the first time I considered how it must have felt for him to see me that way. He had been close to my father too; I wasn't the only one who'd felt his loss.

Images of that day flashed in my mind. My mother trying to catch me as I ran to the treehouse, then giving up to collapse sobbing onto the lawn. She was never the same after that. She checked out of life and remained distant and sad, even after she remarried. Garrett always was faster than me; he caught up and we ran the rest of the way together. We stayed up here into the evening, only realizing later that Becky Lee had spent the entire day sitting beneath us on the spiral staircase in case we needed her while Bill had stayed with my brothers and mother in the house, making phone calls and arrangements for the funeral and the . . . body. Dad had died in his bed of pancreatic cancer. My brother Cameron had discovered him early in the morning, before the hospice nurse had arrived for the day.

"We were only fifteen, Garrett. What else could you have done? You stayed with me. You held my hand. You let me cry and didn't try to make me stop like everyone else always did. That was enough." The words floated out of me as if I hadn't been the one to speak them. Sometimes buried truths felt that way; like they came from somewhere else.

"But, after that—when you finally came back to school—we didn't talk anymore, at least not like before."

"I didn't want to talk to *anyone* after that. Not just you."

"But, Clara and Leo—"

"Clara's dad took off and her mom is a cold-hearted witch. Leo's parents sent him to live with his grandparents after he told them he was gay. I lost my hearing, then a few years later, my dad died. We didn't talk to each other, not really, and if we did, we weren't sober. Look, you and I were on two different paths, Garrett. Yours led to the baseball team and the student council, to college and then the Marines. Mine led to cutting school to get drunk in the woods behind the library with Clara and Leo, then right here back at the inn. I just couldn't deal, with anything. It wasn't about something you did or didn't do. I promise."

"And what about now?" He crossed his arms over his chest.

"What about now?" Too many truths had spilled out of my mouth, like puzzle pieces from the past. I could see him putting it all together as he watched me pace the length of the treehouse deck.

"We still don't talk, Molly. I've been back in town for almost four years and once a conversation between us moves past, *'Hey, how are you?'* you make sure you have somewhere else to be. You're not even subtle about it."

"I don't do that," I insisted. *I totally did that.* He just looked at me as I continued pacing and thinking and pacing some more. Without intending to, I stopped and met his eyes.

He rocked forward on his feet, then forced himself to take a step back, stuffing his hands into his pockets with a frustrated sigh. "You were my best friend. Then you weren't. I missed you—I still miss you," was all he said. But I guess that said it all, didn't it?

I stood there, trapped by his eyes, whiskey brown and earnest. I was a sucker for earnesty. Earnestness? Whatever. Abbie was earnest, and that kid always got four cookies out of me. My guts heaved with the possibility of being spilled. "Maybe I do avoid talking to you," I admitted. "I —I don't like remembering how I was back then, how it felt. I really don't like thinking about the past at all. I don't consciously avoid you. I don't want to hurt you. Now I'm the one to say I'm sorry."

"Maybe we should stop apologizing to each other and lose this awkwardness. Yeah? We don't have to talk about the past." He held his pinky out, bridging the distance between us.

I grinned at the familiar gesture and reached out to link mine with his. "Yeah, okay. But I'm on to you, so don't think I'm overlooking the insomnia thing. I'm just letting it go for now, but turnabout is fair play, my friend." I let the pent-up feels in my chest take the form of a huge sigh and then let it out. "I need a cookie." I let my hand fall from his as I stepped around him to return to the table, right my chair and sit back down. I was full of scones but I was also an emotional eater, so I stuffed a bite of cookie into my mouth hoping my feelings would be stuffed down with it.

"Okay, then I'll eat the rest."

"Should I have Abbie bring out the big bowl?"

He laughed. "No, I'm good. So, about dinner at my place?"

"Not a good idea," I answered quickly, stuffing another bite of cookie into my mouth to avoid saying anything else.

"But, we just—"

"Became friends again. Even more reason not to date each other."

"Who said it's a date?" He winked, effectively mixing his message.

My cheeks heated with embarrassment, yet I was sure I hadn't misunderstood him about the date. "Oh, uh . . . I just assumed, since—"

"Friends are allowed to have dinner together, right?"

"I guess so . . ." I remembered this part of him. The sneaky, twisty word guy. Garrett always won every argument we'd ever had. He was also a master deflector. He liked to be the one to provide help or give of himself. He never asked anyone for anything.

"I have to get back to work. We'll talk about dinner later." He got up to leave, grabbing the cookie container as he stood up.

"Okay, sure, we'll make plans."

Scooting my chair, I leaned on the railing to watch him walk down the stairs and back to the inn, but I failed at being subtle. He caught me looking and waved as he shouted from the lawn, "Bye, cutie!"

"Later, buttface!" I was trying as hard as I could to ignore what was happening—the odd chemistry that had bubbled between us last night and the fact that he definitely asked me out, then took it back to pretend it was a friend thing. He wouldn't play games with me—I believed that. He had to be just as confused as I was.

CHAPTER 5

GARRETT

"*H*ey, man, we're almost done in here. Good thing you'll be the one in charge after Dad retires. He won't fire his protégée for sneaking off all morning." My brother Everett had arrived while I was in the treehouse and just in time to give me crap about missing most of the kitchen demo. My crew had cleared almost the entire space in my absence, and I could hear them outside loading up the trucks to haul away the old cabinets and appliances. It was just Ev and me left in the kitchen.

"No matter what papers we signed or what Mom says, Dad will never retire. He'll run Monroe & Sons forever." I grabbed the broom and started sweeping. "You finished with the cabinets yet? We should be ready to start installing them at the end of next week."

"Yes, sir," he drawled.

"Very funny. You're older—you could have been the chosen son. It didn't have to be just me."

"Nope, I'm happy with my shop and I'll be happy to keep working for you when that day comes."

"Did Barrett leave already?"

"Yeah, he had to meet Dad and Sadie up at the Bandit Lake site."

"I'm glad he's running that one. Do those two ever stop arguing?"

"They don't and it's hilarious. She sure knows how to push old Barrett's buttons."

"'Bout time. Someone needs to push them. Maybe she can get that stick out of his ass while she's at it." My father had hired Sadie as an interior designer. He was always coming up with ways to expand the business. The fact that she and Barrett drove each other crazy was an unexpected and amusing bonus.

He nodded in agreement. "Here's to hoping. Did Mom call you yet? Dinner at the house tonight, six o'clock."

"No, I haven't heard from her today."

"Be prepared. I think you're her next project."

I shook my head. "No. I'm not."

"No? Like you say no and that's it? We all know you're her *special wittle boy*, but good luck with that, bro." He laughed.

"She doesn't boss me around like she does the rest of y'all. I'm not going to worry about it."

"I'll be sure not to laugh too hard when you're left shocked and wondering what the hell's going on—probably on your wedding day." His phone pinged with a text message. After a smirk in my direction, he sent a text back and headed for the front door of the inn. "Later, Garrett."

"Yeah, later." My mother liked to meddle, and was all up in Everett and Wyatt's business when it came to their relationships with their now-wives. She wasn't that way with me though. And yeah, it was because I was the youngest. It hadn't escaped my notice that she still treated me like a baby sometimes.

I pulled into my parents' long driveway for dinner with a grimace. The house in town was an old Victorian sitting on a huge corner patch of prime downtown Green Valley real estate. Since it held the office for Monroe & Sons, the driveway was also a parking lot, and to my dismay, it was full. I spotted each one of my brothers' cars, some cars I didn't recognize, and a few Jeeps, which told me Wyatt's wife, Sabrina, and at least two other Logans—her family—were here too.

Was there a party I didn't know about? I thought this was just a family dinner. Sure, now that two of my brothers had gotten married, the family was bigger, but there were way too many cars to account for that.

"I see one of my favorite boys!"

"Hey, Ma," I called as I slammed my truck door behind myself, wincing at the squeak of the door.

Her hands waved happily as she stepped off the porch in my direction. "I heard the news and I'm so happy!"

I turned around when a red Volkswagen Beetle pulled in next to me. Molly got out wearing a purple sundress patterned with llamas wearing sunglasses and a big smile on her face. "Hey, y'all." Even though the dress was completely ridiculous, she was hot in it. It was all I could do not to give her a thorough up and down and look my fill.

"Hey, honey! A little birdie told me all about the two of you kissing at Genie's and I am thrilled to pieces for y'all! And for me!" A slightly manic giggle escaped before my mother continued. "I had the most terrible day. I was down with a migraine for hours, then your daddy threw his back out at the Bandit Lake house. He's okay now, bless his heart. Your aunt Dahlia called to tell me your uncle Ben broke his leg skiing. But, don't you worry, I'll be calling that brother of mine tomorrow to give him a piece of my mind—skiing down that big mountain, at his age? I don't think so! I think my magnolia tree is dyin' and the toilet in the downstairs powder room is all backed up, so don't go number two in there until it gets fixed. I just have to say, your news was like sunshine on a stormy day! I had to throw a little impromptu dinner party to celebrate it! This is the best day ever!" She clapped her hands once, whirled around with a wave and a flourish, and went back inside the house.

Molly turned to me, eyes huge in her face. "I didn't catch even half of what she said, Garrett. She knows we kissed? How does she know? I mean, I'm only eighty percent sure we even did!" she hissed in question.

I leaned in. "I have no idea how she knows what she knows, other than she almost always knows everything. I'll explain it all to her later, okay?"

"Yeah, okay. I heard the words 'best day ever' and I'm not about to wreck that for her. Not yet, anyway."

I nodded with my hand held out. She took it with narrowed eyes and a determined smile that said she knew exactly what waited for us inside—a bunch of gossiping family members, most of whom had matchmaking tendencies or were just outright nosy. We held hands in solidarity as we crossed the parking lot to the porch.

My mother bustled about in the kitchen, gathering napkins and a pitcher of lemonade. "Come in! Wash up in the kitchen and meet everyone in the dining room." She hurried through the arched entrance and called out, "They're here! Start passing the food around!"

"Uncle Garrett." I bent down, better to hear the whispering voice. "This is the weirdest dinner ever," said ten-year-old Mak, Wyatt's oldest daughter, her eyes big with warning.

"Hey." I looked up to see Ruby, Sabrina's niece, and Gracie, one of the now ever-present Hill sisters, had entered the kitchen to stand behind Mak.

"Looks like y'all are up next." Gracie snickered.

Molly stiffened beside me and her hand squeezed mine once before she let it go to point at Gracie. "Gracie May Hill, no shenanigans. I know about your nosy matchmaking. Clara told me all about what went on with your sister."

Gracie held her hands up. "*I'm* not doing a thing. This one's out of my hands. Plus, I'm still exhausted from our work on the Everett-and-Willa courtship. Aren't you tired, Ruby?"

"Oh, totally. That was taxing on so many levels. So, we're here in a different capacity. Which is weird, but . . ." Ruby shrugged.

"But here we are, warning you that Miss Becky Lee has gone 'round the bend," Gracie finished for her.

"Yeah, she's gone full on *Pride and Prejudice*-Mrs. Bennet-matchmaker, except y'all are brothers not sisters."

Gracie disagreed. "No, she's more like Emma. She's totally bonkers with it."

"How in the world do you know all this?" I demanded.

Gracie rolled her eyes at me. "Duh, because of my sisters, plus I work for Everett and—I don't know—like, basic observation."

Ruby cut in. "I live with Wyatt and Sabrina, and seriously, this is a small town. Everyone always knows everything." She turned to Gracie with an incredulous look. "Like, how do they *not* know everyone's talking about them?"

"Too right. You're lucky we're here to warn you," Gracie agreed.

"You're lucky, Uncle Garrett!" Mak chimed in. She was eating this entire conversation right up.

"It was last night!" Molly's incredulity matched my own. I stood there staring at the girls and wondering what I had gotten myself into by coming over here for dinner.

"This family's gossip phone tree and underhanded planning is legit," Gracie said sagely.

"And none of this even gets into the bizarre smorgasbord in there either. Be prepared," Ruby informed us as an aside.

"If being pregnant means craving that weird stuff, count me out," Gracie said as she turned to follow Ruby.

"Count me out too," Mak agreed and followed the older girls out of the kitchen.

"Holy crap, Garrett. What should we do?" Her eyes were big with worry as she stared up at me. I had to make this better.

"Nothing. Don't worry, my mother will drop it if I ask her to. Come on." I grabbed her hand once again and tugged her behind me to head into the dining room.

The dining room was massive and kind of a sore spot between my parents—not an ugly sore spot, just one that my dad couldn't stop razzing my mother about. Last year, much to my father's dismay, my mother spent a huge chunk of money on wood for a new dining room suite with a table so big it should have its own zip code and we were not allowed to utter one word about how all of it was custom made by Everett. Not until my father moved on from the fact that she'd convinced Everett to clear out his study and knock down the wall in order to fit the dang thing inside the house while he was off on a fishing trip with Wyatt and his kids. Bottom line—she remodeled my father's man cave into an extra-large dining room behind his back and accepted my father's good-natured zingers about it as her due.

"There they are! The happy couple!" my mother cried as we entered.

I froze. Molly bumped into my back and my eyes shot straight to Everett who was grinning at me from the table. *"Told you so,"* he mouthed. I couldn't flip him off because my mother was in the room, so I settled for a weak scowl instead.

Molly's hand in mine tightened into a death squeeze. I quickly turned around to reassure her and bent to speak softly in her ear. "It's fine. I'll explain it to her later and she'll drop this whole thing. Okay?" She nodded and released my hand with a huge sigh.

My mother, an eternal momma bear to all who needed a mother and always the consummate hostess, passed us glasses of lemonade from a silver tray. "Y'all two sit right here," she ordered and pointed. I shot her a look, but we sat down anyway. I was next to Sabrina, who promptly burst into tears and threw her arms around my neck. Since her pregnancy, the normally shy Sabrina had changed, at least with the family. Everything made her cry; we were always on the lookout and prepared to give her a hug at a moment's notice.

"It's okay," I whispered and patted her back as Wyatt rushed up to sit on her other side and take over the hug.

"Garrett, your momma made that lemonade because I love it. I love this family . . ." she sobbed into Wyatt's chest.

"Don't drink that lemonade, man," Wyatt warned me. "It is pure sugar."

"It's the best lemonade in the entire world," she countered. "And I love your mother so much," she cried.

"She loves you too, darlin'," he whispered in her ear.

"So, did she make this pickle stuff for you too?" Hesitantly, I took what resembled a jalapeno popper with a hollowed-out pickle in place of a jalapeno from one of the many pickle-based hors d'oeuvre trays covering the table—fried pickles, chopped pickle-covered devilled eggs, a huge cheeseball studded with diced pickles...

"Pickle poppers," Wyatt answered. "Yeah, Sabrina had a craving for party food. And pickles—always pickles."

"Pickle party food, huh?" I chuckled as I tasted the pickle stuffed with cream cheese and wrapped with bacon. It wasn't too bad. "So, what about you, Willa. Any of this for you?" Willa was across from us, sitting between Everett and her sisters, sipping the extremely sweet lemonade with a grimace. She was not nearly as far along as Sabrina, but I knew crap-all about pregnant women and when they started craving stuff.

Everett lifted a platter full of fried pickles and offered it to Willa, who shook her head no, then to Molly who daintily grabbed one to pop into her mouth. "Nah, she's easy so far," Everett answered for her. "Basically, if it's a cow and it's dead, she wants to eat it. Dad's grilling out back with Barrett. Your brothers are out there too, Molls."

"I can't wait." Willa grinned, then beamed when Everett planted a kiss on her cheek and fed her a potato chip I could only assume was pickle flavored.

"Meat. That's what I'm talking about." I held out my fist and Willa bumped it with a smile.

I turned to Molly, sitting there smiling blankly as she looked around the room. Belatedly, I realized she was probably having trouble hearing us. It was crowded in here and sounds blended together for her when there was a lot of noise in a room. Between Wyatt's kids, Sadie's two boys, and Abbie running around the house playing, the different conversations happening at the same time, and the music coming from the back yard, it was pretty noisy right now. "You doing okay?" I put my arm over the back of her chair and leaned across to ask in her opposite ear—I had sat on the wrong side for her to hear me. "Trade places with me." She nodded and stood up. "Sorry, cutie," I leaned in to whisper once we'd sat down.

She leaned right back into me to hiss in my ear. "That 'cutie' is not going to help your case when you talk to your mother, Garrett."

"Neither is all our whispering right now. Or this," I patted her shoulder with my hand, to remind her my arm was around her. She shrugged her shoulder and scowled at me. I removed my arm with a laugh.

I looked up to see the four Hill sisters, tall, blond, and gorgeous, all sitting in a row across the table next to Everett, their eyebrows raised as they watched Molly and me. And Ruby, sat at the end, waggling hers with a knowing smirk. "What are y'all looking at?" Molly sniped.

"It'll be more fun to watch you figure it out," Clara drawled.

"Okay, y'all, dinner is served. Kids, find a seat. Grandpa is coming in with the food!" my mother hollered as she hurried into the room, then stopped next to Molly. "You're up next, sweetie! I can't wait to see what you're gonna crave!" she said as she passed us to go into the kitchen.

"Ma!" I shouted at her retreating back, shocked at how far she was taking this whole thing.

Abandoning all pretense of keeping things cool between us, Molly yanked me close by the collar of my T-shirt. "What did she say?" she hissed.

I shook my head. "Don't worry. I'll take care of it, I promise."

CHAPTER 6

GARRETT

*D*inner was uneventful except for watching Willa polish off two huge-ass rib-eyes and a couple of cheeseburgers. Thanks to my father's intervention, my mother had dialed it down on the craving talk and her not-so-subtle hinting around about Molly and me. We had just finished enjoying wedding cake for dessert. That's right, wedding cake. Willa's cravings weren't entirely normal after all, and my mother had ordered a double-tiered wedding cake from the Donner Bakery especially for Willa because apparently regular cake "tasted different."

My father caught my eye and motioned for me to join him in the kitchen. "I'll be right back," I told Molly. She nodded, then continued chatting with the Hills. Everett had gone out back with Molly's brothers and the kids, while Wyatt and Sabrina took their brood and went home for an early night after Sabrina had almost fallen asleep at the table.

My mother smiled and patted my cheek as she passed me while heading back into the dining room. "This is wonderful, honey," she whispered. I felt terrible for deceiving her, even if it was only for a day and even if most of my heart felt like, in the end, it wouldn't end up being a deception. More and more I found myself wanting to take a chance with Molly. It had started to feel inevitable that we would.

The look on my father's face told me I would be getting one of his "dad talks." I braced myself because I could take a pretty good guess as to what it would be about. "I'll cut to the chase," he said.

I leaned a hip against the counter and crossed my arms. "Right, I think I know what you're going to say and—"

He shook his head. "No, no I don't think you do. I'm happy for you. I might not be as enthusiastic as your momma is, but I think this could be good for both of you. That girl has been . . . struggling, I guess you could say, ever since her daddy died. It didn't escape my notice that she went a bit wild after his death. Your momma and I did all we could to step in and be there for her. But this? With the two of y'all? Well, I think this could be just the thing to get her back to the happiness she deserves. For you, too."

"Me? I'm fine. I've always been fine," I protested.

Dad shook his head as he opened the dishwasher and started loading it. He wasn't one to sit idle and just talk. I grinned and started sorting through the stacks of dirty dishes on the counter to put them into the water-filled sink to help. "Garrett, I've watched over the years as you put girl after girl up on that pedestal you've always kept Molly on and then waited for them to fall off." I froze with my hands in the dirty dishwater. Dad shook his head and continued, "Except for that last one you were engaged to. She jumped clear off of it her damn self when she left town." He chuckled to himself. "You're a Monroe, son. We're all one-woman kind of men."

I nodded, because it sure seemed that way. Monroes weren't known for divorcing, Wyatt and Barrett were the only ones to divorce in decades and they'd both still be married if their wives hadn't cheated on them. "Yeah, I guess so."

"You met your person too early is all. But it will work itself out, so long as you get rid of that pedestal. You get me? Ain't nothing in this world is perfect."

"I don't have her on a pedestal, and I don't think she's perfect—" And I wasn't sure she was "the one" either. It was way too soon for that kind of talk. I'd missed her over the years, that's true. I wanted to know her again and spend time with her, take a chance on something more. But that didn't add up to what my father just said, did it?

"Yes, she is!" My mother swept into the room to deposit the pickle platters on the counter.

"You have ears like a bat, my love." Dad looked up to wink at my mother.

"She's perfect for my boy and that's all that matters. Maybe now that he has Molly, he can finally get some sleep! Maybe being alone all night is part of the problem—"

"Hey, y'all. I heard my name?" Molly entered with arms filled with dirty glasses.

"It was nothing," I answered quickly. Just like everything else, I would explain later. I didn't want her to get upset. Or my mother to get upset. Hell, at this point, I didn't want to get upset.

"You sure? I feel like I interrupted something," she prodded. I took the glasses from her and set them on the counter.

"Everything is fine, honey," my dad soothed. "We're just doing the dishes."

"Okay . . ." She gave me a questioning look.

I mouthed "Later." She nodded and followed my mother back into the dining room. Sighing, I headed out to the backyard. *Later* would be coming soon and I needed a break.

"Yo." Molly's brother Cameron greeted me as I stepped onto the patio. He sat with Jordan, Everett, and Barrett, sipping beers at the umbrella-covered table, while Abbie and Sadie's two boys ran around the backyard. Landon and Leo hadn't been able to make it because they were running the dinner hour at the inn tonight.

"Hey, y'all." I wasn't in the mood for beer, so I grabbed a Dr. Pepper out of the cooler before I joined them at the table.

Jordan lifted his chin. "So, you and my sister, huh?" *Well, shit.* So much for getting a break from the nosiness.

I gulped. This kept getting deeper and deeper. "Look—"

"You kissed her at Genie's? Leo said y'all kissed last night," Cameron chimed in. Molly's parents were childhood sweethearts who'd had Landon straight out of high school. About seven years later, they had Cameron, Jordan, then Molly all in a row, within a year of each other. Molly was the baby. It started to dawn on me that I should probably be nervous about pursuing a woman with three older brothers. It didn't matter how close I was to Landon, Jordan, and Cameron—Leo too, for that matter. If I hurt Molly, they'd beat the shit out of me first and ask questions later, and I wouldn't blame them. I'd do the same thing if I had a sister. Hell, I'd do the same thing for Ruby, or Gracie, or even Sadie and Clara if they needed it. Maybe it was overly protective and anti-quated, but if sticking up for loved ones is wrong, I did not want to be right.

"Yeah, we—"

"So." Jordan set his beer on the table and glanced over at the kids on the swing set across the yard before continuing with his voice lowered so they wouldn't hear. "Are y'all *together,* together? You wouldn't fuck around with my sister—"

"Nah, he wouldn't fuck around with Molly. He knows better than that, don't you?" Cameron's eyes narrowed on me.

Everett and Barrett chuckled, and I shot them a glare. Some kind of backup. What ever happened to brotherly loyalty?

Cameron burst out laughing and slapped my shoulder. "I can't keep it up, man."

"Yeah, we're just fucking with you," Jordan added with a smile that managed to be both friendly like usual and vaguely threatening at the same time.

"Correction. We're ninety percent fucking with you," Cameron added. "There's ten percent left over in case you fuck this up."

"I'm not trying to—"

Jordan interrupted. "We don't think you'd hurt her deliberately. Just make sure you don't do it accidentally is all we're saying."

"Because then it will be our duty to fuck you up. I'm sure you know how it is." Cameron dealt the final warning.

I gulped down some Dr. Pepper before answering. I couldn't tell them this was fake. Not after they knew I had kissed her. And especially not before I told my mother. One of them would hit me just on principle and I probably deserved it. "I know she's your sister, and I would never—"

The French doors opened behind us and my mother popped her head out. "Garrett, honey, can you move your truck? I need to run up to the Piggly Wiggly and you're blocking the garage."

"Sure thing." I couldn't get up fast enough. I raced around the house to the side gate to the driveway, smiling when I saw Molly at her VW. "You're leaving without saying goodbye?" I teased as I hopped inside. "Wait for me. I have to move my truck real quick," I said through the open window.

"Oh, okay. I sent you a text. We'll set up dinner tomorrow."

My mother stepped onto the porch. "Oh! Am I interrupting you two? Don't stop making plans together on my account!" She giggled. Molly quickly opened her car door to toss her purse inside as my mother crossed over the lawn to hug her and probably ask her a few intrusive questions while she was at it.

"Don't worry," I mouthed behind my mother's back as Molly glared at me. I twisted the key and to my dismay, the engine wouldn't turn over. My truck was an old 1972 Chevy Cheyenne I'd bought in high school I couldn't bring myself to replace with something new, no matter how much trouble it sometimes gave me.

My mother opened my door and shooed me out of the cab. "It's time for a new truck. This one is too unreliable and not safe for you to be running around town in. What if you ended up stranded on the highway? The cell signals are spotty way out there. You could get eaten by a bear! I won't have it. Molly will drive you home and I'll get your daddy to take care of this. We'll have it towed to the Winston Brothers' garage first thing in the morning. Everett or Barrett will pick you up for work if we don't go truck shopping before it gets fixed. Go on, get in her car. Scoot!"

"What's happening?" Molly asked, her face full of alarm. I knew she didn't hear. Mom was facing me and talking so fast that I barely understood her.

"Can you give Garrett a ride home, sweetie? His truck won't start," she shouted from the porch.

"Oh, uh, sure. I can do that."

"Yay! Goodnight, y'all!" With a wave goodbye, my mother turned to go back inside the house.

"I'd appreciate it," I told her after my mother went inside the house. I didn't want to take advantage of her, but I really wanted to get away from her brothers and the family gossip that we'd been drowning in.

CHAPTER 7

MOLLY

*H*ow did this happen? Yeah, I know, truck breakdown, I can't hear for shit, yada yada yada. But in terms of fate, kismet, stars aligning in the universe and crap like that—how? I was already having trouble resisting his sexy self and now here he was, too tall, too broad, too hot for my own dang good, slouched over in my tiny Beetle while I drove him home to his secluded and most likely romantic cabin in the woods. It was probably adorable and charming, and if it was even one tiny bit whimsical, I would be in unimaginable amounts of trouble.

Damn it! I was so screwed. I stupidly thought that dinner with our families would get us back to normal and put an end to this swirly-whirly crap happening between us. Turns out: not so much. I wanted to jump every bone in his body.

"Turn off on that road. Do you see it?"

I squinted in the glare of an oncoming car. "You mean that tiny gap in the trees? That one by the mailbox?" I pointed as I slowed down and turned my signal on, just in case.

"Yup, turn there." He pointed too, causing our fingertips to brush together. *Ugh!* Damn zing-tingles. No more touching. I pulled my hand back like I had touched something hot. *Huh, I kinda did.* I smiled to myself as I turned the wheel. My tires crunched over gravel as we passed a sign that read "Private" to travel down a narrow tree-lined road straight into the forest.

I switched my brights on because *yikes.* It was as spooky as it was beautiful. I mean, I watched the *X-Files.* Serious shit went down in forests and one could never be too careful. "You live in a serial killer's paradise, Garrett. No wonder you can't sleep at night."

He chuckled next to me, low and rumbly. "It's peaceful out here," was all he said.

"Yeah, I'm sure it is . . ." The thought of driving out of here alone after I dropped him off freaked me the eff out. Maybe my car would die halfway out of the woods and an ax-murdering yokel would hack me to death in my VW. And if not, there were always aliens to worry about. I could almost hear the whistling of the *X-Files* theme song in my head. I so did *not* want to believe.

"We're almost there. See the light up ahead?" He pointed again.

"Yeah." I followed the road toward the light. But there was really no other direction to go in unless I wanted to drive up a dang tree.

"Just pull in front of the cabin when you get there. I never use the garage."

"Okay." The tree line widened on either side of the road as the light in the distance grew brighter.

Then I saw it: the most adorable place ever. It was like driving into *Hansel and Gretel*—a totally adorable house surrounded by spooky-as-heck woods, where you just knew a whacked-out cannibal witch was waiting to shove you in her oven to cook you and eat your foot with a bottle of merlot or whatever.

If I kept my eyes out of the murder forest, Garrett's cabin was beautiful and serene. It was made up of stacked, rounded logs and topped by a gently sloped green corrugated roof. A wraparound porch held big wooden planter boxes stuffed full of red roses, while forest brush, ferns, and even wildflowers were dotted about in haphazard, patternless beauty to surround the small front lawn. It was simple and charming with one door in the middle and one window on either side. The cabin's covered porch glowed from a strand of fat-bulbed lights that were strung from one side to the other. This entire property was whimsical AF. All that was missing was smoke coming out of the stone chimney and maybe a few cute Disney-style animals prancing about. *Dammit.*

"It's adorable! You even have a porch swing!" I accused. Flinging out a hand, I smacked him lightly on his impressively hard chest. "Ow, that hurt."

"Well, hitting isn't nice now, is it?" he teased.

"Whatever. This place is the cutest. Did you build it?"

"Of course I did." I glanced over at him as I pulled to a stop in front of a lighted post set halfway between the house and the small garage. He had shifted to sit against the door with one hand on the dash and the other arm across the back of his seat to watch my reaction. There was just too much of him to look at; he overwhelmed this small space. He overwhelmed *me.* I huffed out a sigh and exited my Beetle to get away from him and gather my rapidly escaping thoughts about why I couldn't just take what I wanted and attack him.

My sandals crunched through the gravel toward his porch as I shivered against the chill in the brisk evening air. "It's cold." I jumped at the sound of his door slamming behind me.

"Let's get you inside, then. I'll start a fire." A fire, right. *Get even more romantic, why don't you?*

"*Ugh!* Okay," I yelled, quite unsure of where my attitude was coming from. "Start a fire. Offer me some freakin' tea while you're at it."

"Would you like some freakin' tea, Molly?" The laughter in his voice was so sexy. He had some nerve unleashing it on me. *Hmph!*

"I would love some freakin' tea. But only if you serve it in an irresistibly cute teacup, please," I groused as I stood there glaring at his front door.

"I think I can do that." He chuckled.

"Of course you can! Is there nothing you can't do?" I shouted.

He unlocked the door and stepped aside to let me in. "After you." I scowled up at his grinning face.

What was I even doing here?

"I should just go. This is a bad idea." I took a step to go around him but turned back when I heard the high soft trill of a *meow* echo in my hearing aid.

"You have a damn cat too?" I whirled back to face him with an accusatory finger pointed and at the ready.

"Sure do. He's a cute damn cat, too." He clicked his tongue against the roof of his mouth to call what would most likely be the most scrumptious cat in all the known universe.

There are five things I couldn't resist in this world: kitty cats, pie of all kinds, big shoulders, wicked grins that hinted at delicious possibilities, and all things that sparkle.

So far, Garrett was three out of five tonight—the audacity! I heaved out yet another disgruntled sigh and stepped inside. The cabin was one large room with two doors on the left and an open kitchen on the right. In the center of the kitchen area was a square butcher block island surrounded by padded stools. Copper pots hung from a black iron rack over the island, herbs grew in tiny terra-cotta pots in the bay window above the sink . . .

It was like he'd hired a fairy-tale princess as an interior decorator.

I needed to leave.

Right the frick now.

But another high meow hit me before I could bolt. "Kitty!" I cried.

At the rear of the cabin, a furry black and brown striped head popped out from behind a couch followed by a huge, chunky, kitty-cat body, then a bent bottlebrush tail that swished side to side as he moved. His eyes glowed dark yellow in the dim light of the cabin as he hobbled in our direction. The dang cat had three and a half legs and a crooked tail. He was ugly as could be, yet he was the cutest thing I'd ever seen in my life. I sank to my knees and held a hand out. "What's his name?" I whispered as the cat nuzzled my fingers, then crawled onto my lap. Forget Garrett; I had just fallen in love with this little furry purry.

"Stan," he answered. "He's probably getting hungry, so watch your fingertips. He likes to nibble, and he can be kind of a grouch if I don't feed him on time." I beamed up at Garrett as Stan took a little nip at my finger. It wasn't a bite, just a little touch of his teeth. "Stan, you're a little weirdo, aren't you?" I giggled as Stan purred like a motorboat on my legs.

"He's an odd duck, for sure. He used to hang out on my porch. Took me weeks to get him to trust me. Now he's never gonna leave, right, Stan?" My heart melted as Garrett baby-talked the cat and received a very loud, trilled meow in response. Then Stan snuggled into my stomach and I was done for. I was in this evening for the long haul and I would probably try to smuggle Stan home with me in my purse.

I grinned up at him. "So, you built this cabin, rescued this weird-ass cat, and now you're going to make me some freakin' tea."

"Yeah. Don't forget about the irresistibly cute teacup, cutie." He laughed as he slipped out of his flannel shirt and tossed it to me. "Put this on until I get the fire going." I let go of Stan to slip into the shirt. It was toasty warm and smelled wonderful—like hot guy, clean laundry, and dreams come true. *Again, I say dammit!*

"Thanks. Now all we're missing is pie to make it perfect," I grumbled as I watched him kneel in front of the straight-out-of-a-freaking-storybook stone fireplace to build a fire. If he made pie? Holy crap, I didn't even want to think about it.

He turned to me with a grin. "I can make pie. I made a pate brisée yester-day. It's in the fridge, and I have a jar of cherry filling that my mother made when she was doing her canning. It's cooked, so it's just a matter of waiting for the crust to bake and the cherries to get hot and bubbly. Do you like whipped cream or ice cream?" he asked as my jaw dropped. I envisioned myself falling to the floor legs open and slammed my mental eyes shut with a grimace. I had no tequila to blame it on tonight—just Garrett and his effing four out of five.

"Whipped cream," I managed to answer around my dropped jaw and blown mind. I should have never stepped foot into this lady-trap cabin.

"I'll start some coffee for me and get the teakettle going." He stood up after one more poke at the crackling fire he'd just created.

Gently, I gathered Stan in my arms and stood to follow Garrett to the kitchen. "You can't drink coffee at ten p.m., Garrett. You'll never get to sleep. I haven't forgotten about the whole insomnia thing, you know. The problem with ten p.m. is that it can turn into three in the morning real quick if you don't watch out. No coffee allowed." I plopped onto a black and white buffalo-checked cushioned stool at the island. Stan cuddled his head into my neck like a little baby and purred his fluffy brains out.

"Yes, ma'am. What kind of tea should we have?"

"Chamomile. I have emergency tea bags in my purse if you don't have any." He grinned and glanced at me out of the corner of his eye as he filled a kettle with water at the deep farmhouse sink. *Did he just look at me with amused and flirty masculine indulgence? Not allowed!* "What about it?" I snarked with narrowed eyes. "Everyone in the world is obsessed with coffee. Tea drinking is underappreciated. One must always be prepared." This vital fact was one he must be informed of.

He chuckled—again with the flirty indulgence. *Ugh!* He was making me feel girly and cute and he needed to knock it the heck off before I blushed or something else equally lame.

"I do have chamomile, but its powers are wasted on me," he said as he gathered stuff from the refrigerator.

66

"Bummer. I'll sit here and brainstorm about it. Oh! What did your mother say earlier?" I didn't even look up at him. I was too busy ogling his perfectly veined forearms as he rolled out the pie dough on a slab of marble that he'd pulled from beneath the island. He had a tattoo of a rose slithering up his arm, and it was a sexy one too, the big, hot jerk.

His head did that tilty-dip thing guys do, and his eyebrows rose as he answered. "Don't go nuts. She said, now that I have you, maybe I'd finally get some sleep." He paused his dough rolling to make air quotes around *have you*. A nervous laugh escaped as I squirmed in my chair at the thought of him *having me* and what it would take to wear him out enough to get him to sleep. Obviously, that was not what Becky Lee meant, but holy heck it was all I could see—and I have to say, it was quite an enjoyable naked mental image. I shook my head to clear out the porn before I answered.

"No, no, I'm good. No going nuts. I've decided to stay sane. And you do *have me*—we're back to best friends, right? And yeah, your eyes are definitely dark and circley. So! Challenge accepted!" I slapped a hand on the counter, startling Stan. "After tea I'll get you to sleep and then I'll go home."

"What do you mean, 'get me to sleep'?" He chuckled.

"I'll lie down with you until you go out. I do that with Abbie all the time, when Jordan is working and she can't fall asleep. Do you want a story? I could sing you a song?" I flirt-smirked—flirked—at him. I couldn't help myself. But at least I didn't add a jaunty wink—if I had jinked at him, we'd end up in his bed for sure and *not* to sleep . . . "If those don't work, I'll rub your head. Head rubbing has never failed with Abbie."

"Very funny." He shoved the tray with the pies in the oven, then reached up to grab a bowl hanging from the rack above, treating me to a glimpse of his abs and the glorious happy trail that led below them into his jeans.

I slammed my eyes shut. Because clearly, I couldn't speak words that made sense and look at him at the same time. I knew my limits. "Do you doubt my skills? I'll bet you right now that I can make you fall asleep tonight." That's right, I threw down, just like I used to do with him. Something about him had always felt like a dare—exciting and fun.

"Odds?" His deep voice rumbled with laughter. I opened my eyes.

Flexy pecs.

Bulgy arm porn.

Whipping cream by hand was no joke.

Ohmygod!

I quickly looked down at Stan, sweet, sweet Stan, before I answered. "The odds, my friend? The odds are that I'll win, and you'll take me to The Front Porch for steaks. Boom! Those are your odds, buttface."

Wait, did I just ask him out to the fanciest date-night steak house in Green Valley?

Did I want to win? Or lose? Losing a bet went against everything I believed in as a human. But was winning losing in this case? Or was winning winning? What the hell had I just done? I got up and wandered into his living room shaking my head while he laughed at my ridiculous antics. I had to sit down in a place not quite so near him. *He* was the tequila tonight, and here I was, already drunk like a dumbass.

Choosing a denim-covered wing chair in the corner next to the fireplace, I took a load off. I was out of Garrett's view over here, so I felt free to frown in consternation at will. Stan squirmed to get down when he heard the top *pop* on a can of kitty-cat food, so I released him to brood alone in my chair.

Soon the whistle of the teakettle broke my reverie and I stood up to make sure Garrett knew how to handle the tea. I refused to drink a bad cup; life was too short for that nonsense.

"Is this cute enough for you? My mother brought it over to use from some shop in Nashville. She's not a coffee person either."

I smiled at him and took the cup to examine its cuteness. "I know," I informed him. "I discovered the joy of tea-drinking from her. We go to that shop in Nashville every year for her birthday and mine. Mother's Day too, after she's done with you boys. We drink tea and eat tiny sandwiches and talk about life." His return smile was soft—another manly, indulgent one—but I didn't want to get into the meaning of it, so I looked away.

"I made mini pies. They won't take long to bake."

"This is nice. You don't look like a man who bakes."

"What kind of man do I look like?" he laughed.

"The kind who . . . uh, does badass stuff. I dunno, ax throwing? Ride motorcycles on the Tail of the Dragon with the wind in your hair? Race cars at The Canyon like you used to do back in high school when you hero-worshipped Duane Winston? That's not quite as badass, but his racing skills are legendary, so I don't blame you. We all have our heroes." I shrugged.

"You knew about that back then?" He seemed surprised.

"I did. Clara, Leo, and I watched all your races." For some reason, this felt like a confession and not simply an innocuous statement about our not-so-innocent youthful activities.

"I wish I had known you were there," he murmured. I had to read his lips to know what he said, he was so quiet.

"Why?" I asked. But did I really want to know the answer?

His soft eyes met mine and I couldn't look away. "Don't you know by now?" *Did I?*

Bing!

The timer on the oven went off and I stood up to get the kettle for our tea while Garrett grabbed potholders to get our pies out of the oven. He plated them and opened the fridge for the whipped cream. "We can sit on my deck out back. Take the kettle and I'll get a tray for this stuff. Go switch on the lights and I'll meet you outside."

"Okay," I whispered and turned to cross through the living area to do as he asked. I flicked the switch on the wall, then opened the heavy wooden door, laughing as I stepped outside. After placing the kettle on a tile-topped table, I spun in a slow circle to take in what had to be a thousand tiny lights strung across the top and down the posts of the covered deck to sparkle in the dark like tiny stars.

Holy crap. He was five for five tonight.

CHAPTER 8

GARRETT

*W*e drank the tea. We ate the pie. We did it in silence, but it was comfortable. Where I would normally feel compelled to talk, or flirt, or entertain, with her I could just relax. There were few people in my life who made me feel free to just *be* with. It had always been my family, her brothers, and her. Through all the time between us, I'd never had another friend like Molly.

"You ready for bed? Let's do this thing." She clapped her hands together and grinned. I chuckled when, yet again, she grew startled by one of the random forest sounds.

"You don't have to do this. I've managed going to bed for years on my own, you know."

"I know. But why should you? I know you think I'm being silly, but sleep is important. I don't like the thought of you alone in the dark, staring at the ceiling. It makes me sad. We used to have sleepovers all the time, remember?"

"Uh, we were children, Molly."

"Yeah, okay. You have a point about that, I guess." She looked like she was trying to convince me of something—or maybe herself.

"You guess? It's a good point," I argued. "Sleeping in the same bed as adults is . . . well, it's intimate. Don't you think?"

"It can be. But it doesn't have to. It can be just one friend helping another friend fall asleep. Then that friend gets up and drives home or maybe the friend sleeps on the couch because the thought of going outside alone into that dark forest full of murderers, rabid animals, probably aliens, cannibal witches, or other assorted spooky *X-Files* bad guys scares the holy ever-loving shit out of her and she doesn't want to be alone in her car driving out of your dark-ass, haunted, horror movie excuse for a forest, okay, Garrett?" Her little tirade started off calm but ended up shrill and panicky in a hurry. Why did I find it so cute?

"Ah, I see now." I grinned at her red cheeks and scowling mouth. I wanted to kiss that scowl off, but I refrained. Now wasn't the time.

"You do not see anything!" An animal howled in the distance and she jumped. "Ahh!"

"Maybe you should stay here tonight. I don't want to be responsible for you crashing into a tree on your way home if another animal makes a sound out there." Suddenly the idea of having her in my bed felt comforting instead of sexual. The idea of holding her, keeping her from getting scared of the dark, then just innocently falling asleep beside her was impossible to resist.

And why should I resist it? We were both free. Our families may have placed expectations on whatever they thought was happening between us, but in the end, what they wanted had nothing to do with what actually occurred between Molly and me. We were adults; we could make our own choices.

Her sigh of relief told me I'd made the right call in telling her to stay. "Good. Let's go inside now. I'm done pretending all that dark out there isn't freaking me out. You need more exterior illumination, Garrett. Put some lights in those trees out there."

"I used to have motion-detecting lights right off the deck, but there's too much going on outside. The lights went crazy all night long."

"Oh my god! I'm going inside right now. You clear the table. I'm done with nature and I think I hear Stan." I couldn't help but laugh as she slammed the door behind herself.

"No laughing!" She poked her head out of the door. "I didn't hear it, but I know you're doing it! Don't forget, we sort of bet on this anyway. I'm getting the steak *and* the lobster, buttface."

I gathered everything I could fit on the tray and started to head inside behind her. Despite my mental insistence that this would be a platonic, friendly sleepover, my stomach was turning somersaults as anticipation flooded my veins with so much adrenaline I doubted I'd be able to sleep any time in the next week.

Her head popped back out. "I'm sorry I keep calling you a buttface. You make me feel a little crazy sometimes, Garrett. Let me help you." She grabbed the kettle and carefully took the teacup from my other hand.

"Hey, as long as you're not calling me Gawwett again, I'm fine with it."

"Ha ha ha. It took me awhile to fully embrace the letter R, didn't it?" Her sideways smirk was both familiar and new. My feelings for her were also familiar and new and I didn't know how to wrap my brain around it. Being with her was as comfortable as when we were kids, but there was a physical aspect to it now that had never existed before. I wondered how I should handle it tonight. There were no rules to this game, and there was so much more than just the two of us involved—our families, our history, all of it would be put on the line. Crossing that line was absolutely a risky move.

Despite my trepidations, I turned to grab the tray from the table to follow her inside with a smile on my face.

"So . . ." Her voice was whisper soft in the moonlit dark of my bedroom.

"Yeah?" Face scrubbed clean, hair in a ponytail, wearing one of my T-shirts, she faced me on the other side of my bed. She was pretty as could be, lying there looking at me the way I sometimes dreamed about. Her rosy cheeks and big brown eyes were gorgeous in the moonlight and the idea that I could fall asleep right now was insanity.

"Flip over so I can get you to sleep," she bossed.

"I'm not a kid and I'm twice your size. You should flip over."

"I'm the one helping you fall asleep. I should be the big spoon. Flip." She put on a mask of annoyance but the smile she was trying to hide from me destroyed the effect.

"I'll flip, but only because I want to see you try to be the big spoon. You're barely the size of a demitasse spoon."

"You know what a demitasse spoon is?" She laughed at me while shoving at my shoulder to move me to my side.

"You've met my mother, Molly. Don't make fun." After flipping over, I went stock-still as I felt the press of her full breasts against my back and the warmth of her leg hooking over my hip. Her arm went around my shoulders and the hiss of her breath on my neck sent a shiver down my spine.

Friends. We were friends right now, nothing more . . . not yet, anyway.

I could do this.

No, actually I could not.

My dick got hard. I slammed my eyes shut and thought of my mother's laundry drying on the clothesline in the backyard when I was growing up, granny panties as far as the eye could see . . .

Stan's hairballs . . .

That dead raccoon he'd dragged onto the deck as a gift before he moved in . . .

Dr. Pimple Popper on YouTube.

Ahh, that did it. There was nothing like the mental image of a big-ass cyst erupting to get rid of a boner.

"Dammit, Garrett. You're too big. This is like trying to comfort a brick wall. I can't even fit my arm around you right. This is much easier with Abbie."

"Well, she's a tiny little girl and I'm a large, strapping man. And you are just a little shrimp. You flip over."

"I can't be the little spoon! I'm the one helping you fall asleep, remember? Plus, you look warm and cozy and if you cuddle me, I'll go out like a light. I've never had problems sleeping."

"I remember. You could never make it through my parents' movie nights. They'd put a blanket on you, and it was lights out, like Pavlov's dog. Fine. Alright, lie on your back and you can be the spoon rest. You know, the one that sits in the middle of the stove?" I felt her nod against my back. "You be that big spoon and I'll put my head on your chest. And if this is a bet, why am I helping you win?"

"Because, you'll win too. You'll get a good night of rest, and then we'll eat steak and lobster at The Front Porch next weekend to celebrate my victory and the fact that I'm never wrong when it comes to sleep. Duh, Garrett." She let go of me and turned to her back. After fluffing the pillow behind her head, she patted her chest. "Come on, I'll rub your hair like I do for Abbie. You'll be out in no time and then I'll go out to the couch with Stan."

"Stan is a bed hog. Have fun with that," I warned as I scooted closer and allowed my head to rest on her ample chest—was I a pig for noticing how soft she was? Probably, but I'm only human and this situation was unprecedented as well as completely crazy. I heaved out a sigh and tried to relax but it was impossible.

"He's so floofy." She sighed, causing her chest to rise and fall beneath my head. "I'll be Stan's big spoon when I'm done with you," she whispered as her hand went into my hair. My eyes rolled back as her little pink fingernails lightly scratched my scalp in a heavenly massage. "Relax. Let me help you, Garrett. You deserve to get some rest," she soothed as she used her other hand to caress the back of my neck and the top of my shoulders. It was impossible not to do as she said. My body grew heavy with exhaustion as I succumbed to her magic fingers, her softness, her sweetness and care. Not to mention the fact that she smelled like heaven and I wanted to lie here and inhale her forever.

I awoke hours later to the warmth of her snuggled next to me, curled on her side with her head on my chest, one hand under her cheek and the other on my stomach. My quilt wrapped around us both, cocooning us in warmth like we were in our own little world right here in my bed. Sunlight filtered through the slats of my blinds to cast striped shadows over her sleeping face. Lightly, I traced the bridge of her nose with a fingertip. It turned up at the end with exactly seven freckles decorating the bridge and one tiny crescent-shaped scar left over from the car acci-dent that had taken her hearing. When we were kids, I used to tell her the scar looked like the moon and the freckles were her wishing stars. I also used to run Hot Wheels over the top of her head and down the bridge and pretend the upturned tip was a jump-off to make her laugh.

I should move.

A good guy would slip out of this bed and let her be. But really, a good guy probably wouldn't have let this happen at all.

I did not move.

The feeling like I finally had everything I'd ever wanted forced me to stay and look at her a little bit longer. Her face was shaped like a heart and I had the inescapable feeling that she may have just stolen mine. Looking at her like this, sleeping and peaceful, gave me an odd ache that made my heart beat faster the longer I stared.

Blinking to clear the remaining haze of sleep from my eyes, I reached out again to make sure I wasn't dreaming. Her cheek was soft beneath my fingertips, a sweet smile crossed her face as her eyelids fluttered open. "Garrett," she murmured turning her face into my touch. "I knew I could help you sleep."

I could roll away and not kiss her. I could get up and make coffee or tea. I could do so many other, smarter things right now but . . . *this was everything.* My whole world, the air in my lungs, the beat of my heart, every thought in my head centered around her at this moment and I didn't want it to stop. She was so warm and soft pressed against me, so real, so perfect, and always, *always,* mine.

"Molly," I murmured, tightening my arm around her waist as I shifted to my side to face her.

"Yes," she whispered. Our past flowed into the present like a river while memories skipped over the surface like stones, each one a reason why this was always meant to happen.

With her hands in my hair, she pulled my head down to hers. Her sweet pink lips were an invitation I could no longer resist. But she pulled away before I could get a taste of her. "I don't know how to do this with you, Garrett."

"Do what?" I asked anyway, though I knew what she meant.

"Kiss you . . ." Her whispered breath on my skin urged me closer.

"Don't you like this anticipation? It's going to feel so good, Molly." I brushed her hair back to cradle her beautiful face in my palm, dipping my head low to place a kiss on her forehead.

"It already feels too good to be true." Her hand pressed against my chest above my heart. "You feel it too, don't you?" Her eyes flitted to mine, wide and golden brown like amber in the sunlight. Her dark eyelashes fanned over her cheeks as her eyes drifted closed.

"Yes, I feel it." My voice was hoarse, thick with emotion and barely leashed need, while my heart beneath her palm raced out of control.

She surged up and met my mouth with her own. Her lips, soft and full, parted beneath mine as her hands threaded into my hair and her tongue met mine for a soft, quick caress just once before she took it away with a moan.

I was so wrapped up in her I didn't immediately recognize the sound of my front door opening and closing until I heard heels clicking over the hardwood floor, rapidly approaching the bedroom door.

This moment was over before it had a chance to really begin.

I broke the kiss with a groan and pulled away, throwing the covers back to stand up. My chest heaved as I watched her sit up to clutch the blanket to her neck. "Stay here. Someone is in the house." She nodded once before I stepped out and shut the door behind myself.

CHAPTER 9

MOLLY

I fumbled around on the bedside table for my hearing aid, then stood up, looking around for something murdery to grab so I could assist. I'm not one of those horror-movie chicks who's gonna hide out and let her, well, whatever Garrett was to me now—best? Boy? Because were we dating now? Whatever-friend—be chopped up by some serial killer or eaten by Bigfoot. And let's not forget about the *X-Files* aliens lurking about. Locating a baseball bat in the corner, I snagged it and threw open the door.

What I saw made me want to dart back into his room and hide in the little bubble we'd created together overnight.

"Molly? What is she doing here, Garrett?" Garrett's ex-fiancée stood, in all her freaking gorgeous strawberry blond glory, with her arms around his neck, in the middle of the living room. She was tall, thin, elegant, gorgeous—in other words, everything *I was not*. He fit with her in a way I would never be able to match.

She had broken his heart. The word around town was that she left a note on his kitchen counter while he slept. Obviously, I had never talked to him about it myself or mustered up the courage to ask Becky Lee if that's what really happened. After she'd gone, her momma told everyone she just wasn't ready to be a wife.

I hated her.

For no good reason, I had always hated her, like, at-first-sight, wanted-to-punch-her-face-off hatred.

Belatedly—as in, just now—I realized why.

Garrett had always been *mine*, even when he wasn't. His engagement to her had meant there was no hope left for me.

So, it was never hatred.

It was pathetic, out-of-control jealousy instead.

The bat slipped from my hand to clatter to the floor as I dashed to the front door. My purse and keys sat on the table next to it. I grabbed them and ran out, slamming the door closed.

To my horror, I burst into tears. I almost never cried. I was so very good about nipping my feelings in the bud, burying them, or denying I even had feelings at all. But seeing her here, arms thrown around Garrett's neck, his hands at her waist, hurt too much to contain it. With a rough swipe of my arm beneath my eyes, I wiped my tears, but it didn't stop the flow. In my haste to slam the door shut, I dropped my keys. "*Ugh!* What the hell?" As I bent to retrieve them the door opened, and Garrett stepped outside. With a lurch, I hauled myself up, abandoning my keys to run off toward the forest, wincing as dried pine needles pricked at my bare feet.

"Molly, come back!" I stopped at the tree line. I had no plan. Was I going to run off into the forest like a crazy person? With no shoes and wearing nothing but Garrett's big T-shirt and a pair of undies?

What was wrong with me?

The usual was wrong with me. All drama, no plans, reacting to stuff before I thought it through.

"I don't want to." I stood there facing the trees and probably a few ax-murderers, and maybe a rabid squirrel? If there were aliens out there, I wished they would just abduct me right now and get me the hell out of here.

"Come on, Coop. Please come back." He called me *Coop*. Not cutie, not even Molly. Coop, just like when we were kids, just like when we were *friends*. Just like the last time I saw him in town *with her*. My body swiveled in place before my mind could force myself to run away from him. I needed to get my keys and I needed to get the hell out of here. I also did not need to be here for their joyous reunion. He bent to pick up my keys and stepped off the porch to head in my direction. "I'll get rid of her. Let's go back inside."

"We both know this whole thing was a bad idea. This just proves it."

His head jerked back in surprise. "What are you talking about? This? It's nothing. She barged in. I didn't invite her here. I didn't even know she was back in town."

"I know you love her. You were always with her, you were—"

His jaw clenched with frustration. "And you always had a boyfriend, didn't you, Molly? She left me, remember? She is in the past, just like your Chrises. Don't go." He reached out as if to touch my face, but I backed out of his reach. "Please don't cry, this is nothing to—"

"Right, she broke your heart. Everyone knows that! I guess you got her back now." I held my hand out and gestured for my keys.

"No, we should talk about this. I want you to stay—"

"Not now. Not when she's still here. Please, Garrett, I need to leave. Please give me my keys and let me go."

His eyes softened on my—most likely bright red and tear streaked—face. "I understand. I'll get her gone, then I'll come find you."

The keys dropped into my outstretched palm and I darted to my VW to get the hell out of here. Once I made it to the highway, I realized once more that I hadn't dressed or put on shoes. And one look in the rearview mirror at my puffy, red eyes and blotchy face told me I couldn't go home like this. My brothers loved Garrett, but they loved me more. They'd take one look at me and be out the door like avenging angels to either beat the shit out of him or threaten him until he cried. And don't even get me started on Leo. The last Chris I dated was a cheater who called me a *see-you-next-Tuesday* when I dumped him; he probably still rued the day he'd ever met Leo, and I'll just leave it at that.

Once I got into town, I pulled into the nearest parking lot to dig out my cell and call Clara. It was Sunday; she should be at her mother's farm. Ever since Sadie's husband had left her and she'd moved back in with their momma, Clara had been down every week for their regular Sunday dinner as a show of support.

"Where are you? At your mother's?" I dove straight in with no preamble.

"We're all at Willa's place," she answered.

"Damn it! Shoot! I'm in my underwear and my face is a mess. I need clothes before I can go home!"

"No, sugar, you need to back this story up because it feels like you left all the interesting parts out. Come on over, we got clothes. But more importantly, we've got *you.*"

"But Everett—"

"Is at his shop for the day. It's just us girls here, so come on."

"I'll be right there." I had nowhere else to go. The only other option I would have had was to call Becky Lee and I couldn't do that—once again proving that attempting to date Garrett was a bad idea and kissing him had been a huge mistake.

I found Everett and Willa's place, parked at the curb and looked around to make sure the coast was clear before I ran to the door and banged on it. Clara threw it open like she'd been waiting for me on the other side, which she probably had done.

I dashed inside because even though Garrett's shirt was long, I was still in public wearing nothing down below but panties. I held up two fingers. "So, two things—I need some pants, and I don't want to talk about it."

Clara laughed. "Three things—you are so gonna talk about it, we have pants for you upstairs, and what direction are we going in, food or booze?"

"Gosh! Food! It's morning!"

"Yeah, and that's what mimosas were invented for," she shot back at me with a smirk.

"I'm not drinking anymore. Drinking is what got me into this stupid mess in the first place," I declared.

"No, it wasn't the drinking, but we'll get into that later."

"Hey, Molly. Don't say anything juicy until I get back. I'm doing a doughnut run to Daisy's. Want me to pick up a coffee for you?" Gracie hugged my neck, then moved around me toward the door.

"You're a doll, Gracie, thank you." I followed Clara through the foyer and up a staircase to what I assumed was Willa and Everett's bedroom. She waved me inside with a pair of leggings in her hand.

"I found these, Molly. They're capris on me, so they should be normal length on you."

"I really appreciate this, thank you."

She tossed me the leggings with a smile. "We've all been there—a dramatic, tear-filled escape in a man's too-big T-shirt is a rite of passage every woman goes through at least once in her life. Am I right?"

Clara shrugged. "I had two last year alone."

"We need to talk about your taste in men, Clara." She deserved better than the losers she always ended up going out with. She was a beautiful, blond tower of awesome and she should have it all.

"Well, we don't all get a shot at a Monroe," she sniped.

"Well, my shot at one is gone. May I flop?" I gestured to the bed.

Willa laughed. "Flop away."

"I haven't told you how glad I am you're finally home, Willa," I mumbled into the mattress. Willa had run away from home with her boyfriend when she was seventeen, but now she was back, and to use the words Garrett had kept haranguing me with, we needed to *catch up.*

"Thanks, Molls. But probably not as glad as I am to be here."

Clara plopped down next to me and nudged me to my side. "Y'all are so sweet. Yay for reunions and all that. But what happened? Start from the beginning and leave nothing out. Go." She clapped her hands and stared at me expectantly.

Willa sat at the head of the bed with her knees tucked to her chest. "Get it out, you'll feel better. Then we'll all eat doughnuts together and feel wonderful."

"I spent the night at Garrett's cabin—"

"Oh my god! Was there stamina involved?" Clara burst out.

"No, our clothes stayed on. He can't sleep sometimes, and we sort of made a bet about it. I helped him fall asleep and accidentally crashed next to him. We woke up, we kissed a little bit, then Lacy showed up. She had a key. She let herself in."

"No! Boo, Lacy!" Clara turned to Willa. "Garrett's ex-fiancée and we hate her. Team Molly for life!"

"Gotcha," Willa confirmed with a grin. Obviously, she was on Team Molly. She was out of town for the Garrett Monroe/Lacy LaRoe engagement of doom. I mean, imagine if they actually got married. Her name would have been Lacy LaRoe-Monroe. *Ugh!* Nauseating and adorable.

I sat up, realizing that I may have overreacted just a bit.

Clara pulled me into a side hug. "What else, sugar pie? Why are you here, pantsless and morose? Tell us all about it."

Why was I sad? He hadn't actually done anything wrong. *Uh-oh . . .* "He called me Coop?" I was digging for anything to make me seem less irrational.

"And?" Willa encouraged with a gentle smile.

"And, there is a chance I may have jumped to some conclusions . . ." Pulling away from Clara, I reflopped onto the mattress, stole one of Willa's pillows and buried my head for good measure. I was such an idiot.

I peeked out to see Clara studying my face with her head shaking side to side. I uncovered my ear to hear her. "So, what you're saying is, you took one look at her and your denial jealousy activated your fight-or-flight response and you flighted out of his house like a big ol' weenie?"

"Denial jealousy?" Willa questioned. I could hear the amusement in her voice, and I couldn't blame her. I was totally amusing right now, all red-faced and pantsless, flopped over and hiding in her bed like a wuss.

"I'm not in denial!" I insisted before reentering the pillow fortress I'd built over my head.

"Denial jealousy occurs when you refuse to acknowledge your feelings, which our girl Molly does in regard to almost ninety percent of her life. Hence the use of the word *denial*."

"Oh god," I moaned. "I wrecked everything."

"No, I don't think so." Clara pulled the pillow away from my head. "If this were a normal dating situation with a regular guy, then I would say yeah, you probably did. But this is Garrett and he's known your wacky ass since birth. You've got a lot of slack to work with when it comes to him."

"You think so?"

"I know so," Willa interjected. "Those Monroe boys can tolerate a lot of nutty behavior. Honestly, I think on some level, they like it. Plus, normal is so overdone. It's boring."

"Let it all hang out, I always say," Clara agreed.

"Y'all are so right. And Becky Lee isn't exactly what you'd call normal, as you know. Plus, she is their first example of womanhood!" I was starting to feel a little bit better. The hope that had been dead only moments before started to rekindle in my heart.

"This gives me hope for Sadie's eternal Barrett crush," Clara laughed. "Talk about a whack job."

"Y'all! Oh my gosh! Y'all come down here!" I heard the shout from downstairs, but I couldn't make out what was said.

"Gracie is downstairs." Clara lifted my pillow to inform me. "Let's go." I slipped into Willa's pants and followed them down to the kitchen.

"Sadie has news!" Gracie hollered as soon as she saw us. Sadie stood beside her holding a cardboard cup holder full of Daisy's take-out coffee.

"Hey, y'all. Kitchen," Sadie ordered. We all followed her in a hurry. Her raised eyebrows, wide eyes, and sideways smirk were all dialed to the "big news is a'comin'" setting, and I could use some better news than what I'd got this morning. Or even a good dose of someone else's bad news.

With a grand gesture toward the table, she sat down with the seriousness of a CEO at a board meeting.

Gracie plopped a huge box of doughnuts in the middle of the table and handed me a Daisy's take-out coffee. "Thanks, honey," I said and yanked out a chair to sit.

"I heard some things from Barrett," Sadie started. "As y'all know, Lacy dumped Garrett about a year and a half ago. She left a note on the counter and took off in the dead of night, leaving a sleeping Garrett to discover it in the morning. Her momma said she had to work on herself, but really—"

"We already know this, Sadie," Clara interrupted. "Get on with it."

Gracie was still in her chair, eyes focused with rapt attention on Sadie. "I don't know any of this. Keep goin', Sadie."

Sadie stuck her tongue out at Clara, then addressed Gracie. "The official story is that she wasn't ready for marriage. Cold feet and all that crap.

But my sources have always said that Garrett didn't make enough money. He wasn't climbing up the Monroe & Sons' ladder fast enough and that's the real reason why she dumped him. And despite everyone's encouragement"—her derisive gaze shot to me—"Molly refused to swoop in and make her move. Finally, they were in the same town at the same time, both single, no more Marines, no more Chrises, but noooooo . . ." Her eyes landed on mine with a sympathetic gleam as she patted my hand. "Anyway, Barrett said Lacy found out from her momma that Garrett will be the one taking over after Bill retires."

"He told you all this?" Clara sounded surprised.

Sadie curled up her lip and snorted. "No, he doesn't tell me that kind of stuff! I overheard him talking to Wyatt on his phone in line at Daisy's just now. Wyatt saw Lacy talking to your cousin Samantha at the Piggly Wiggly late last night—Sabrina ate all the pickles and he was on an emergency run—and Lacy was trying to get information from Sam about you, Molly. Asking if you were dating anyone, if you'd talked to Garrett lately, stuff like that—"

My nose wrinkled in confusion. "Why would she ask about me?"

"Stick with me, Molly, okay?"

I nodded. "Okay . . ."

"I know you don't like to think about—" She exchanged a glance with Clara before continuing. "Things . . . but it's time to start thinking and land your man."

"My man?"

"Garrett!" they all shouted.

"Okay, sheesh. But he's not—"

"Shush!" Sadie held up a hand. "He is, and that is only part one. Part two is that obviously she's here to dig for gold. I mean, she's back in town and staying with her cousin Gretchen almost immediately after she finds out Garrett will take over Monroe & Sons? Hello?"

"But she's not a gold digger. She's a nice person which makes me a terrible one for hating her! And everyone already knows he's taking over the business," I argued.

Sadie shrugged. She'd made her mind up about Lacy and I was just along for the ride. "Sure, people know he's the one taking over, but as a rumor or like a '*maybe it will happen, maybe it won't*' kind of thing. But they signed papers at the office on Friday. It's totally official now. And you're not terrible, Molly. Jealousy is not the same as hate, and that's what you've been feeling. Hush."

"Oh, snap!" Gracie smirked.

Sadie lifted her chin with a sly grin. "You're damn right, oh, snap! And Lacy's momma was the clerk who filed all the Monroe & Sons paperwork. At least that's what I heard. It all adds up, doesn't it? Lacy 'found herself' once she found out that Garrett will be rolling in Monroe & Sons money one day and probably living in that big old house in town, and now, suddenly, she's ready to see him again? I don't buy it."

"Garrett is too smart to fall for that," Willa said.

Sadie agreed. "Yeah, he absolutely is. But—" She turned to me. "Don't get mad, Molly. You're going to let her mess up your head again and we are not going to let it happen this time."

I shook my messed-up head and stood up to leave. All of this was too much. It felt like a competition—one that I knew I could not win. "None of y'all have to worry because no one is getting in my head. I'm keeping everyone out, because I can't do this. There's too much to lose. Thank you for the pants, Willa. I'll wash them and bring them back. I love y'all, but I'm going home." I slipped my feet into a pair of flip-flops I found sitting by the door, grabbed my purse and got the heck out of there.

CHAPTER 10

GARRETT

I wanted to hop in my truck and go after her and I resented the fact that I couldn't. The thought of her off somewhere crying and upset made my heart hurt. Lacy needed to leave.

For years I'd felt like part of myself was missing, a nagging little hole in my soul that left me with the feeling that something big was out there waiting for me. Nothing I ever did filled that hole. Not racing cars in high school or enlisting in the Marines. Working for my father didn't fill it and no woman had ever come close—until last night with Molly. Whenever I was with her my only thought was *more*. I wanted more of her time; I wanted it all. As a kid, she was the most fun, even more fun than my brothers. She made me feel like the person I wanted to be.

She had a wild heart and she used to live her life with it right there on her sleeve. By contrast, I had always hovered somewhere in between wild and staid; the pendulum never stopped shifting as I grew up and I liked it like that. I could be steady and safe with bursts of excitement whenever I needed them. After years in the Marines, the pendulum had swung heavily to staid. I had forced it to stay there and I hadn't yet figured out why. Maybe I had become risk averse or maybe I was scared? Maybe I needed a spark to set me off again. Maybe Molly was the spark I needed.

"Garrett! Is she gone yet? I need to talk to you," Lacy called from my living room. Why was she here now, after all this time?

I had built this cabin with my father and brothers, back when I'd needed peace and quiet. I thought I had found it here in this cabin with Lacy. She was easy to be with and we'd had a good time together, but after she left, I found myself not caring she was gone. It was then I knew what we'd had together hadn't been right. Ask anyone and they'll tell you she broke my heart, but when she left, it was a relief. It meant that I hadn't had to end it myself.

Opening the door, I stepped inside to find her fraught with emotion, wringing her hands and pacing back and forth which was more emotion than I had ever seen out of her when we were together. "We need to talk."

"It's been almost two years, Lacy. You left a note and took off in the middle of the night for who-knows-where. I can't imagine what we would have to talk about. Why are you here?"

Her eyes filled with tears. "I—aren't you happy to see me?"

"Sure? I guess. How are you?" I stepped around her toward the kitchen. Stan needed his breakfast. And I just wanted her to leave. He came running when he heard his food hit the bowl. I gave him a pat and stood up. Unfortunately, she stepped in behind me and tried throwing herself at me again and, once more, hands at her waist, I set her back.

"I missed you. I think we should try again. Or maybe we could have one last time together for old times' sake?" Her words burst out in a nervous rush. "We were good for each other, Garrett. Can we try?"

"No, we can't try again, and we weren't good for each other. Stop and think about it and you'll see the truth. We weren't meant to be, and I think you know it. It was why you left, wasn't it? After leaving like you did, I can't understand why you'd even come here."

She studied my face with narrowed eyes. "Is this because of Molly? Are you with her?"

"No, not—"

We both turned as the front door opened and Barrett stepped through. "Hey, y'all." His expression was set to solemn and suspicious. It had been his default ever since his divorce. He had been against my engagement to Lacy and had tried to talk me out of it.

"Barrett, hi. I'm going to go . . ." With a sharp pivot she marched toward the door to leave.

"Wait!" Barrett called to her. "He needs the ring back. It's a family ring." He had also tried to tell me not to give her an heirloom, but I hadn't listened.

She struggled with the ring. "It's stuck!" With a final glance in my direction, she dashed to the door, clearly embarrassed. "I'll see that you get it. Goodbye, Garrett."

"Take care, Lacy," I said, sick with the idea of hurting her feelings even though she was the one who had left me. I hated confrontation and I would never want to cause someone pain.

Barrett looked at me, eyebrows up and shaking his head. "Willa texted Everett about Lacy being here. He's at the shop. Was I in time? Did it get ugly?"

"No, just weird. Confusing. What the hell was she thinking?"

"She was probably thinking she could charm her way right down your pants again. I'm glad you didn't fall for her shit."

"She didn't give me any shit. She never gave me shit, even when we were together. We just weren't right for each other is all."

"You need to be more careful about who you trust, Garrett."

"And maybe you should be less careful, or less pessimistic at least."

"I've earned my attitude," he threw back. "You got home looking to settle down. She found you when she was looking for—" He stopped and turned away.

"What? Say it," I demanded.

"Security, money, someone steady and safe? I don't really know. But it wasn't *you* she wanted; it was whatever she thought she could get out of you. I'm not trying to be harsh and I'm not even judging her because she gave you what you needed, too. You weren't ready to be alone when you got back. People do that shit all the time out of convenience. But then you went and proposed to her when it should have been a fling. Deep down, you knew it. Don't deny it."

"Yeah, well, I didn't want a fling. I guess I thought of it as the next step."

"You want to be like dad," he said in an unreadable tone that put me on the defense.

"Why *wouldn't* I want to be like him?"

He held up his hands. "That wasn't an insult. I wanted that too, but sometimes it doesn't work out, for whatever reason."

I drug a hand through my hair. "I need to find Molly."

"She was at Everett's with Willa and her sisters."

"That's just great. Half of them are nuts." I threw up my arms. "Who knows what they're telling her."

He shot me a look. "They're all nuts. But at least they're upfront about it."

"True. What you see is what you get with them. Why can't everyone be like that?"

"I wish I knew. It would have saved me a lot of trouble in my life. But, enough about me. Your truck is at the Winston Brothers' garage, so you need a ride. Dad is going to let you borrow his until they're done with it. But first, let's go find your girl."

"I'm not so sure she's my girl." The words were a lie, considering the memory of holding her all night and our kiss this morning kept hammering into my brain that she would absolutely end up as my girl, and that maybe she always had been. I couldn't stop picturing the stricken look on her face when she ran out of here. I felt compelled to fix it. To fix her.

Barrett studied my face. When he put his mind to it, he could figure us all out. "She will be," he said with a grin.

CHAPTER 11

MOLLY

*W*henever I was upset there was one thing that never failed to make me feel better, aside from Abbie's hugs, of course. And that one thing was pie. Any flavor—it didn't matter. I always got it from the Donner Bakery instead of Daisy's Nut House because when I needed pie, I required the whole pie, not a slice of pie, and no one questioned buying an entire pie in a bakery the way they did in a diner. Been there, done that and bought the mother-effing pie anyway. I refused to be pie-shamed by anyone.

Eating my feelings was way better than feeling them and I was about to have pie for breakfast, lunch, and dinner. And freaking dessert and snack time too, because I had a lot of feelings right now, dammit. I might even need two pies.

Currently, I was parked at the downtown bakery location contemplating if I was decent enough to go in. I mean, at least I had pants on now. As I flipped open the visor mirror, I cringed at my reflection and slammed it shut. I opened the glove box to grab my oversized sunglasses and a hair clip. One messy bun later, I exited my vehicle, tied the hem of Garrett's at-least-four-sizes-too-big T-shirt into a huge knot at my hip and marched through the parking lot with my stolen flip-flops slapping angrily over the pavement. I was officially on my quest for emergency pie. I may even buy three pies; I was seriously perturbed and might need a midnight snack or maybe second breakfast. Come to think of it, elevensies sounded like a winning idea too. If my life plan now had to include adopting the eating habits of a Hobbit, so be it. I could adapt and buy bigger clothes. I already had this damn T-shirt, right? It was a start.

I would get my pie, go home, eat some pie, send Garrett an "I'm sorry for running off on you" text and go back to avoiding him like I had been subconsciously doing all this time. Things were easier when they remained stuffed into my subconscious. I hated conscious feelings; they were harder to fight. Avoiding him would make everything go back to normal. Except this time the avoiding would be conscious and deliberate, well thought out and surreptitious. I was about to get tactical up in this bitch and no one, especially Garrett, would see it or me coming. Molly Hazel Cooper would become a ghost in this town. Ghosts were dead, and nothing could hurt them. I needed to go back to being dead inside.

Problem solved.

The end.

Except he would be working at the inn for the next few weeks. In and out, all day long, looking sexy with his tool belt, big muscles, and crew of hot guys. I couldn't take a vacation, not with construction going on, and it was too late to cancel the renovation or hire someone else. I wrinkled my nose and shook my head in dismay. *Ugh!*

Why did I ignore my instincts? I knew getting close to Garrett again would be a bad idea and I was correct. Now I had feelings that were probably too big to bury, I was doubting the power of pie, and people were looking at me. I had stepped through the bakery entrance beneath the adorable striped awning and I was garnering stares. Was it because of the gossip going around town about me, Garrett, and the kiss at Genie's bar? Was it my weird attire? The huge round sunglasses indoors? Or the fact that the story going around had become juicer with the arrival of Lacy? I didn't have time to care. I needed pie and solitude. I needed to be alone with my thoughts so I could silence them one by one with each bite of pie I shoveled into my face.

I stopped and stood in line in front of the counter. It smelled wonderful in here, all cinnamon and sugar, coffee and chocolate. Heaven on earth in the form of delicious baked goods. Honestly, it was better than therapy and just as effective. Or maybe it was just easier and more fun to eat my feelings instead of talking about them.

"Hey, Molly." I jumped at the interruption of my thoughts, because that was totally sane. No wonder I was getting so many looks. If my expression matched what was going on in my brain, someone would end up calling 9-1-1 while I was here.

"Oh, hey." It was one of the Tanner twins behind the counter today. They were most notable in the Green Valley gossip circles for having dated and then been dumped by Jethro Winston, who was notable for *a lot*. Among other things, being married to Green Valley's only movie star, Sienna Diaz. I never could tell which Tanner was which, but that didn't matter since both twins had been with him. I checked her name tag; this one was Blaire.

I sighed. It was heavy and dramatic, and it tickled my sinuses until I sneezed.

"Bless you. I guess you'll be needing a pie? More Chris troubles?" She smiled, both with sympathy and empathy—she'd been there. We had both been scorned once or twice over the years. Viva la sisterhood, girl power, and all that crap.

I shoved my sunglasses up to sit on the top of my head and leaned an arm on the counter with three fingers up. "Yes, and obviously, my man trouble will be eternal and devastating. I'll take three pies to go, please, and I'm not particular about which kind, so feel free to surprise me. And a slice of that lemon cream to eat here while you box them up."

Her eyes got big while her smile got sweet with commiseration. "Sure thing. Coffee?"

"Why not? I should live a little, right?" I tapped the counter and grinned at her to hide my discomfiture at the fact that she was on to me and my pie-eating ways.

She slid a cup of coffee across the counter. "I'll get your slice of pie and meet you at the register." I paid, gathered my sweet bounty and looked around for a table. Spying one in the corner, I raced through the maze of tables, chairs, and faceless bakery patrons to snag it, beating a mommy/daddy/baby-in-a-stroller combo on the way. I didn't even feel bad; I needed immediate pie in my face more than they needed this table. They had each other, and what did I have? Nothing but heartbreak and pie. That, plus three older brothers and a Leo who would be all up in Garrett's business if they ever found out my feelings had been hurt. It wouldn't matter whose fault it was, either. I shoved a bite of pie in my mouth with a scowl on my face. *Disgruntled, thy name is Molly.*

As I ate and sipped and waited for my boxed-up pies to go, the bell over the door would occasionally *bing* and someone would come in. I could hear it better than the conversations happening around me. All the voices blended together into one big background word smudge, but that freaking little *bing* popped my head up every time.

After my last bite of pie, the *bing* happened again and Lacy walked through the door. My first instinct was to dive under the table and hide, but that would be neither tactical nor surreptitious since she had spotted me the second she crossed through the doorway. Did she know about me and my pie? Was nothing sacred in this town? I couldn't help but feel like she was looking for me.

"Molly! Hey, girl!" Her smile of greeting was huge and so sweet it had to be faux, as per usual with every interaction we'd ever had. Her wave was exuberant and done with her left hand. She excitedly flashed her ring finger at me with a little "*squee.*" I saw the sparkle on *that* finger, and it made me want to barf up the pie I had just consumed. "It's been so long since I've seen you around town!" she said cheerfully, like she was happy to see me. As if she hadn't just witnessed my mortifying and pantsless escape from Garrett's cabin this morning. As if she didn't have her engagement ring back on her finger and was quite obviously here to taunt me with it. I had never realized she had an inner mean girl. How silly of me. "Can I sit with you?" she sing-songed as she claimed the chair across from me.

"It's a free country," I answered and sipped my coffee. I decided to be breezy. Easy-breezy Molly could handle anything. Easy-breezy Molly was going to be cool and collected until she could go home and dive face-first into a pie, or cuss and break stuff. At this point it could go either way.

"I think it's so great that you and Garrett are friends again. Friends are so important, especially to Garrett. He's so happy to have you back as a friend."

Friend. Friend. Friend.

I was growing to hate that frickin' word. "Yeah, well, we've known each other forever. Bonds like that never die, you know what I mean? It will always be there no matter who comes and goes." I decided to channel some Hill sister sass and throw it back at Lacy. "Funny how he didn't mention you coming back. What a fun surprise."

"Pity you had to dash off like that. We didn't get a chance to chat." Her eyes glittered in the overhead lights as she glared at me until I flinched. I had the feeling she hated me.

"Well, I had places to be and people to see, crap like that." She wasn't the only one who could fake a smile, dammit. I pasted my best fake sparkler on my face and let her have it.

"Molly, your pie is ready!" Blaire called from behind the counter.

"I gotta boogie! Maybe we can do lunch sometime?"

"Oh yeah, sure. Bye now!" She took her phone from her pocket and started furiously texting someone.

I had made it through my encounter with Lacy without violence or tears, which was a win in my book. "Thank you." I took the pies carefully; I was short and busty, and this was a tall stack of pies. It would be tragic if my boobs knocked the pies out of my arms.

She leaned over, arms on the counter. "Watch out for Lacy, Molly. She's full of crap. I would take everything she just told you with a grain of salt."

99

"I've already forgotten the entire conversation. I'm good, or at least I will be. Thanks, Blaire." I hiked my purse up my shoulder and hugged the pie boxes to my chest to leave, sparing one glance behind myself to see Lacy ordering at the counter.

Halfway to my car I felt a hand at my elbow. Spinning around, I found Ruby with her little brother Harry. She reached out to steady my boxes with a smile. "I heard everything," she said. I hadn't even seen them in there. Maybe I should take sneaking-around lessons from her.

"What did you hear?"

"There's no time for games, so I'll cut to the chase. Ever since Sabrina married Wyatt, I've gotten to know the Monroes. They don't do this. They don't spend time with one woman, then give a ring back to another the same morning. Something is up with Lacy."

"How do you know about this morning? Already? How does this keep happening?" If I hadn't been holding boxes of precious pie, I would have thrown my arms out in a frustrated mini-tantrum.

"Gracie told me. Plus, that one nosy waitress from Daisy's Nut House who lives across the street from Everett saw you on the porch this morning in just a T-shirt and told all her friends, one of whom is Mrs. MacIntyre, who called Sabrina to check on you. I don't know about anyone else." I slammed my eyes shut to reboot my easy-breezy-Molly vibe. In this town, someone always knew your business, and apparently, it was my turn to be the spectacle.

"Uncle Garrett is nice. He wouldn't trick you," sweet Harry helpfully added.

"I know he wouldn't trick me. That's not the type of person he is. Thank you, Harry." I didn't think that was the type of person Lacy was, either. Garrett wouldn't have been with her if she had been one hundred percent bitch. Would she try to trick me? I didn't know if I had it in me to fight that kind of battle—or if I even wanted to.

"I'm okay, Ruby. Thank you for watching out for me. I'll see y'all later."

Halfway to my Beetle, I spotted Garrett, waving at me from the passenger side of Barrett's truck. Since I was now only hanging on to my sanity by a thread, I started hauling butt to my VW, shuffling rapidly over the parking lot on my pilfered flip-flops. I couldn't deal with him right now. Plus, I had pies to put in the fridge, dang it.

Even the fact that I was leaving him at the bakery with *her* inside of it didn't stop me. A girl can only take so much. "I'm okay now! I'll text you!" I shouted before I got inside my VW and took off for home, where I would most likely *not* text him. And I was definitely *not* okay. I was such a liar.

CHAPTER 12

GARRETT

"Now what do I do?" I sat back in my seat, dejected.

"Maybe she needs some space." Barrett pulled into a parking spot and shut off the engine. He turned to me with a sympathetic smile and leaned back into his seat.

I stared out the front window, wondering what I should do. "She's had nothing but space from me for years. Maybe she's just not interested."

"She spent the night with you, didn't she?"

"She was scared to drive home in the dark. I was probably wrong for thinking it was her excuse to stay." But that kiss couldn't have been a one-sided thing. Could it? She had been the one to pull me in.

"Don't worry, you'll see her tomorrow morning at the inn. And every weekday plus two Saturdays after that for approximately five weeks as long as nothing arises to complicate things, of course. You have time to figure this out and get a read on her. Dial it back, Garrett, and give her some space." His attention to detail was annoying. He memorized the schedule for each one of our projects and almost always had the right answer for everything.

"How do you know what my dial is set at?" I sniped. I felt annoyed that he seemed to always have it together when I was stuck here feeling a bit lost and hopeless while I wondered what to do.

He shoved my shoulder. "You never were very good at waiting, now were you?"

"I guess not. I'll give her some space. She was crying when she drove off this morning. You know, when we were kids, I always knew why and exactly how she was upset or angry, with me or anything else. I don't feel that way right now." Feeling dismal, I ran my hands into my hair, shoving my palms into my eyes. An epic headache was forming.

He started his truck and backed out. "Y'all ain't kids anymore. Women are a whole different kettle of fish. Hell, I quit understanding Lizzie when she turned thirteen and she's my daughter. We'll stop by Everett's house and talk to the Hill girls before I take you to get Dad's truck. We'll find out how she's doing from them and you can decide what to do from there. Look, she told you she'd text you. And if there's one thing I know for sure about Molly, it's if she's not in the mood to talk and you push her, you'll set her off. Molly isn't one to hide her feelings, or at least she never used to be. Also, don't forget about her temper." I chuckled. Molly's temper was adorable but I could admit it was also kind of scary. It probably wouldn't be a good idea to piss her off at this point, not right after the Lacy thing this morning.

Seeing the merit of his argument, I agreed. Respecting her wishes was the way to go. "You're right. I'll wait for her to text me. Probably. Or I'll wait until morning to call her. And are you saying you'll voluntarily put yourself in the same room with Sadie Hill on your day off?"

"Yeah, and now you owe me a favor, don't you?" he chuckled as he turned off onto Everett's street.

"Don't start an argument with her and it'll be okay."

He chuckled. "I'm not the one who starts them. It—it just kind of happens with her. She gets under my skin sometimes is all."

"Yeah, I bet she's under your skin. Word has it she's been trying to get under *you* for years."

"Nah, I'm no good for her. She'll get over it." My head whipped to his. That was not what I expected to hear.

"That's crazy." Barrett was a good man and a great dad. I couldn't believe he thought of himself that way.

"I'm divorced. I failed at—"

"Well, she's almost divorced too," I shot back.

"Her husband left her. That's not her responsibility."

"Your wife cheated on you. How is that yours?" I countered.

He shot me a "shut up" look. "We're here." He pulled up to the curb of the old Colonial house Everett inherited from our grandfather.

The front door flew open before we even got to the porch. "What are y'all doing here?" Clara yelled. "Where's Molly?"

"We passed her at the Donner Bakery. She said she's okay and she'd text him," Barrett answered, gesturing back at me with his thumb.

"And you believed her?" She let go of the door and stormed off into the house.

"Why wouldn't we believe her?" Barrett answered when I reached the porch behind him. I followed him inside and shut the door, slowly resigning myself to the fact that I was in the oddest situation of my life. I had feelings that were rapidly growing out of control and no idea what to expect.

"She was at the Donner Bakery. She's about to get loaded up with pie and eat her feelings. Maybe it's better if he stays away," we heard Sadie say as we approached the living room. Three of the Hill sisters were sprawled on Everett's sectional couch, *The Transporter* was paused on the television, and takeaway cups and a doughnut box from Daisy's Nut House covered the surface of the coffee table.

"I see you mentally counting us," Willa joked. "Gracie is closing the shop today. Everett will be home any minute."

Sadie scooted to the center of the couch and patted the cushion next to her with an evil-eyed gleam directed in Barrett's direction. He shrugged and sat down. Willa was in the corner of the sectional, sitting with her legs crisscrossed and wrapped up in my papaw Joe's favorite afghan. I smiled at her and sat in the recliner by the window. I looked expectantly at Clara, who rolled her eyes in response. They were like the Graeae, all knowing and scary as hell, sitting in a row on that couch. Except the Hill sisters were hot, blue-eyed blondes instead of old gray witches sharing an eyeball. I shuddered and looked away. Somehow, I knew whatever I said would be wrong.

I shouldn't even be here; I should be checking on Molly. I got up to leave. I sat back down when Everett appeared in the arched living room entrance. "That ex of yours did a number on Molly at the Donner Bakery," he declared before bending over the back of the couch to kiss the top of Willa's head.

"I knew this was coming! I called it the second Molly told us about her skank face showing up at your house this morning." Clara burst out yelling and stood up in a rage. "I'm going to fight her. I haven't smacked down a bitch in years. I'm due for a good brawl."

"No, you're not!" Sadie grabbed her wrist and tugged her back down. "We're adults now. Fighting is kid stuff and you could get arrested. We'll just start posting shit about her on social media—keep it classy, you know. Act like ladies for a change."

"Y'all calm down," Willa, the Hill sister voice of reason, ordered.

"Calm is for wimps!" Clara said this as she cracked her knuckles ominously. "Molly is my best friend and she'd do it for me!"

"No fighting. No posting. Let Garrett handle this," Barrett interjected. "He will talk to Lacy. He'll tell her that it's over, get the ring back, and that will be the end of it."

"God, Barrett. That's the least fun way to handle this," Sadie griped as she side-eyed him.

"It makes the most sense," he countered.

"Making sense is for weenies," Sadie shot back. Barrett shook his head and chuckled under his breath.

"Yeah, here's what's happening," I cut in. "I'll tell her to back off when I get the ring. Problem solved. All I care about right now is Molly."

"You're right. She wouldn't like it if I beat the shit out of Lacy." Clara sighed and flopped back against the cushions.

"She hates drama too," Sadie agreed. "I mean, she's full of drama, but not the bad kind."

"Well, okay. I need to get Dad's truck so I can go home. I'll see Molly in the morning. That's my plan."

"You can take my Bronco," Everett offered.

"Thanks. Keys?" He gestured for me to follow.

"Don't listen to what any of them tell you." He was serious as he pulled the keys off the hook by the fridge. "You know her, and you know how you feel when you're with her, don't you?"

I nodded. "I do. Or I thought I did—"

"You do. Trust your gut, Garrett. And trust *her*. Molly's always been a sweet girl. Remember what Papaw Joe used to say to us whenever he was missing Grandma?"

I grinned. "What?" Everett and our grandfather had had a special bond; they were two of a kind. Loyal almost to a fault and everything you could ever want in a friend or a brother.

"You'll know she's the one when she feels like everything, and everything else becomes just everything else. Don't forget that."

"I won't forget it, Ev. Thanks, man."

"Just talk to her. And be patient—you know how she is."

"I know. Patience isn't my strongest trait." I sighed.

Molly was already starting to feel like everything. Was I ready for that?

I awoke to the sounds of stupid birds chirping and stinking fresh air wafting in through the window. After Jordan got off work and picked up Abbie from my house, I hightailed it over to the tree-house to spend the night. I figured not being home would be a good idea just in case anyone had any big ideas about coming over to check on me. But no, the big old buttface didn't call, text, or stop by. So, who needed him? Not me! I brought a pie with me, so I was fine alone up in this tree-house all by myself, without him.

This wouldn't be the first time I drove a man away and clearly it would not be the last. Chris number two couldn't run far enough away after our third date. Apparently, dramatic outbursts and effusive enthusiasm freaked some guys out. So I got excited about things—was that wrong? Second Chris required a sedate woman with whom he could feel comfortable in a public setting. One who could control herself around dessert carts, for example. I was not that woman. We were still friends; I didn't blame him. I felt it was fair to blame Garrett though, because he knew what he was getting into with me and he should have known better. So, for now it would be just me and my pie. I had to be okay with that.

Speaking of pie, it was time for breakfast. Or rather, first breakfast—the Hobbit diet seemed like an inevitable life choice based on the feelings I'd woken up with. I mean, I was already short and I hated wearing shoes; I was halfway there already.

I rolled over with a groan and yanked the pillows over my head. Hiding sounded better than working. And who was I trying to kid about the pie anyway? It hadn't worked last night. I cried myself to sleep up here like a lovesick chump. I hadn't bawled like that since way back during the first few weeks after my father died. In fact, I couldn't even remember the last time I had a good cry. That couldn't be healthy.

Anticipation and sorrow caused a lump to form in my throat and tears pricked behind my eyelids as I thought of Garrett and Lacy. I'd see him around here today; it would be unavoidable. No matter how much effort I put into hiding, the inn was not big enough for total avoidance. And Lacy had been wearing the ring he had given her: his great-aunt Jade's ring. I used to admire it on her finger when I was a little girl. It was beautiful and unmistakable with its trio of diamonds and ornate band. For the life of me, I couldn't reconcile everything I knew about him, the night we'd spent together, our morning kiss, and that damn ring on her finger.

Something didn't fit.

I sat up and fumbled for my hearing aid on the bedside table. I had to get a move on. Being late for work was terrible when you were the one in charge. And since we were in the middle of the remodel, I had to be there on time.

"Molly!" Startled, I almost fell out of the bed. It was Garrett. He'd made it up the stairs and through the hinged floor door before I had put my hearing aid in. I'd heard nothing. I should rig the treehouse like my house. I had door dingers and alarms all over the place. Landon had hooked me up when he'd remodeled my little carriage house. Being caught unaware was one of my biggest fears and a real concern, considering my hearing. "You up here? I brought you coffee from Daisy's. I sent a text and I tried to call you, uh, a few times." I picked up my phone to check and, sure enough, there were two texts and three missed calls. I grinned to myself as I got up and slipped into my robe.

"Yeah. I'm here. Give me a minute," I called back. My heart raced as I stood up. Memories of the way his lips felt and the way he tasted when I slid my tongue along his consumed my mind and I could hardly think of anything else. That was until the image of Lacy flashing Great-Aunt Jade's ring in my face glimmered into my thoughts and I stomped out to greet him. Why didn't he call me last night? He had known I was upset.

"So, you found me. Here I am. The jig is up, isn't it? How's Lacy?" Knowing was better than not knowing—probably. I headed out to the deck area to sit at the little table. If I developed a feels overload and got sad or mad, I could always push him over the side. He'd survive; it wasn't that high.

He followed me to the table, his gaze steady and sure as he sat across from me. "I didn't invite her into my house yesterday. You do know that, right?"

"Yeah, I guess I know it." I wanted to ask about the ring, but I was afraid of what he would say.

"I know she flashed Great-Aunt Jade's ring at you in the Donner Bakery. She didn't give it back to me when she left. I asked her mom a few times to get it back and she'd always put me off. Eventually, I just called it a loss." My mouth formed an O of surprise as I felt myself shrinking in my seat with embarrassment. "Ruby told Everett what happened at the bakery and he told me. I'm so sorry she did that to you. I—I almost came by last night, but you said you'd text me and I thought you may have needed some space. I hope I did the right thing."

"I don't know what to say. I jumped to conclusions and ran out of your house yesterday with no pants on and prayed for your forest aliens to abduct me. That's crazy, Garrett. You don't need that in your life. It was good you stayed away last night."

"You're wrong, Molly. I do need that in my life. I've smiled more with you over these last few days than in the entire time I've been back in Green Valley. You make me feel alive again."

"Bull crap." I huffed. "No way."

"Stan missed you last night," he said, and his voice was sweet. I knew when I was being cajoled; I wanted to stay mad and therefore protect my heart, but dammit! I never could resist a cute kitty cat.

My eyes snapped to his. "Aww, he did?"

"He sure did. I think you should come over tonight. You left your clothes in my bed."

I reached over the table to cover his mouth. "Shh! Why would you say that? Out loud? Do you want someone to overhear and draw conclusions and tell your mother? For the love of god, Garrett! My brothers are so freaking nosy. Any one of them could be lurking about outside."

He took my hand and kissed my palm with a wink. I sunk down in my chair and stopped thinking. When my brain finally came back online, I snapped. "We shouldn't be doing this. We should just tell everyone the truth. The kiss at Genie's was fake and there's nothing going on between us."

"There's a lot going on between us and you know it. We should absolutely do this. In fact, we should do even more. Don't forget, you won the bet. Dinner at The Front Porch on Saturday night. I already made reservations."

"Ugh! I forgot how bossy you always were. Funny how when you're missing someone, you only remember the good stuff—"

"So, you missed me, then?"

I blew a curl out of my eye with a heavy sigh. "Yeah, fine, I did but—"

"I missed you too."

"But that doesn't mean we should—"

"Look, you eat pie to cope. I bake pie to cope. You're wearing pants now, and lately I want nothing more than to get inside your pants. We both have lips, and obviously we enjoyed the kissing yesterday. I fail to see the problem here. I think this thing could work, cutie."

"Is that it, then?" I demanded.

"Is what it?"

"Cutie? My nickname? Your endearment? Is that our secret code word?"

His chuckle was adorable, but my resistance was still strong. "What's wrong with cutie? It's way better than buttface," he teased.

"What would you rather have me call you? Sexy pants? Hot tamale? Sugar booger? Schmoopaloo? Baa-aabe?" I pointed right in his smug and adorable face. "You don't get to choose the nickname, Garrett, the nickname chooses you!" My voice rose and grew more high-pitched after each endearment. I never could tell how loud I was being. I usually had to judge by the stares I attracted. Lucky for us, no one seemed to be around.

"None of those," he murmured, the quiet, deep pitch of his voice drew my eyes to his mouth to read his lips. "Say my name. When I get you good and crazy, promise to say my name." *Ugh!* How was I supposed to resist that? His hot eyes, sexy smirk, soft luscious beard, and muscles galore were like those super strong magnets that could hold up an anvil. Each one of my feels was pulled right to him, *bam, bam, bam!* Dang it, he wasn't playing fair.

"No flirting allowed!" I shouted and stood up. "I promise nothing!" I waved a hand in front of myself as I yelled. I mean, really? If he couldn't tell by looking at me, I would just have to spell it out. "I'm already good and crazy, Garrett. Don't forget that fact on Saturday night at The Front Porch when I do something bonkers that draws a crowd. I've been known to get very excited by their dessert cart, okay? Some people find that embarrassing."

"I won't forget it. You're completely unforgettable and I never, not even for one second, got you out of my mind. You're the best friend I've ever had, Molly, and I want you in my life any way I can get you."

With that, the winds of fury, sadness, and embarrassment blew right out of my sails. "Garrett . . ." was the only thing I could think to say as I all but collapsed into my chair. But my face must have said everything because he took my hands, linked our fingers together across the table and smiled at me. "Okay, I'll have dinner with you at The Front Porch on Saturday night," I conceded.

His whiskey brown eyes twinkled in the early morning sunlight as he grinned his irresistible, slightly crooked grin at me. "I know you will. Like I said, I already made reservations."

I almost twisted in my seat, blushed, and reacted like a girly girl. Instead, my eyes involuntarily rolled as my snark won out. Sometimes I lost control of my attitude. I simply couldn't help it. "Well, no one likes a know-it-all and I *did* win the bet. I'm ready to taste the sweet flavor of victory in the form of lobster and filet mignon."

"You got it. And I'll make sure the dessert cart rolls by our table once or twice too."

"But this isn't a date. I'm through with dating, Garrett. I'm through with love, and I'm way over men and all of the varieties of crap they always seem to dish my way," I insisted.

"Of course it's not a date. We made a bet and I always pay up." His agreement was swift, and he was unsurprised by my declaration. Like he was familiar with my ways or something.

I narrowed my eyes. "Okay, good. I won't wear my best dress and absolutely no sexy high heels will be on these feet."

"I'll ditch the necktie and I won't use aftershave."

I gasped in alarm. "Oh no! Don't shave your beard off!"

"You like my beard, do you?" His smile was smug.

"I mean, I guess it's alright." I scoffed as I shrugged at the sexy-man arrogance in his expression. "Also, I have to get ready for work. I still need to shower, wash Willa's pants and return her stolen flip-flops. Big plans—you know how it is."

"I do know how it is. And for the record, I *like* how it is." My eyes flew to his and a small smile crossed my face. "So, I'll catch you later, Molly. I'll be around." He got up, flicked two fingers out in a wave and left.

"Later," I whispered to his retreating back. I took a sip of coffee and watched him walk across the lawn.

Maybe I did bottle things up too much. I swallowed a lot of feelings last night along with my pie. I swallowed the truth about Lacy and forced myself to believe it was a lie. Deep down, I knew he didn't give her back that ring; there should have been no question about it. I had been so afraid of how he made me feel that I used the first thing I could find as an excuse to run away from him. Lacy and the ring were just an opportunity for me to escape.

There was no reason for the way I acted yesterday. My tears last night were meaningless because I had no actual cause to cry them. I owed him a real apology.

CHAPTER 14

GARRETT

"*H*ave you talked to her?" Everett asked. We were in his store in town on Main Street, Twenty Sides and Sundry. It was a gamer shop where he sold everything one would need to become fully immersed in the geek lifestyle. Occasionally I watched the shop for him so he could have a day off, saving him from hiring someone else since he rarely needed the extra help. His sister-in-law and sole employee, Gracie, was behind the counter texting on her phone in between helping the customers who were trickling in and out while Everett and I sat at one of the tables near the front window facing the street.

"No, she gets crazy busy at the inn. We haven't had a chance since she agreed to go to dinner with me." It had been a few days; we were both too busy with work. All I had managed was the smile-and-wave combo I used to get out of her before our Genie's breakthrough.

"Oh, to The Front Porch dinner-date thing?" Gracie asked without lifting her head from her phone.

"Yeah. But it's a bet, not a date," I answered. I wasn't willing to be honest with anyone about my feelings. No one needed to know that I planned on doing my best to make sure the bet ended up as our first date.

"Sure, okay." She snickered. Gracie, even though she was only about seventeen, was just like her sisters—a little bit scary. They always knew everything, and I couldn't quite figure out how. "Don't end up like one of her Chrises, Garrett," she warned with a quick glance my way.

"What's that supposed to mean?" I questioned as Everett sat there carving a miniature dragon and chuckling to himself at my expense.

She held up a finger as she finished ringing up a customer. She answered after the patron left the shop. "Don't get dumped, blown off, or let her chase you away. According to Clara, Molly is oblivious to male attention unless it's super obvious. So be obvious, Garrett. That's all I'm saying, because that's all I know. So far, anyway."

I ran a hand into my hair, covering my eyes with my palms against the imminent headache. "How do you know? Why does everyone know everything? This town is ridiculous."

Everett glanced up at me. "There's a Hill sister dinner at my place once a week, man. They poke through all the Green Valley gossip while they eat my spaghetti. You and Molly were the topic the other night."

"Everett makes the best spaghetti. Maybe you should make Molly some spaghetti," Gracie added with a sage nod. I nodded back, because yeah, he did, and maybe I should. "Okay, it's seven. I'm off. See y'all tomorrow."

"Thanks, Gracie. See you at home." Willa had taken Gracie in when she came back to Green Valley, so she was like a little sister to Everett and, by extension, to the rest of us.

"Oh, snap! Look!" I opened my eyes to see her pointing at the window of Stripped, the dance studio across the street, owned by Suzie Samuels.

Everett looked too, then laughed at my expression when I caught an eyeful of Molly hanging upside down on one of the poles set up in the window—Stripped also offered pole fitness classes. "Wow, that looks pretty difficult," he remarked and set his carving down to watch.

"It is," Gracie answered. "It's a basic invert, but not easy to do. I almost fell off last time Suzie tried to teach me. Dang, look at her go! Well, bye, y'all!" She opened the door, flipped the sign to "Closed" and locked the door behind herself.

"Fuuuuuuuuuuck." My stomach dropped and I tugged at the collar of my T-shirt. She was dressed in tiny black shorts that hugged all her curves and a tight black tank with crisscrossed straps. I couldn't look away even though I was certain my eyes had bugged out. Everett was going to give me so much shit for this and I deserved it. Not too long ago, it was him staring out the window at his now-wife Willa on one of those poles with me dishing out the shit.

This was the last thing I needed to see. I was always up at night because of my insomnia, but lately the reason for it was her—the way she looked at me and the secret smile that would cross her sweet face when she thought I didn't see her. I couldn't tear my eyes away. She was not grace-ful; she was powerful as she moved. Strong, like a wild cat, jumping, attacking, moving up and around that pole with fierce purpose. I admired it. It was sexy as hell, but also aggressive and athletic and I had no idea she had that in her—it was one more thing about her to discover and admire.

Then my mother stepped up to the pole next to her and swung around it in a circle. I shoved my chair back and blinked several times before Everett lowered the blinds with an abrupt crash. "We never saw that. That never happened and we won't be scarred for the rest of our lives," he declared.

I slumped in my chair. "Give me some of that denial, man. My eyeballs were in paradise and now I need therapy."

"You and me both. I still can't decide if that place is a blessing or a curse."

"Right now, it's a curse." He laughed and picked up his carving while I contemplated calling Molly.

We both jumped at the knock at the door.

"Yoo-hoo! I saw you through the window! It's your momma!"

"Shit, man, I need a few hours to get that out of my head. Don't let her in," I said under my breath.

"We can't ignore her. She knows we're in here." He laughed and got up to go to the door. She burst in wearing a bright pink track suit with a headband wrapped around her forehead like something out of an old eighties movie. Grabbing Everett's face, she kissed each cheek. Trailing behind her was Molly, wearing the same tiny shorts with a hoodie on top. *Damn.* Seeing her standing there doubled my pulse rate and made me want to stay seated at this table to hide my half-hard cock. It was a testament to how hot Molly was since the image of my mother on that pole was still hovering somewhere around the perimeter of my brain.

"Garrett William, get over here and kiss your mother," she demanded after letting go of Everett's face and stepping back. Her voice took care of the boner—it deflated, and I got up to say hello.

"Hey, Ma." I hugged her and let her manhandle my face before turning to Molly with a grin. "I saw you flying around that pole, Supergirl. Impressive."

Her cheeks heated. "Thanks. I took pole classes with Clara years ago, back when she was in college and still stri—never mind. Anyway, hi . . ."

"Hi," I returned, wishing my mother and Everett would get out of here so I could be alone with her.

My mother's beaming face passed over Molly, then mine. "Oh, you two! So cute together—"

"They're not together," Everett interrupted her. He shot a sympathetic smile to a red-faced Molly.

"That doesn't mean they won't be. Take her out to dinner, Garrett." She was not to be deterred.

"Ma! Give it a rest, please?" If I didn't nip this in the bud, she would never quit, and I did not need a lifetime of her pushing her way into my relationship with Molly. I loved my mother with all my heart, but when I finally got my shot with Molly, I wanted her far, far away from it. Especially since she was so important to Molly and a big part of Molly's hesitation when it came to being with me.

"Oh, fine. I'll quit pushing. I just love you both so much and I want you to be happy. With each other—"

Everett held out his arm. "Mom, I'll walk you to your car. It's time to lock up, I have a pregnant wife at home in need of Christmas cookies, and I'm not sure where to find those in the fall."

She took his arm. "I'll make her some tonight."

He tossed me the keys to the store with a grin. "Don't forget the alarm. Later, Molls."

I caught the keys with a matching grin. "I won't forget." He was now my favorite brother.

"Bye, y'all," Molly added before Everett shut the door. "She's never going to give up, is she? Everett flat-out said we weren't together, and it was like she didn't even hear it."

"Yeah, I'm sorry about her."

She laughed. "Why? You don't control her brain. I'm the one who's sorry. I never really apologized for acting like an idiot about Lacy. For making assumptions about the two of you. I should have known better."

"There's nothing to be sorry for—"

"Listen, I overreact sometimes—or, really, kind of all the time. I even know this about myself and I still do it. Here's your chance, Garrett. Get away while you still can. I won't stop you." She puffed out a breath of air and brushed a bit of non-existent lint from the sleeve of her hoodie.

"Hey, I'm not going anywhere except to Front Porch with you on Saturday night," I reassured her.

"Be sure, Garrett. I . . ." An unexpected hint of vulnerability entered her voice as she drifted off, her thought left incomplete. It raised my protective hackles, because who had hurt her?

121

"I'm sure. Six o'clock, The Front Porch, steak, lobster, you and me. No pressure, casual. It's a done deal."

A slow smile drifted across her face. "I'll meet you there." I had a lot of hope invested in that smile. I'd missed it over the years, so much that seeing it again on a regular basis had become somewhat of a life goal. I never wanted to lose her again.

"Good. I'm looking forward to it, Molly. More than I think you know." I held the door of the shop open so she could exit, then turned my back to set the alarm.

I walked her to her car and stood there as she drove off. I'd given away too much again. I wanted to spend time with her tonight, but I had the feeling that pushing her about it would only push her away, so I let her go instead.

CHAPTER 15

MOLLY

*D*espite what I'd told Garrett the other day at the treehouse, I *was* wearing my best dress. It was one of the few normal ones I owned. Nary a kitty cat or other cute critter was printed upon it. It was a silky black wrap dress that tied at the waist and ended above the knee with a slit up the side. Cut in a low V-neck with spaghetti straps, this was the kind of dress that skimmed over your bad parts and made the good ones look better. I paired it with my highest black pumps— four-inch, pointy-toed, sharp stiletto heel, and sexy as hell. This outfit was magic. It made me look like a long-legged hourglass, when in reality, I was an ample-racked shorty who happened to be packing a fair amount of jiggle in her wiggle.

With a sideways turn, I examined myself in the mirror. I'd gone with full makeup and minimal thinking about why I was making these choices in attire. Berry-stained lips to match my freshly painted nails, black eyeliner with the cat-eyed swoosh at the corner, and pink rosy cheeks. I left my hair down, allowing it to flow in soft waves over my shoulder; the memory of him running his fingers through it at the treehouse had dictated that choice. The way I had dressed and my insistence that this was not a date were in direct conflict with one another. Clearly, I was in the mood to tempt fate—or at least Garrett—tonight. Or maybe I was tempting myself into taking what I wanted by forcing my own hand. I stuffed my pink leather clutch with my going-out necessities and grabbed my pink pashmina in case it got cold. My stomach flipped with nervous anticipation at the thought of seeing him tonight, and I couldn't fight my grin when I imagined his reaction.

I didn't have to imagine it for long, because when I opened the door to leave, he was standing on my porch with a bouquet of pink peonies in his hand. My favorite. How sweet! But also, excuse me, and what the fudge? We were supposed to meet at the restaurant.

"Ahhh! Flowers aren't allowed! Especially my favorites. You, sir, are nothing but trouble," I declared. Shocked at the flowers, shocked that he was here to pick me up, and most of all, shocked at him standing there looking suit-and-tie-sexy and all dressed up just like he wasn't supposed to be. Only one of us was allowed to break the rules and that was meant to be me. My eyes were on a nonstop trip up and down his tall, fine form in his black suit, crisp white shirt and black tie. His gorgeous, dark hair was swept back off his face and his eyes were smiling at me—lazy with heated perusal. He knew he would get me all worked up and he had meant to do it, the turd.

"You look stunning," he said as he took my hand and kissed the back of it.

"Thank you," I huffed. "And you look devastatingly sexy in that stupid suit, dammit. Let me go put these in a vase before we go. Peonies are my favorite and I love them. Why are you so sweet?" I left him chuckling in my doorway while I tossed my bag and wrap to the couch to stomp to the kitchen. I yanked my step ladder out of the pantry with a glare aimed his way—my vases were in the cupboard above my stove and it wouldn't be dignified to just climb onto the counter like I usually did. This dress was too short and my panties were too sexy. All the while, he just followed behind me with an amused expression on his face, like he thought I was cute or something. *Pfft.* I'd show him cute.

"Need a little help?" he asked, stepping behind me and putting a hand at my waist as I climbed up the ladder.

"I got it, thanks. I've had a lifetime of being short. I'm used to it." I snagged the vase and stepped down; my booty slid against his hard chest and down his abs until I was on the floor. He tugged me against him to kiss the top of my head.

Holy, holy, holy, crap, crap, crap.

This felt way too good already.

We needed to get out of my house. There were way too many comfy horizontal surfaces to get into trouble on in here and he was wearing Mollynip, a.k.a. a sexy James Bond suit. He had me shaken *and* stirred, thank you very much. My favorite thing about going out with a handsome man in a suit was taking it off his hot bod later, and Garrett was the hottest man I'd ever seen. Not to mention, the sweetest and nicest.

He took the vase out of my hand with a smile and turned to the faucet to fill it. Silently, I placed the peonies in the water. "Ready to go?" he asked.

Hell yes.

All I could do was nod up at him. Even though I had been the one to win this bet, I had the feeling that he didn't consider it a loss. I ducked my head and grinned as he found my pashmina and held it out for me to slip over my shoulders and I thanked him when he handed me my clutch. He held my hand the whole way out to the Bronco and helped me up into the seat, the freaking gentleman.

We drove through Green Valley, chatting about the inn, our work, Stan and other small-talk stuff that I would absolutely not remember a word of later. Being with him was easy, talking to him was fun, and looking at him as he drove was doing things to my insides that were dangerous to the walls I had built around my heart. Plus, I had to be a total weirdo because watching him drive was making me hot. Was it his large hands holding the wheel? Or maybe the eyeful I was getting of his muscular thighs, or how beautiful his flawless profile looked in the golden early evening light? Or maybe it was just everything about him.

I fidgeted in my seat, becoming acutely aware that I had dressed to tempt. I knew it had worked when he ran a hand down my thigh at a stop sign and said, "You in that dress . . . fucking gorgeous." The grin he shot in my direction held promise. Loads of it.

My nerves started to get the best of me the closer we got to The Front Porch, and by the time he'd pulled into the parking lot, I was kind of a wreck. It was too late to go home and change into something else, and like an idiot, I didn't pack an alternate wardrobe choice in my bag in case I lost my bravado. No matter. I could do this because I was great at denying my feelings—or so I've heard. And in that spirit, I inhaled a huge breath and raised my hot-guy shield.

After one last stalling makeup check in the visor mirror, I got out. I loved this place; it was a grand old Victorian house with a huge wraparound porch for outdoor dining. My dad used to take me here for dinner the day after Valentine's Day every year. He took my mother here on Valentine's Day itself, of course. He wanted me to know how a gentleman was supposed to treat a lady. He'd always said I shouldn't settle for anything less. Gosh, how I missed him. I couldn't help but smile as Garrett offered me his arm just like a gentleman would.

"I can't believe you can walk in those shoes. Careful, cutie." He chuckled as he helped me keep my balance as we made our way to the entrance.

"Well, I can't go very far in them. They were really only made for one thing, you know." Oh crap. I blinked, frustrated with myself. Again, with the not thinking before I said stuff! *Ugh!*

He stopped right before we reached the porch. "Oh, yeah, and what's that?" His sly smirk was knowing as he bent his head down to look at me standing in front of him like a dummy, mouth agape, in my best dress and stupid fuck-me shoes.

I poked him in the stomach. "Your expression says you already know what I'm talking about and you just want to hear me say it out loud," I said as I rolled my eyes and flopped my clutch against his arm.

He dropped a kiss on my forehead with a chuckle. "You don't have to say it. Knowing you're thinking about it is enough." He had to quit kissing me like that—top of the head, forehead, all of it. Every time his lips touched me, I lost more of my will to fight the attraction between us. And probably some IQ points along with it.

He held the door for me, then took my elbow as we followed the hostess to our table. She escorted us to a dark wooden booth in the corner—the most cozy and intimate spot in the entire restaurant, because, obviously, this was so not a date. We weren't each dressed to the nines in our sexiest attire and giving all the hot looks to each other—insert eye roll here.

Why do I do these things to myself? What had possessed me? God, that had to be the eternal question of my whole entire dang life.

Of course he helped me out of my pashmina and made sure I was comfy on my side of the booth before he scooted into his side—just like my dad had taught me to expect and just like Becky Lee and Bill had probably taught him to do. "Thank you," I whispered, then immediately scooched all the way over to the wall and slunk down in the booth, trying to blend into the wood as he ordered a bottle of wine for us to share.

"What is it?" he asked after the hostess left, scanning the restaurant before shaking his head with a laugh. "One of your Chrises is with Jackie, the poor guy."

I shook my head. "Yeah, number two is with Jackie, over by the window. But that's only kind of the problem—look at us!" I hissed. "We're both dressed up and you're acting like the most gentlemanly man in the history of the world. No one will ever believe we aren't on a date. What were we thinking coming here? We should have gone to Knoxville or literally anywhere else."

"Who cares?" he hissed back at me. "I'm about to buy you steak, lobster, and your choice of whatever dessert you want on that cart." He pointed at the cart that had just rolled out to the dining room and, oh my gosh, it looked like they had a few new selections . . . "Relax," he advised.

"Look! They have new stuff, Garrett. Is that a tiny cupcake tower?" It was sad how easy it was to distract me.

His lips twitched before a huge smile split his face. "Yeah, it sure is."

"We'll each need our own. I don't share dessert, Garrett. I don't know if you remember that about me but it's pretty important." I was talking to him, but my eyes were still on the cart.

"How could I forget? I once took an elbow to the ribs when I tried to take a Ding Dong from you back in second grade, even though there were two left."

I turned back to him. "Well, stealing is wrong. You should know better."

"Sharing is caring," he shot back, eyebrows raised in amusement as he grinned at me.

I held up a hand. "Dude, not when it comes to chocolate."

"Point taken. I don't particularly enjoy sharing desserts either, come to think of it."

"Right? Someone always tries to get their spoon into the best part. Eff that," I grumbled.

"Yeah," he agreed. "Sabrina is always taking the cherries off whatever Wyatt orders. And I'm sorry, I need my cherry."

"I would never take your cherry, Garrett." And because I was totally ridiculous, my words came out sounding like a vow.

His smile shifted to the side as his eyes warmed on me. "I respect that about you. You're a good woman, Molly."

"Heck yeah, and you might be the best date I've ever had." *Did I just say that out loud?* He grinned at me so big that I could see his dimples through his beard. "Uh, I mean . . ."

He grabbed my hand across the table, lacing our fingers together. "Shh, don't wreck this moment for me."

"'Kay," I murmured. We both looked up as our waiter arrived to take our order. I dropped his hand like a hot potato and let my eyes drift across the restaurant, grimacing when Jackie waved her phone at me. I was trying so hard not to care what she or anyone else in this town or anywhere else thought about me. Trying to impress people was a waste of time. I didn't want to change myself anyway—what you saw is what you got, and I was okay with that. What I cared about was this getting back to Becky Lee. If she found out how close to a date this evening had been, she would never stop matchmaking. And I would end up letting her down because the more I found myself wanting this match to happen for real, the more I also knew that it never could. The risk was too high, and I had too much to lose.

CHAPTER 16

GARRETT

I tried not to get lost in her tonight but failed spectacularly. She was hilarious and funny. Beautiful and smart. Most of all, she reminded me of our past together as kids while at the same time showing me some of who she had become during the years I'd missed with her. I was burning with the need to kiss her, dying to feel her body next to mine like the other night, and hoping I could make her feel the same way I did by the time we were finished with dinner. She had no idea what she was doing to my heart as she sat across from me, smiling and laughing as we ate.

"So, how's Stan?" she asked. Besides being gorgeous, she was also great company, asking about my day, my life, *me*, like she wanted to get to know me again as much as I wanted to know her. Our conversation flowed, effortless and smooth. It struck me that we weren't that different than we used to be. We liked most of the same things and hated the same things as well. We caught each other shoving the tomatoes in our salads to the side and had a laugh over it.

"He's fine. He left a dead spider on my bath mat this morning. It was disgusting."

"Aw, he loves you, Garrett."

"I like it better when he shows his love by purring or curling up against my chest. Come to think of it, I liked it when you did those things too." She blushed bright red and smiled at me through the fall of her hair.

"Garrett . . ." she whispered. "I liked that too."

I glanced out the window, away from her. I needed a break from her eyes on me. An anchor to hold on to before I became swept away entirely and made a fool of myself. It was way too soon for her to see this side of me. In fact, it was far too soon for me to feel this way at all. I'd never fallen like this before, like I was already halfway gone before I even got to know her again. *Again*—that was the key word. I already loved everything I knew about her from before and each new discovery made my feelings grow exponentially.

Maybe I should give her space. Something told me we needed more time, but there had already been so much lost time between us, and I didn't want to waste a minute more.

I looked back to study her face in the glow of the candlelight as she told me about something cute Abbie had done. Even though I was torn between not wanting to waste time and protecting my heart, I had to be truthful with her. I felt too much to keep it inside. "I want to be honest with you. I'm having some feelings, Molly."

Her eyes shot to the table. "Then I should be honest too," she murmured, looking everywhere but at me. "Feelings scare me, Garrett."

"I know they do, baby. So, here's what's going to happen." She inhaled a deep worried breath, in anticipation of my words. "I'm going to drive you home after dinner. I'll walk you to the door. I won't ask to stay, and I promise I won't ask you to go home with me. We'll say goodnight on your porch, and you can kiss me goodbye if you want to." A relieved giggle escaped her as she smiled at me. I decided to stop rushing, quit worrying, halt my hurrying, and put the brakes on trying to race to the finish line with her, because for now, she was here with me and that was enough.

"That sounds just perfect. Thank you, Garrett." Her smiling eyes shined on mine in the soft light as she squeezed my hand across the table.

Lately my world had been turning for nothing but her. She had become the center of my universe and everything else had faded into the background.

I've spent my whole life getting ahead of myself, like my heart was always a mile ahead of my brain. I'd never met a risk I hadn't wanted to take, and it seemed like Molly would be the biggest risk of all. I should go slow for her sake, but probably for myself too. We had all the time in the world. I knew I shouldn't want her this badly. Not yet.

We finished our steak and lobster, the dessert cart rolled by, and we added mini cupcake towers and smiles to our table. I forced myself to let this unfold at its own pace. Slow, like we both needed. For now.

Molly

I caught my smiling reflection in the passenger window on the way home. Having a smile on my face and hope for the future had never been a big part of my dating life—until tonight. He pulled into my driveway, then darted out of the Bronco to rush around and open my door, helping me down and tucking my pashmina around my shoulders. Garrett had always been good to me. I should have known he would make this night a special one.

He was doing exactly as he said he would do, walking me up to my porch. But I was doing the opposite of everything I had intended to do. The only thing I could think of was how to get him to kiss me goodbye. Flat-out asking for one felt a little desperate.

"Goodnight, cutie," he whispered. I swallowed hard. He looked so gorgeous in the dim glow of the porch light—irresistible. I shivered in the suddenly cool breeze as he took my keys from my hand and opened my door. "It's getting cold. You should go inside."

"Not yet." I tossed my purse to the porch swing behind me and traced his necktie with a fingertip.

His hand came to my face to trace my cheek with his thumb as a small smile unfurled across his face. "You have no idea, Molly. No concept of what you're doing to me right now." His voice was a low growl, but the still silence of the evening allowed me to hear it, and believe me, I felt it everywhere.

"I want—"

"You want a kiss, baby?" I could only nod in response as his face dropped to mine, nudging my forehead with his—softly, sweetly. His beard brushed against my cheek as his mouth moved toward mine and my eyes fluttered closed. The press of his lips was gentle, even tender, but it wasn't enough for me.

Wanting something I couldn't even begin to define, I wrapped my arms around his waist and pressed closer to his big, warm body. I wanted him to absorb me, hold me tighter, never let me go. I was falling into a dream, forgetting myself entirely until I was nothing but a breathless, confused mess of sensation and completely lost in his arms.

His other hand went to the back of my neck, then drifted into my hair as he backed me against the wall next to my door, dipping low to press his hips against me as he deepened our kiss with a touch of his tongue. I couldn't think anymore. I'd forgotten how to breathe. I pulled back with a gasp, but not away from him.

Pressing my cheek against his broad chest, I sighed. The lapel of his jacket was soft against my skin as I stood there with my heart pounding in my ears. He wrapped his arms around me, cradling me against his warmth.

"I've never been kissed like that," I whispered. My ear rested right above his heart and I could hear it beating against me, steady and strong. I had the odd thought that my confession was spoken right to it.

He inhaled deeply before pulling me tighter and darting his tongue out to trace the shell of my ear. "I want to be the one to make you feel things you've never felt before. The only one," he murmured, causing goose bumps to rise over my flesh.

Once I found my voice again, I whispered back. "I hope we can both do that for each other."

He pulled away, his eyes burning into mine as he confided, "You already do." I loved hearing that, so much so that I wanted to throw all my trepidations out the window and invite him inside with me. But before I could, he stepped out of my arms, bent to hand me my clutch from the porch swing and held the door for me to go in. "It's cold out here. Go get warm and I'll see you soon, cutie."

I gazed up at him with big eyes, and for the first time in years, my heart was wide open to him. "Goodnight, Garrett. This was the best night I've had in a very long time."

He took my face in his hands again and bent low to whisper. "For me too, Molly. Get inside before I get too weak to let you go." After one last kiss that seared into my soul, he let me go and stepped off the porch.

He didn't leave until I had gone inside. I knew because I peeped at him through the blinds. He'd waited there for a second, hand to his mouth as he watched my door. Much like the way I stood on the other side watching him until he drove away.

I was restless, not ready for sleep and not ready to let this night end even though he was no longer here to share it with me. I filled a glass with wine, then stepped onto my front porch to sit on the swing and let my mind wander through the memories of tonight.

I turned as a light went on behind me, from Jordan's house. "Molly—" Jordan wasn't that much older than me. But he sure could get bossy sometimes. I was not in the mood for bossy. I was more in the mood for a bubble bath and some alone time. How dumb of me to sit out here when his nosy butt was just right next door.

He plopped next to me on the swing. I shot him a glare as the wine sloshed in my glass. "The idiot is into you, Molly. Try to not break him, okay? That's all I wanted to say."

I set the glass on the porch rail and stood up. "Are you saying he'd have to be an idiot to be into me? Rude, Jordan." I was about to storm off and leave him out here, but he tugged on my arm, so I turned around to listen instead. His look of surprise hurt my heart. Was I really that stubborn?

"No! I'm saying that he's had it bad for you for years. Everyone knows it."

"That's crazy, Jordan. No one knows such a thing, because such a thing isn't true or even possible. And I would never hurt him."

"I know you wouldn't, not on purpose. You're just kind of oblivious to, uh, the way he feels about you, and you always have been. I shouldn't even be saying this. He's my friend, but you're my baby sister. I love both of you, and yeah. Just open your eyes a little bit, okay?"

He looked at me expectantly, waiting for me to yell at him, probably. Or stomp off or any of my other usual reactions to his advice but I just stood there with my mouth slightly agape. I stared at him as memories crashed into my head showing all the reasons why he was probably right about Garrett's feelings and why I was such a dumbass. "I need to sit down," I finally said as I stepped down and sat on the steps. "Why am I like this?"

"You've got a lot on your mind," he answered sagely as he got up from the swing to sit next to me, folding his big body in half to hog most of the space on the top step.

I dropped my head into my hands. "I do not agree. Sometimes I think I have very little in there. Or at least nothing useful."

"That's not true. Your problem is you have too much on your mind. But when it weighs you down, you let it go before you think about it or ask yourself why you want to let it go."

When did he get so wise? I decided to ask him the question that had been nagging me all night. "Do you think I played a mean game with him tonight? By wearing this dress to make him notice me when this is just a bet I won? I kept telling him it wasn't a date. But I don't know if even I believed it." I turned my face to his so I wouldn't miss any of his answer.

"Why couldn't it be a date?" he questioned with a gentle smile on his face.

"Because we agreed that it wasn't. I insisted it wasn't."

"Sometimes things change, Molls. Maybe you didn't start out on a date tonight, but that kiss on your porch changed the ending. And no, I wasn't spying on you. I was doing the dishes and I saw it by accident through the window. You wore the dress for a reason, didn't you? Now pay attention to what comes next. Try that. Just be honest with yourself."

"Okay, I will pay attention. Promise not to say anything to anyone about this conversation. Keep it between us, like it never happened."

"I won't say anything." He chuckled, his brown eyes twinkling as he nudged my shoulder with his. "Your brain is always at least three steps behind your heart, little sister. Let it catch up for a change."

I shot him a glare. "I'd get mad at you for that, but it made too much sense and kind of explains a lot about my entire life."

He grinned at me and stood up. "Abbie is asleep inside, so I can't stay out here too long. Goodnight, Molly. Promise me you'll listen to your heart."

I stood up to go inside. "I will, I promise. But, Jordan?"

"Yeah?" He turned back to listen.

"You listen to yours too." He lifted his chin with a grin, then he went inside, leaving me alone again with thoughts I was afraid to examine too closely. Everything he said about me was correct. I knew it; I just needed to decide what to do about it.

I grabbed my wine and headed inside to get ready for bed.

CHAPTER 17

GARRETT

*T*he rest of the weekend flew by. Then Monday, Tuesday, Wednesday blew past in a hurry and I hadn't had one single moment alone with Molly since our Front Porch experience—I still wasn't sure if I should call it a date. But it wasn't for lack of trying on either of our parts. Every time we got close enough to say hi, someone would come around making demands. My crew and I were busy in the kitchen and she had been swamped with her guests. I had never realized what a pain in the ass people on vacation could be. They had all known before they booked that the kitchen would be under construction and all meals would be catered by The Front Porch. The inn's rates were even discounted, but all I heard from every guest I happened upon was a complaint. The construction work was too loud. Where were the famous scones? Why was dinner not being served in the dining room?

Every time I crossed paths with Molly, she was on the run, off to soothe an upset guest or offer yet another discount to placate a whiner. I would have thrown the whole lot of them out to get some peace and quiet. But not her—Molly was born for this job. She never stopped until even the crankiest jerk-weasel had a smile on their face. Her crazy sense of humor and fun-loving spirit brightened this place and people were drawn to her like moths to a flame.

Watching her at work off and on today was like being smacked in the face by every single thing I'd been missing about her over the years. She had made my childhood fun. Whether it was playing *The Princess Bride* in the treehouse—she was always Inigo and I was usually Fezzik—or playing (fighting over) video games in my parents' basement, or simply sitting around talking about nothing, being with her had always made me feel alive. After her father died, her light dimmed. As a kid, I didn't know how to light her up again, but as a man, I think I can.

We'd made good progress today, my crew had left, and I was in the kitchen space clearing out the mess from the day so I could leave too—or try to find Molly. I hadn't decided yet. I glanced up as Leo appeared in the doorway. "I am beside myself without my big beautiful kitchen and nothing to do." He sighed. "So, I did a little somethin' somethin' for you and Molly. Take pity on me and share it with her. Pretty please?"

I glanced warily at him. The matchmaking tendencies of my friends and family revealed as of late were more than slightly terrifying. "What did you do?"

"Well, I don't quite feel like Cupid, but I did go up to my tiny kitchen upstairs and make y'all a cheese soufflé and spinach salad to have for dinner. All you have to do is invite her. It's cheese—she won't say no."

"Oh, okay." I laughed with relief. "Out of all the crap everyone has been pulling lately, this is almost normal. Thanks, Leo."

"Ooh! Speak of the devil. Molly, come here! Garrett didn't sleep at all last night. Look at those dark circles! He was thinking of taking a sick day tomorrow to sleep. You must work your magic upon him again. I need my new kitchen and he has got to be in tip-top shape to build it for me. I cooked dinner for y'all! It's on the console table in the lobby. Later!" I took back everything I said about him being normal as I watched him haul ass up the stairs.

"I'm fine. You don't have to—"

140

"I had a day, Garrett. Get me out of this place and take me home with you. I want to cuddle Stan and eat massive amounts of cheese. I'll bring a pie for dessert. I have apple crumble and peaches and cream. Choose."

"Uh, apple crumble. I made vanilla bean ice cream last night." As usual, I couldn't sleep last night. My ice cream maker had borne the brunt of it.

"Perfect. I'll meet you at your house." She turned on her heel and marched out of the kitchen. What just happened? I stared at her retreating back as she left, wondering how she could be so distant and *right there* at the same time. She was all over the place. It was exciting and it was terrifying. She scared me in the best way possible.

A burst of adrenaline shot through me as I grabbed the packed cooler of our dinner. "Thanks, Leo!" I shouted up the curved staircase.

I laughed when his head popped around the corner. "I got you, Garrett. Sometimes people need a little push. I lied before. I am totally Cupid and don't y'all forget it. You can save me a dance at your wedding to thank me." His smile was contagious and full of hope. I returned it with my own hopeful grin.

"You got it, man." My smile faded. "I mean if we ever—" I shouldn't agree to that. It was probably bad luck. We hadn't even been on a real, fully acknowledged date yet. So far everything she'd agreed to was "not a date." I'd never in my life had feelings like this. My feelings were strong and only getting stronger as days passed.

"Hush. Leo knows all. I'm never wrong about true love!" He waggled his fingers in a wave and dashed the rest of the way upstairs.

I doubled back to leave through the kitchen so I could lock the side door and set the alarm.

The golden glow of early evening soothed my nerves as I turned onto the highway toward home. I'd never been with someone like Molly before—someone I already knew so well. But I had to rethink my knowledge of her. We had both changed over the years and it was important I recognize that fact or I was doomed to fail with her. I wanted so much more than our friendship back; I wanted everything she had to give.

I parked in front of the garage, saving the lighted post spot for Molly. After running into the cabin to put our dinner away and say hi to Stan, I headed to the garage to dig out the solar spike lights I'd bought when I first moved in. There was probably enough sunlight left to give them a charge. Quickly, I placed them along the edge of the front yard area and along the road so she would have more light to guide her out when she left—if she left. I was hoping she'd just stay here.

Around the back of the cabin, I unlocked the breaker box to turn on the motion lights as well as the perimeter lights I had forgotten to mention to her the other night. The dark had never bothered me. I found it soothing.

Kicking my shoes off and shucking my clothes on the way, I headed to the bathroom for a shower. Halfway through, I heard a knock. "I'm in the shower, come in!" I shouted before I realized that if it were Molly, there was no way she would be able to hear me. After a quick rinse off, I wrapped a towel around my waist and ran to the door, skidding over the wood floor on the way. It was Molly, of course. Who else? "Hey. I tried to hurry but you caught me in the shower."

She just stood there, staring. I had never seen eyeballs move so much. Up and down they roved. Over me, in my towel. I leaned an arm high on the doorframe with a grin. "Molly. Hi there." I didn't plan this. But I should have.

"Uh. Um. Uh, hello, Garrett," she said to my abs.

I flexed them in response, why not? The blush that rose up her neck to cover her cheeks was adorable. *How red could I make her get?*

"Would you like to come in?" I grinned at the top of her head since she had yet to meet my eyes.

"Yeah. Come in. Okay," she said to my chest. I flexed that too because the towel seemed to be working for me and I should probably exploit it. I stepped back and waved her through.

"Thanks, Garrett. Holy crap, I like your towel." Her eyes slammed shut. "Dammit, I mean, I brought my pie to eat. For dessert. The pie." She thrust the box into my chest and wandered off into the living room.

"Where's Stan? Stan! Staa-aan!" she called as she headed to the couch at the rear of the cabin.

"He's probably in my bedroom. You can check if you like." I turned to go in because I needed some clothes. The towel was working for the moment, but it would probably be awkward if I tried to work it for dinnertime too.

"I'm not going in there! With you and that towel? Nuh-uh, nope. I need a drink. Can I get a glass of water? Do you have ice? I'm hot." Her voice was breathy and high, her cheeks were flushed and adorable, and I wanted nothing more than to jump ahead of everything that was proper and kiss the hell out of her. But I didn't. I couldn't. I wanted it all, and I'd never get it if I acted like all the Chrises she used to date and jump all over her. Plus, she had insisted we couldn't date anyway. This wasn't a date—it was another weird un-date thing.

"I'll just go get dressed. Help yourself to whatever you want in the kitchen. I have tea in the fridge, or beer. Whatever you like."

"Thanks," I heard her reply, and judging from where her eyes were before I turned around, I was pretty sure she had just thanked my ass. I flexed that too because I'm no fool.

I donned my clothes in a hurry. She was cuddling Stan on the couch when I found her again in the living room. "Sorry about that, I had drywall dust all over me from work and I felt gross."

"It's okay. Stan and I are just fine. Aren't we, Stannypie?"

"Stannypie?" I scoffed. "He's too tough for a nickname like that. He's a forest cat, he survived wild hogs, raccoons, and who knows what else out there in order to find his way to my deck."

"You rescued him from outside? I had assumed you got him from a shelter or something." She looked Stan in the eye before she addressed him. "Stannasaurus Rex, you're a fluffy little badass, aren't you?" He purred and butted her chin with his head.

I laughed. "You don't choose the nickname, the nickname chooses you, right?" I teased.

"Exactly. I don't make the rules, buttface." The sparkle in her eyes and her wicked grin were adorable. She was full of sass and snark and everything I never knew I needed in my life. "So, what's for dinner? I didn't hear what Leo said before—something about cheese, right?"

"Yeah, cheese souffle and spinach salad. I don't know if it held up through the drive home, though. I haven't opened the cooler."

"If it has cheese, it will be good no matter what. And Leo puts lots of bacon in his spinach salad. Cheese, bacon, and pie are my three favorite foods. If you put cheese and bacon in a pie, I might marry it."

"Huh. He gave me a quiche recipe to try that you might fall in love with. I'll make it for breakfast if you spend the night again. You're invited to stay, you know, if the aliens are acting up when it's time to go . . ."

"Ha ha ha. And I might take you up on it. I am the sleep whisperer, after all. And we can't have you missing work. Leo will be devastated if his kitchen gets delayed."

I stood up. "Let's eat on the deck. I have a surprise that might help you love it back there like I do."

"Unless it's exterior illumination or you tell me Fox Mulder is joining us, then I doubt it," she teased.

I chuckled. "It's option A. I turned the breaker on. Exterior illumination will be served alongside the souffle."

"Be still my heart, Garrett. I love nothing more than outdoor lighting."

"I have candles too. Come on."

"Candles make me swoon. Coming." She set Stan down to follow me to the kitchen. We gathered candles and the food. I snagged a bottle of wine from the rack with a wink. "Wine too? You've got it going on, Garrett Monroe."

"What can I say? I try to make every un-date an unforgettable experience." I slid the door open and placed the candles on the deck railing while she placed the cooler on the table.

"Un-date?" Her giggle was like little bells. "I love that. I'll un-date you anytime."

I could only manage a smile in response. I found myself lost for words as I stood there looking at her. She wore a sunny yellow dress patterned with tiny calico cats; it showcased her bare shoulders dotted with freckles. The low cut of the dress was the best/worst and now I was the one who couldn't put my eyes in the proper place.

"Uh, do you want some music?" I stupidly asked. For a second I forgot about her hearing. If we played music, then we wouldn't be able to talk. But maybe that would be a good thing right now . . .

"Sure, but play something soft so I can still hear you."

"You got it." Great thinking, dumbass—add soft, romantic music to the occasion. She was already impossible to resist. I was about to be trapped on a candlelit deck in the dusky moonlight with a dinner full of cheese and the most beautiful woman I'd ever seen in my life. I would be lucky if I could get through this evening without popping an inappropriate boner. My only consolation was knowing for most of the night the table would hide it. I heaved out a sigh and found a slow playlist on my phone.

"In spite of the horror movie qualities, it is beautiful out here," she said as she set the table. I reached for the cooler bag. The soufflé had fallen but it still looked tasty. "But I still don't understand why you'd want to be out here all by yourself. Come on—you had to have had at least one freak-out, right?" she prodded as she dished up the salad.

"Nah, nothing really scares me anymore. Focus on what you like about it out here. Try to forget about all those *X-Files* episodes that used to scare you. I'll show you my hammock after dinner if you want."

"Hammock? Is that a euphemism?" She laughed as I shook my head no with a grin. "No, thanks, Garrett. Hammocks freak me out. I've never managed to get into one successfully."

145

"Well, then, I double-dog dare you to join me in my hammock after dinner. I promise you'll love it. We'll look at the stars and drink wine. It's one of my favorite things to do when I can't sleep, aside from baking." Great move—mix a kid's double-dog dare with wine. *Real smooth, idiot.*

"You mean, we'll make ourselves drunken bait for whatever is living out there in your murder woods? Seriously?"

I burst out laughing. "I do it all the time. I'm still alive, right?"

"I guess so. And hammocks are almost as intriguing as they are terrifying. So, I accept your dare as long as you don't laugh at me when I fall out of it."

"I won't let you fall. I promise to catch you—always."

"That felt like flirting. People on un-dates don't flirt," she murmured.

I shrugged. "I can't promise not to flirt. It's kind of my thing."

"So I've heard. That twenty-five percent reputation thing, right?"

"My twenty-five percent is down to zero, just so you know."

"Oh yeah?" she breathed.

"Yeah, and I don't see any Chrises around, so how about we only un-date each other."

"Like friends who don't go out with other people, and may or may not have benefits one day?"

"Exactly like that."

"I don't know, Garrett. I might like that idea a little too much."

"I might love that idea a lot," I returned.

Her fork clattered to the table. "Show me your hammock."

With my hand held out, I stood to lead her off the deck to the rear of my yard. Silently she took it and followed, her expression inscrutable in the dimming glow of the sunset. "Here it is." Strung between two tall pines

146

and made of a swath of wide, tan-colored canvas, the hammock was big enough for two people to get real close in. I sat on the edge and once more offered my hand. "I got you."

"I know." She hadn't just given me her hand to hold—I felt that down to my bones. I shifted my hips and threw a leg over the side, giving her a gentle tug of encouragement to follow me. When we were side by side, I let go of her hand to slide my arm around her. She came to rest against my side with her head on my chest just like the night we had spent sleeping together in my bed.

"Look up." I chose this spot for the hammock because there was a clearance in the trees. From right here, if you looked straight up, you could see the sky.

"My goodness, that's beautiful. The treetops look like candles burning in the sky," she murmured. The setting sun made the tops of the trees glow like flames in the dark, but that was not what caught my eye. She did, with her gorgeous Cupid's bow lips I was dying to kiss.

"It's not so bad out here, is it?"

"Not as long as you're here." Her arm tightened around my stomach as she leaned further into my side. My heart raced and I wondered if she could feel it against her cheek. We stayed in contented silence for a few minutes, just holding each other while the sun went down. "Aren't you afraid this will ruin our friendship?" she asked, breaking the silence. "This doesn't feel like an un-date."

"Honestly?" I felt her nod against my chest. "No. Our friendship was ruined when you broke my Wii back in third grade. I haven't felt the same about you since then."

She snorted out a laugh and lightly smacked my side. "Oh my god, Garrett! It's been what? Twenty-math years? It's time to get over it."

"Okay, okay. We're still friends and I'll always be your friend. But yeah, it's a little bit ruined because I kind of want to kiss you right now and I can't stop thinking about it."

147

"That probably isn't a good idea. I mean, we really shouldn't keep kissing each other. It confuses things." She settled back into my side. Still close, but at the same time further away than ever.

"I had a feeling you'd say that." I tried to turn away, but dainty fingers slid along my cheek to turn my face.

Her eyes blazed into mine. "How can we be friends if we kiss? How would that work?"

"I guess the same way it works right now only sometimes there would be kissing involved."

"Maybe we could kiss again. But not right now. Let's wait a bit, to see if we really want to go there."

"Whatever you want, Molly." Her eyes held mine. She didn't turn away, or even blink.

"I don't know what I want. I'm afraid to let myself think about it. I mean, what it would be like to date you for real, not a bet, not an un-date or an accident of timing or whatever. I'm not just afraid to lose you. I'm afraid to lose your mom and dad and your entire family—"

"You'll never lose any of us. No matter what happens between us." If somehow I screwed this up and lost my shot, I'd be the one who was lost. I would never allow her to take responsibility for it. I'd even leave Green Valley if I had to. "We can't be like we were before. We can't go back to that. Yeah, we were best friends when we were kids, but as adults we aren't. We still have to get to know each other again. I feel too much—"

"I know. You're right, and I feel it too, Garrett."

"So, what do we do?" I asked. The question hovered between us for a horrible minute before she finally answered me.

"Let's un-date, like you said before."

"You mean, be like friends with ben—" I didn't want to do that. I wanted more.

Her hand pressed into my chest as she rolled her eyes. "No. Not like that. Let's keep this thing between us. No one needs to know; they already know too much already and it's like this huge pressure that is making me crazy. And you know me, I'm already crazy enough."

"So, you're saying you want us to date but keep it a secret?"

"Yeah, exactly like that but let's call it un-dating. It sounds more fun that way." I didn't like keeping secrets. But at this point, I would take what I could get.

"I can work with that," I agreed.

"Okay, let's look up at the stars and get back to the mood we were in before."

"I don't know if we can just switch moods midstream again, cutie," I teased. In spite of the secret, I was thrilled with the possibility of dating her, of having a real chance to make this work.

"Fine, then, let's talk about *cutie*. How do you feel about darlin' instead? Or sugar?"

"You can't choose the nickname, cutie. The nickname chooses you. Also, Wyatt calls Sabrina darlin' all the time. It's sweet but it's theirs, and there has to be a law against using the same nickname your brother uses written down somewhere."

"Well then, I guess you're in for an as-yet-undetermined period of time dealing with buttface, then, buttface."

I laughed. "I can work with that too. But I reserve the right to throw in a *baby* here and there when the mood strikes."

"Fine. I've always been partial to honey bunny and hotshot, but I've never had adequate motivation to use them."

I held my hand out for her to shake. Her lips quirked sideways as she took my hand. "This is fun. I like being with you, Garrett. I always have."

"I like being with you too. So how was your day, cutie?"

149

CHAPTER 18

MOLLY

"*My* day was hectic and busy and my feet still hurt from running around. And yours?" An exhilarated rush ran through me. I felt like I'd just taken a huge step forward. I hadn't been one hundred percent honest with him yet. Meaning, I hadn't confessed that I wanted to date him for real but was too scared to do it. I figured ninety percent honesty would be good enough until I got braver as long as I stayed honest with myself, like Jordan said.

"Better now that you're here with me. And I have a fix for your feet too. Everett and I just put an old copper claw-foot tub in the bathroom. It'll stay hot for hours. I could run you a bath? My mother brought by a bottle of lavender bath oil from the Hills' farm stand. It hasn't helped me sleep but it feels nice after a hard day."

"That sounds wonderful." I enjoyed picturing him naked in a tub of hot water, so much so that I shivered against him and wondered if it was too soon to ask him to get in there with me.

"Are you cold?" He rubbed his hand up and down my arm to warm me up.

"No, I'm fine. You're like my own personal space heater. And I would love a bath. I only have a shower at my place. I can only take a bath if we have a vacancy at the inn." I felt the rumble of his chuckle in his chest. Being close to him like this was almost too much to handle. His body was hard with muscle and he smelled so good.

"You got it."

"What about you? You worked hard all day. Do you need a bath too?" *What are you doing? Don't invite him into your bubble bath fantasy! It's too soon! RETREAT!*

"I had a shower right before you got here, remember?"

"Of course. How could I forget that towel?" My only problem with the towel had been that it had never fallen off. But it had been low enough to give me a clear view of the gorgeous V that led down to the good stuff. So, I guess the towel and I were on good terms.

"Do you want to watch a movie and eat pie after your bath? Are you staying tonight?" He poked my side to give me a little tickle as he teased, just like he used to do when we were kids. Actually, that's not right; when we were kids, he would hold me down and tickle me until I squirmed. He only quit doing it after I peed my pants and kneed him in the balls by accident. Good times.

"Hmm, I dunno. Like a sleepover? Or an overnight un-date?" I poked him back, but unfortunately, he wasn't ticklish. He was hard as a rock and it made me want to feel up his abs.

"Let's mix it up and see? I would never have expectations of you. I'll let you know that up front, right now." He was earnest. He didn't need to explain himself; I knew him enough to trust him with my body. He would never take advantage of me or pressure me. But it was still great that he said it anyway.

"Thank you, I appreciate that. And I would never have expectations of you either. You can give it up whenever you're ready, hotshot."

He laughed so hard it almost rocked us out of the hammock. But he managed to swoop both arms around me and rock us back to center in a last-second save. "Oh god! Holy shit, Molly. I almost forgot about the crazy stuff that always comes out of your mouth."

A smile flickered across my face at his laughter. "I am unable to censor myself. It is a huge character flaw," I confessed.

"Hell no, it's the best thing about you. What you see is what you get. I love it—always have."

Good thing it was dark because I was blushing something fierce. Sometimes the bravado of my words didn't reflect the way I felt on the inside. In other words, I often wrote checks my butt simply could not cash. "Well, I'm glad to hear that. Some would consider it my worst quality," I joked.

"*Some* are just boring assholes. Fuck 'em." He hugged me close and kissed the top of my head. I hugged him back and held on. I was suddenly emotional because of how good he had made me feel, not physically, but about myself as a person. Okay, not *only* about myself as a person. It felt pretty awesome to be wrapped up in his big arms like this and pressed up against all those muscles. I kind of never wanted to get up. He smelled good from his shower and he felt strong and solid against me. There were ten different kinds of feels coursing through my body right now and each one had its own sub-list of minor feels just waiting to be categorized and sorted into something that made sense. *Ugh!* I was like a periodic table of feelings or a horny science project.

I wasn't even scared of the Yeti or the rodents of unusual size who were probably lurking beyond his little backyard picket fence. Aliens hadn't crossed my mind even once. I felt safe with Garrett. I'd never felt safe like this with any other man before. Not once in my whole, entire dating life. Maybe this un-dating thing had merit; maybe he could be my non-boyfriend next.

"Should we go in?" I asked, finally breaking out of my thoughts.

"I don't want to move. You feel too good in my arms." He propped himself on an elbow to watch my face as he traced a fingertip down my hairline, ghosting across my chin to end up pressed gently against my lower lip. I pressed my lips together in a kiss and his eyes heated, blazing into mine with an intent I wanted to explore.

The starlit halo in the trees and the lights shining from his deck were our only illumination. His brown eyes glowed gold, while his straight nose and the sharply defined angle of his jawline were cast in a fascinating mixture of shadow and light. He was so beautiful; more beautiful than any man I'd ever seen. I reached up to brush the hair back from his face and he turned his lips into my palm to place a kiss there.

He wanted to kiss my mouth; I could tell. His lips had parted, and his gaze was unwavering and hot as he studied my face.

Did he wonder if I would let him?

No longer did I want to avoid his kiss, to avoid temptation. I wanted his mouth on mine, his hands on my skin. Everything about him was perfect, especially the way he made me feel. My heart raced as out of control as my thoughts, while wonderful ripples of desire spread through my body. "Garrett?"

"God, Molly. How I want you . . ." The words were a tortured groan. It was truth mixed with a warning.

My eyes drifted closed as the sensations he caused in my body gradually overwhelmed me. "I want you too," I whispered. "Please—"

His head lowered but stopped before our lips could touch. My eyes flew open. "Are you saying you want me to kiss you?" he asked, breath against my lips, eyes locked to mine.

"Yes. Kiss me, Gar—" His mouth slamming against mine stole my remaining words. Rough at first, a declaration of intent. Then gentle as our lips and tongues swirled together, melty hot like a gooey caramel sundae and just as delicious.

This was everything a kiss should feel like: consuming, powerful, essential. I wanted nothing else because right now I had it all. His hands cupped my face as he pulled out of our kiss, thumbs stroking my cheeks as he held my gaze. "We're moving fast. Do you want me to stop?" he ground out. His jaw clenched as he held himself back, hovering above me as the hammock swayed side to side and the night breeze tickled my skin.

I shook my head. "No stopping." Nudging him to his back, I took over the kiss. His response was immediate and glorious acquiescence. He relaxed beneath me and let me kiss him how I liked, slow and deep, soft and wet. This was finally my chance to take what I had wanted from him ever since I knew what a kiss could be. Somewhere in the back of my mind I had always known my feelings were more than what I had ever been willing to admit.

His hand traced circles up my thigh as he moved over me again, pushing my dress up on the way. With a shift of my hips, I turned to my back and slid my bent knee up his leg as he pulled me up with his hand at my bottom. The undeniable rhythm of his hips as he pressed his hard length between my legs rocked the hammock, teasing what was to come and I could not wait.

"This is where we start. Secret or not, you're mine now," he whisper-growled in my ear, then gently bit the lobe below my hearing aid, leaving no doubt in my mind he wanted his meaning to be clear.

Unfortunately, his urgent kisses, searching fingers, and my enthusiastic response to all of it did not belong in a hammock and I squealed when it suddenly rocked sharply to the side. Valiantly, he tried rocking in the other direction to counterbalance, but it was no use. It had swung too far, and we tumbled to the ground.

Unlike the morning we woke up together, I was right on top of him. There was no big spoon, little spoon, or spoon rest. He was like a solid-wood cutting board underneath me. Both hard as in a sexy, muscular hunk of man and, also, *hard*. The wood analogy was apt, and I was about to freak out because it felt plentiful between my legs. I wanted a heaping serving of what he was cooking up in his jeans and I wanted it real bad. I slid up and down once, rubbing myself against him to try it out. He groaned and grabbed my hips to still them.

"God, Molly, are you okay?" His hands were everywhere, running up and down my body as he checked for injuries. Upon first thought, falling out of a hammock would not seem like a romantic thing to do, but Garrett made it so. "Are you hurt?"

"No, I landed on you. I mean, you aren't soft by any stretch of the imagination, but you're probably much more comfortable than the ground. Are *you* okay?" He chuckled, grabbed my ass, shifted to his knees, then stood up. Holy hotness, he just picked me right up off the ground. I wrapped my legs around his upper abs as he bounced me higher and wrapped an arm beneath my bottom to hold me. I had never liked being short, but right now I could see the smoking hot potential of it.

He grinned as he walked us across the yard, stopping to set me on the deck's wide, flat railing. With a hard press of his body to mine, he wrapped me in his arms and kissed me. "We can stop anytime," he murmured against my lips.

"Or you could take me to bed . . ." He drew back with a smile, shifting my hair over my shoulder and placing a kiss on my nose.

His hands ran down my legs, dusting them off and brushing dirt from the hem of my dress. "Or I could run you that bath?" His head dipped to mine; our foreheads touched, and his sideways grin was full of wicked promises. "I'll wash the forest off your knees for you."

"I might have gotten forest in other places too," I whispered, and pulled him in to steal another kiss.

"Well, I promise to be thorough. It was my fault we fell out." Suddenly, instead of imagining us together, naked and slippery in his bathtub, I flashed back to age five, the two of us in bathing suits, sitting side by side in Becky Lee's tub as she washed mud out of our hair. We had wanted to look like those stupid Troll dolls.

Garrett and I, despite the distance between us at times, had bypassed the "getting to know you" relationship phase and slid straight into the "shared memories, intimacy, and inside jokes" phase. We had history together, lots of it. We had a vibe, a dynamic. Our past threaded through every word we said to each other. But even with all the history between us, this still felt new. He was a good kisser. I didn't know that before. He liked to bake pie and drink wine in his hammock—also new information. I froze as I stared off into the forest, contemplating all I could lose when I screwed this up.

"What's wrong?" It was beginning to freak me out how well he could read me.

"Huh? Nothing," I lied. Sometimes memories were the worst form of torture, even the good ones.

"Bull crap. How can you be so impulsive and scared at the same time? Like your heart is being held back by—what are you afraid of, Molly? What scares you? Tell me, baby, please. Let me in, just a little bit—"

"I can't. I'm not even sure what it is." Another lie.

The heat went out of his eyes, replaced with the warmth of understanding. "Do you trust me?"

I tightened my arms around his neck and pulled him close. "Of course. You know I do." That was the truth.

He pulled away and took my hands, kissing the back of each one as he stepped back. "You trust me because of our history together," he deduced. He was far more insightful in matters of the heart than I had ever been.

"Yeah . . ." My whispered answer was another truth.

"But you're not ready to trust me with this yet." His palm pressed against my chest, above my heart.

"I—"

"You don't have to answer. We're not in the same place right now and it's okay. I can wait."

"I—" *Don't know if I'll ever be ready but I want to be.*

"Shh. I'll run the bath, and while you're in there, I'll make dinner. Let's agree right now that we won't tell Leo we didn't eat his soufflé," he joked, lightening the mood and lightening my heart, which had become heavy and burdened with my stupid fears.

Hands at my waist, he lifted me from the deck rail to set me gently on the ground. He kissed my forehead before bending low to nuzzle my neck. "Let's go inside. Let me take care of you, Molly." His voice was a rumbly whisper against my skin that filled me with both comfort and lust. Garrett put me at ease, he had snuck up on me in ways my ex-Chrises never could. It was disconcerting and awesome, but I couldn't let myself go enough to decide which side to go with, or even how to cope with my feelings.

CHAPTER 19

GARRETT

*A*fter pulling to a stop in Molly's driveway, I started to get out to walk her to her door, but her hand on my arm stopped me. "Let's say goodnight right here," she murmured. "I don't want Jordan or Abbie to see us kiss or anything."

I turned to her with a smirk. "Who says I'm gonna kiss you?"

"Who says I can't kiss you first?" she shot back as she grabbed a handful of my T-shirt at the chest to pull me across the console. Her other hand sank into my hair as she rose to her knees and pressed her mouth to mine.

I fought the urge to pull her into my lap or carry her into her house and show her how good we would be together. I couldn't rush her, no matter how blue my balls would be by the time I got home. Rushing would scare her away, and at this point I wanted her more than I was willing to let her know.

"Thank you for driving me," she pulled back to tell me.

"Well, I didn't want you getting scared on the way to the highway or abducted by aliens."

She gave my shoulder a gentle shove. "Ha ha ha. Google it—it's not a completely irrational fear, you know."

"I know, that's why I'll wait right here until you get inside your house," I teased.

Her eyes got soft. "How are you so sweet, Garrett?" If only she knew what was really in my head.

I shrugged and drew her in for one more kiss before I left. "You make it easy. Goodnight, cutie." Lies. This wasn't easy. Leaving her here was the last thing I wanted to do. I'd gotten a taste of what it was like to hold her all night and I'd been jonesing to do it again.

"'Night. I'll see you tomorrow."

Halfway to her door she looked up at the sky, turned back to me with a ridiculously fake look of fright, then ran the rest of the way to her porch.

She needed me as much as I needed her. She just didn't realize it yet.

———

Sunlight through the slats of my blinds and the weight of Stan sitting on my chest staring at me in a silent demand for breakfast woke me up, along with a raging hard-on. I'd slept off and on all night, feeling restless, frustrated, and horny as hell since every dream I'd had involved the two of us having sex. All kinds of hot naked sweaty sex, running the gamut from sweet to rough and everything in between. I'd never seen her naked, but I'd touched enough of her body last night that I was pretty certain my mental image was accurate. When we fell out of that damn hammock and she'd rubbed herself against my cock—so soft, so hot—I had lost my mind and I still hadn't found all of it. I shooed Stan off my chest.

"You'll get your breakfast after my shower, like usual." He sniffed and darted out of the room.

I glanced down at the tent I had created with my sheet and sighed. I couldn't seem to bring myself to take care of it. I felt guilty because all I could see was her gorgeous body—naked, begging, and willing—and she wasn't mine yet to think of that way.

I slid my hand down my abs to get some relief, then jerked it back like my dick was on fire.

With a huge sigh I stood up to head to the bathroom. A cold shower was in order, and maybe some introspection.

Pulling the curtain back I started the shower—nice and cold. Maybe the frigid water would get my libido in check so I could control myself around her later. Throwing a leg over the edge of the tub, I stepped under the icy spray and shivered as goose bumps rose over my skin.

Fuck introspection.

With a crank of the handle, I decided on a hot shower and some masturbation instead.

Life was too short for guilt that was pointless. Plus, how would anyone know who I jacked off to anyway? I relaxed under the hot prickly spray and let my head drop forward. As the water ran down my shoulders, I imagined it was Molly's fingers with their cute little pink fingernails scratching their way down my back and over my sides to grab my cock and take what I knew we both wanted.

I was so hard it almost hurt to touch. But, after a few seconds, sweet relief blazed up my spine and I leaned my forehead against my hand on the tiled wall of the shower to draw it out, stroking slowly at first, then picking up speed as images of her flicked through my mind like a thumb on a phone screen full of fantasies. Bent over, legs spread, on her knees . . . her back . . . pictures and possibilities burst like fireworks in the sky the closer I got to release. I squeezed hard, thumb sliding over the tip, and let it all go. Her sweet smile and beautiful eyes, her soft supple curves, the feel of her in my arms, and her body beneath mine were all I could see and feel as my chest heaved, and I threw my head back with a silent groan stuck in my throat.

She had wrapped herself in my thoughts and tied me in knots that I didn't know how to undo. I didn't even want to undo them. Something had ignited in me the second my lips touched hers at Genie's. Something primal—an awareness of her that I knew would never leave me alone as

161

long as I lived. If I never got to have her, it would fucking haunt me. I should have kissed her years ago.

I shut the water off and grabbed my towel from the hook.

It was good that I'd taken her home last night. It would have been too hard to sleep next to her with my feelings growing as fast as they were. Kissing her goodbye in the front seat of Everett's Bronco instead of walking her to the porch like I wanted to stung, but I was willing to wait her out. At this point, I feared I would do anything for her, whatever she asked.

I sat at the edge of my bed and let my head drop into my hands as I contemplated how to handle seeing her today at the inn. How in the hell could I keep the way I felt to myself? Secrets were dangerous and my feelings for her had become impossible.

Stan wound his way through my legs, forcing me out of my somber thoughts. I scooped him up, giving him a snuggle as I stood up to feed him and start my day.

I spotted her through the window as I pulled into the still empty parking lot at the inn, looking gorgeous in jeans and that snug baby blue polo that drove me crazy every time I saw her in it. With a wave she approached, and I slammed my eyes shut. Was I doomed to picture her naked every time I saw her? Probably. Damn it, I knew I would imagine it incessantly until I *actually* saw her naked. I should have stuck with the cold shower since I was now associating her with orgasms, and it fucked with my head. All I could think of was her sweet little body straddling mine when we fell out of that damn hammock and how her legs had wrapped around me when I picked her up.

"Hey, Garrett!" she called. Big smile. Sparkling brown eyes. Big secret. We hadn't acknowledged our—well, whatever we were doing before, but now that we were un-dating, now that it was a real secret, I felt awkward

162

and unsure of how to act around her. What had seemed like a good idea at the time, now felt like a lie. I didn't know if I could do it.

"Molly." The hesitation I felt as I greeted her hurt my heart. Her face fell as I turned away to open the back of the Bronco and grab my tool belt and supplies from the back. I inhaled, swallowed deeply, and fought to get these warring thoughts out of my head. I wanted to stake my claim right now, what anyone else thought about it be damned. But at the same time, I wanted to do what she wished and protect her from her fears.

"Is something wrong?" The soft tremor in her voice was unacceptable. I had to fix this.

I set the supplies down and tried to be reassuring. "No. Everything is fine. Why?"

"You don't seem fine to me . . ." Her head tilted as she studied my face. I hadn't been mentally prepared enough to see her. This was, at worst, too much too soon with a catastrophic secret hanging between us. Or, at best, a dream come true, and all I had to do was wait for it.

I sucked in a breath and sucked it up. "I'm sorry, cutie." I grinned. "I didn't sleep well last night."

She grinned and shoved me back until we were behind the Bronco and out of sight since I had fortuitously chosen the deserted corner spot to park in. A tall hedge blocked the view from the rear. "Can I steal a kiss?" she asked with a devilish grin lighting up her face.

I resurfaced from the negativity I had sunk under this morning and pulled her close. "That depends . . ."

"On what?" Her eyes were on my mouth. Her parted lips and half-mast eyes beckoned me, and I forgot what I was going to say. With a hand beneath her jaw, I dropped my head as I raised her face to kiss her. I invaded with my tongue, claiming her in secret, taking what I couldn't take out in the open. She would be mine, even if no one else knew it and that had to be good enough for now. "Oh, god . . ." Her breathy voice against my mouth shot straight to my cock and I grew abruptly hard as her body melted against me.

"Molly, baby. We should stop. We shouldn't do this out here."

Her breath hitched. "I don't want to stop yet. Another minute." I let her pull me close again. I let her slip her sweet tongue in my mouth as she shoved me against the tailgate of the Bronco with her body.

I licked into her mouth as I wound my arm around her waist to get a handful of her ass. She arched her back and flattened her breasts to my chest as I sat on the tailgate and lifted her up to straddle my lap. She ground herself against me as I pulled her down. The only way we could get any closer would be if I slipped inside her.

No, I couldn't have her right now—but I could sure as hell show her how much I wanted to. She moaned into my mouth and slipped her arms around my shoulders as she buried her face in my neck, nuzzling the neckline of my T-shirt aside to lick at my skin and pepper me with biting little kisses. Everywhere we touched burned like a brush fire. We were out of control and wild with lust. We could be caught at any minute and damn if that fact didn't wreck everything I had been moping over before and make this even hotter. Maybe secrets weren't all bad if it led to this kind of sneaking around. "I want you so much. I need to get inside of you," I groaned in her ear as I pressed my hand between her legs to cup her over her jeans.

"God, yes." Her hips swiveled against my palm. With a reckless grin, she reached between us to unsnap her jeans and lower the zipper. "Touch me," she whispered.

In this moment I was powerless to do anything other than what she wanted. Also, holy fucking shit, this was a surprise. I slid my hand down the front of her jeans, gasping when I encountered her soft, wet heat— there was no doubting how much she wanted me now. "Ohhhh," she said as her forehead fell to rest against mine. A dreamy smile drifted across her face and I swear I fell halfway closer to in love with her, not because I had my hand down her pants but because she trusted me enough to give me this moment of pure vulnerability. She let herself get swept away in her feelings, and I knew how hard it was for her to let go like this.

She rose up higher on her knees so I could have better access, shaking her hips with a grin on her face so the jeans would slide down a bit. I scooted us back, further into the Bronco as I slipped two fingers inside and thrust up gently, seeking that spot I knew would drive her wild. "God, god, god . . ." she panted against my mouth as she writhed against my hand.

"You have to hurry," I ordered. Then I bit her lower lip and pressed my thumb against her clit, trying as best I could within the snug fit of her jeans to make her come. I wanted so badly to strip her naked and get a taste of her, but I'd settle for this—she was about to fall apart right here on my lap.

"Garrett . . . I'm gonna—" Her head flew back as she arched over my thighs and pressed down hard against my hand.

"Shh, baby," I breathed while pressing my lips hard against hers and kissing her to keep her quiet. Tiny moans filled my mouth and headed straight down to my cock; it was all I could do not to roar as she collapsed against my chest, then pulled back with a start.

Her eyes met mine, wide and full of alarm. "That was—I didn't plan that. I, uh—" She tucked her face into the side of my neck. "Oh god, I don't know what got into me," she mumbled into my skin. "I mean, aside from your fingers, of course. Oh jeez, I'm making it worse. I'm so sorry. That was totally impulsive—"

"Shh. Baby, you can be impulsive with me anytime you like," I whispered in her ear, ruffling the curls that had escaped her ponytail and taking a nip of her earlobe just so I could make her shiver again.

"I meant, yeah, I get excited easily and I can be impulsive sometimes, but not fingerbanging-in-the-back-of-a-Ford-Bronco impulsive," she confessed. "I've never done something like this before. When I get carried away, it's usually about pie or when I see a cute kitty cat, or something like that. Oh! Or when I'm in line for a new *Avengers* movie. I get very excited about Captain America." Her face crinkled up as she pulled her head back to look at me. "Now that I mention it, you sort of remind me of Chris Evans with the beard, except your hair is a bit darker and—" I placed a fingertip to her lips.

"It's okay. You're fine, so stop trying to change the subject. You're beautiful when you come, and I loved watching it happen. There's no need to feel awkward with me, but there is a need to get you buttoned back up because my crew will be here any minute."

"Holy crap, Garrett. What did we just do?"

"Had a lot of fun in the back of Everett's Bronco?" I suggested with a grin.

Her lips quirked to the side as she rolled her eyes and buried her face in my chest. "I guess I owe you one. I'll let you decide when and where and also *what* to collect." With a hop, she stood up and fastened her jeans. "I gotta boogie. Duty calls."

I would now be thinking of nothing else all day and I was so glad I'd rubbed one out in the shower before I got here. Going home to change clothes didn't fit into my schedule. Sometimes accidental good choices can save the day. "Will do. See you later, cutie."

"Later, buttface!" Her mercurial personality had always been one of the things I loved about her. She could turn on a dime—sweet to sassy, timid to wild. You never knew what you'd get when Molly was in the room. But at the root of everything was her honesty and unfiltered reactions and that made the unpredictability irresistible.

"Molly Hazel Cooper, will you stop calling him a buttface? He's going to quit if you keep picking on him. Then what will we do about the kitchen?" I poked my head out from behind the Bronco to see Landon muss the top of her hair as he mock-scolded her.

"Whatever, Landon." When she made it to the door, she turned to me with big eyes. Yeah, that was a little bit too close for comfort. The next time I got my hand anywhere near the inside of her pants, we would definitely be somewhere private.

"What about lunch, Molly?" I hollered before she could get inside the inn.

"Can't! I'm having lunch with Clara and the girls today!" she shouted back.

"Lunch, huh?" Landon sent a smirk my way as he walked to the dumpster behind the hedge to throw away a bag of trash.

"Yeah, lunch. Friends have lunch together, don't they?"

"Sure, they do. I see that we're sticking with that for now."

"Sticking with what?" This slippery slope of secrets was getting slicker by the second.

"Just be careful, Garrett. I don't want either one of y'all getting hurt. I know how you feel about her. We've always known it. She's special to you. You have a soft spot for her, and you always have."

"Well, yeah. And I'm always careful. But with her—I would never hurt her, Landon. I swear it."

"I know that. I mean *you* need to be careful. You need to be willing to give her a lot of understanding and cut her a lot of slack. I shouldn't be saying this about my own baby sister, but you have to understand if you want to be with her someday. She'll hurt you without meaning to and you're just going to have to forgive her for it when that time comes—"

My blood turned cold in my veins. "I don't understand what you mean."

His eyes gentled as he answered me. "It's impossible to say how it will happen, only that ever since our dad died, big emotions hit her in strange ways sometimes. Just don't give up on her when she can't let them out. You'll know they're there. You'll even see it in her eyes, but she'll deny it to your face and run away."

I smiled at him, relieved. "I think I get it." I already knew this about her. She was skittish, but that didn't scare me.

CHAPTER 20

MOLLY

On shaky legs, I rushed through the empty kitchen to the downstairs guest bathroom to clean up and recover from my erotic escapade in the back of Everett's Bronco. I slammed the door and checked myself in the mirror. I couldn't wipe off the satisfied smile. I pulled a sad frown, then stuck my tongue out at myself but the residual smiley O-face would not go away. I sighed and splashed water on my face to cool the hot flush of my cheeks. Garrett had strong hands and he knew how to use them. I'd gone off like a rocket in under three minutes. Unless I was using one of my Lelos, that was unprecedented for me. It was also kind of embarrassing, kind of like premature ejaculation. Was there a female equivalency? Whatever—I'd been in a long dry spell. My last Chris and I broke up almost a year ago. Apparently, wearing a dress patterned with cats and ordering two desserts was unacceptable when meeting a man's parents. I still didn't get why it was such a big deal; I paid for them myself. Alas, it had been me and my trusty toys ever since. With a sigh, I left the bathroom to get to work. I'd rather spend the day exploring the various and sundry ways Garrett could put his big hands to use, but a girl's gotta make a living.

The morning sped by. I'd left the inn's day-to-day in Landon's capable hands and now I was sporting my favorite merkitty—that would be a mermaid cat—sundress and on my way to the Piggly Wiggly to try and scrounge up a last-minute baby shower gift for Sabrina Monroe, since my lunch with Clara and the girls was really a surprise lunch hour baby shower for Sabrina. She had insisted she didn't want a party, but now that she had missed her due date and was ready to pop like one of those little red buttons on a Thanksgiving Day turkey, Willa and Becky Lee had decided to throw her a quick little party anyway. If you thought about it, it was really just lunch with presents and cake. She should be okay with the attention since there wouldn't be any baby shower games or hoopla. I wished I could end every lunch hour with a present. How much better would working be if you got a gift every day?

I'd become pretty good friends with Sabrina since Willa had come back to town and brought her into the Hill sister circle of trust—which previously had only included me and Leo as non-sisters. She was adorable, sweet and shy, and an assistant librarian at the Green Valley Public Library. She was one of those rare people who, despite being my opposite in every conceivable way that existed, did not judge me for being such a loudmouth weirdo. I would punch anyone in the face who dared to speak a negative word about Sabrina Monroe, and that was a fact.

Supposedly there was an eggplant parmesan recipe that would put a woman into labor—Sadie swore it was the thing that finally worked when she had her twins. We'd be eating that for lunch, followed by a nice drive in Sadie's minivan over the brand-new speed bumps in the Piggly Wiggly parking lot. Rumor had it the speed bumps had been installed on account of those Winston boys' propensity for semi-regular peel outs. I'm just glad it wasn't because of me. I'd been known to speed out of there too, on occasion. Green Valley was a small town and ex-Chrises had to buy groceries just like we all did. Well, except for Chris number one, whose mother still shopped for him—don't even get me started on that.

I parked, hopped out, and found myself a buggy. Even the Piggly Wiggly had a baby section, so I was sure I could find something awesome. Sadie was supposed to meet me here so we could pick out the present together. After taking a cruise through the gift wrap aisle for a big bag and a bow, I headed to the baby section. I was running out of time; Sadie was running late, and I figured diapers and wipes would work. Not so fun, but always necessary. I tossed in a variety of sizes, some wipes, and a few cute little bottles, then turned and crashed carts with Jackie. Lacy was right behind her, chugging along with her purse hooked over her elbow—no buggy. *Freaking great.*

"Expecting already? Didn't you and Garrett *just* start dating? Easy doesn't even begin to describe you. You do know that condoms are at the end of this very aisle, don't you?" Jackie had that mean girl look on her face—she was ready to take me for a ride in her bitchmobile. Nothing I had ever said to her would sink into her tiny little brain and stop her, so I rarely bothered trying to defend myself to her anymore.

I looked past her to Lacy who, upon closer inspection, was still wearing Great-Aunt Jade's ring on her finger. *What the hell?*

I was stuck in what was surely about to become a rumor cyclone. A perfect storm of bullshit that all revolved around poor, unsuspecting Garrett.

I decided to continue ignoring Jackie. She wasn't worth my time.

"You need to give that ring back to Garrett, Lacy," I declared, because why not? I had the upper hand now, *literally*. I'd just had it in the back of a Ford Bronco and now I didn't have to be jealous of stupid Lacy anymore.

Jackie piped in, as always *not* minding her own business and keeping her nose firmly planted in mine. "Oh yeah, Lacy. Molly's gonna need that ring since she's in the family way. Such a *slut.*" She tossed her hair behind her shoulder and smirked at me like she just scored a point, as if I were still playing her stupid childhood games.

"Hey, y'all!" Sadie swanned into the aisle, tossed her purse into my buggy and faced Jackie with a huge smile—the scary one that reminded me of Harley Quinn that said she was about to *go off.* "Did I just hear my old high school nickname? Oh, how I miss the sound of the word *slut* echoing down the hallways of Green Valley High . . . I missed you too,

Jackie Oh No!" Yeesh, she dropped Jackie's hated nickname, which meant it was *on*. Unless Jackie ran away, like she always did from Sadie.

"I'm not talking to you, Sadie," Jackie huffed. "In fact, I have to go." Jackie was afraid of Sadie. Honestly, a lot of girls we went to high school with were afraid of Sadie. She didn't mince words and she could—and did—kick anyone's ass who crossed her back then, even dudes.

"What exactly is your problem with me, Jackie?" I hollered to her retreating back. She ignored me, as usual. Calling her out only made her retreat. I shouldn't have bothered. I watched her shove her buggy down the aisle while simultaneously texting on her phone. I should lay odds on how fast the news of my nonpregnancy spread across town and make a few bucks.

"She is such a bitch," Lacy complained.

My head whipped to Lacy because *what the heck?*

Sadie's head jerked back on her neck. "Uh . . . I literally don't know what to say right now," she huffed. "That was the pot calling the pot a pot. My work here was done for me and honestly, I feel a bit lost."

Lacy stuck her hand with the ring on it in Sadie's face. "The damn ring is stuck, okay?" she griped. "I've tried everything to get it off, well, every-thing except for lube. I'm here for the KY. I just called and they finally restocked it today. Hang on a sec, because if it works, you can take this freaking cursed-ass ring back to Garrett. The ding-dong dummy jeweler in this Podunk, nosy-as-hell town wouldn't cut it off for me. He recog-nized the stupid thing and didn't want to ruin it. Do you believe that shit?"

"What the hell is going on?" Sadie's face scrunched up in confusion. "Why are you being so nice, Lacy? Don't make me apologize for calling you a bitch, or a pot, or whatever. Jackie wouldn't let me blow my rage wad and I'm about to get blue balled with suppressed anger right here in the gosh dang Piggly Wiggly."

"Look, y'all, I just got a divorce and I was feeling lonely. Garrett is nice, hot, and extremely skilled, if you know what I mean." We stared at her blankly, both of us too shocked to snark. "I wanted to get laid—duh! So I took my shot. I wore the ring to like, blast him to the past or something. It failed, obvs. Right, Molly?" I just stared at her since my gast had been flabbered. "Molly was there," she addressed Sadie. "It was a huge embarrassing thing. I didn't get to blow my wad either, Sadie." She snickered at her own joke.

"Uh, okay. I feel that deeply," Sadie commiserated. She too, was divorced and apparently horny.

Lacy smiled at me and spoke as if we were friends and I hadn't secretly hated her guts for years. "Molly, for future reference, Garrett is an absolute sucker for tears. Hence the waterworks at his cabin." My jaw dropped a little bit. "Don't try and tell me you wouldn't do the same damn thing. You know he's worth it, just for the dick alone. I won't even get into what else he can do." She stuck her tongue out and wiggled it around. Sadie and I locked wide eyes before turning back to Lacy. "God, y'all, I have to pause and reflect on that memory." She held a hand up and took a second before continuing. "Okay," she said with a shiver. "Now that stupid cow Jackie has been spreading it all over town that I'm after his future Monroe & Sons' money. I don't want, nor do I need his money," she scoffed. "I got a killer settlement in my divorce. I'm never getting married again. Oh, and yeah, I was still pissed off and horny when I saw you at the bakery, Molly. I'm so sorry about all that. It was super rude of me. But I have since banged one of your ex-Chrises, so now I'm all good down below and my mood is way improved. Green Valley is a small world after all, ain't it?"

"Holy shit," was all I could think to say.

"That about covers it," Sadie agreed. "Give me your hand." She took Lacy's hand, squirted on a huge dollop of KY and gave the ring a wiggle. It slipped right off. I guess KY could help get anything off. Huh.

"Yes! Thanks, Sadie! I've got to motor. Y'all, can you buy the KY? I'll do a round at Genie's next time I see you there. I'm in town for good now. Toodles!" She waved and hightailed it out of the store.

I watched Lacy leave, too shocked to say goodbye, then turned to Sadie. "I—I mean, what the frick was that? I almost feel guilty for hating her all that time."

Sadie shook her head side to side as she stared me down. "Never feel guilty for that. She deserved it. Garrett is your property, and everyone knows it."

"You're crazy as hell, Sadie."

"I know. Sometimes I wonder if I'm still in a weird place in my life or just a natural-born pain in the ass." She shrugged. "So, what are we getting Sabrina?" She nosed around in the cart, then tossed in some diaper cream and a few bibs. "That oughta do it. Let's go pay. Oh! Wait." She took my hand and slipped Great-Aunt Jade's ring on *the* finger. It was a perfect fit, just like Cinderella and the shoe.

"You do know that I'm waiting for Clara before I ask you about the dick skills, right? Don't think you're getting away with anything."

I nudged her shoulder with mine. "Yeah, I know." I was not one to kiss and tell and she knew it, but there was no point in arguing now since I had no knowledge of the dick skills—not yet, anyway. I could write a freakin' sonnet dedicated to his finger skills though, but I'd be keeping that happy bit of information to myself.

"Let's get out of here." She took charge of the buggy and headed to the front.

Once more I had found myself in Becky Lee's dining room, but this time the table was decorated with white lace and pink roses instead of grilled meat and pickles. Pink streamers, flowered bunting, and balloons festooned every windowsill, archway, and chair—because obviously Sabrina and Wyatt were having a girl. But the piece de resistance, from the Donner Bakery, created and delivered by Green Valley's own Banana Cake Queen herself, Jennifer Winston, was the most gorgeous pink and white confection I'd ever seen. "Welcome, Cora Louise" was piped across the center. Everything was stunning—it made me wish I actually was pregnant so I could have a party like this of my own.

"This is gorgeous, Becky Lee! You outdid yourself." I hugged her neck.

She hugged me back, then pulled away to pat my stomach. "Oh, honey! I'm all aflutter today. I can hardly even think straight. If I were any happier, I'd drop my harp plumb through a cloud! Being able to throw this party for Sabrina and the baby is all such a blessing. Then I got a call from Jackie. She told me your wonderful baby news and accidentally let it spill that you'd been secretly seeing Garrett for months! I'm not even mad that y'all didn't tell me! And I'm thrilled that you and Jackie finally made up. She was so happy for you and Garrett!" She took my hands in hers to give me a squeeze, her eyes got big when she looked at my hand.

Oh snap, the ring!

"Oh! My god! And you're wearing Auntie Jade's ring too! Ahh! I don't have time to properly congratulate you now! Another party is coming up and this one has your and Garrett's names on it!" She grinned huge before hurrying off to the kitchen.

Oh shit oh shit oh shit . . .

I did not have enough IQ points to process this. Why was I such a dumbass?

How long before all of this got back to Garrett?

Damn that Jackie. I should just forget that she's Leo's twin and beat the crap out of her.

I wandered out to the back porch to plop on the porch swing and sort through the sudden burst of mental images of me and Garrett *making* a baby that had just popped into my head. What would that be like?

Get out of my brain, sexy distractions!

I shivered at the awesome prospect of the baby-making but shuddered at the thought of having a real baby. What if something happened to me? Or to Garrett? Whenever someone was at the center of your world, they ended up going away somehow. Nothing ever lasted and I could never do that to a kid.

My thoughts shifted to how to explain to him what was going on when I didn't even understand how all of it had happened myself.

"Molly! Girl . . ." Clara ran up the walkway from the side fence, eyes big, hands waving, and her blond hair flying behind her. "Where's Sadie? We only have like, ten minutes before Willa gets here with Sabrina and we have got to talk."

"I do not even know where to begin right now, Clara—"

Sadie darted out the back door, sliding it shut behind herself. "I'm here! Do not start without me! I had to tinkle—"

Clara rolled her eyes. "Ew."

"Everybody pees, Clara."

"*Blech!* Back to Molly." Clara sat across from me on a deck chair while Sadie joined me on the swing. "I just got a text from freaking Lacy of all people, warning me that Jackie is on a tear. I do not know how she got my damn number."

It occurred to me that maybe, hopefully this was all just a dream. I closed my eyes real tight, then opened them to see Clara and Sadie laughing at me.

"That never works. Haven't you learned that by now, Molly?" Sadie laughed and shoved my shoulder.

"It was worth a try," I protested. "So, we don't hate Lacy anymore. I guess that's the first bit of news—"

The door swung open and Garrett poked his head out, his face an unreadable mask. "We have to talk," he said.

"Oh shit," Sadie mouthed, her back to Garrett. She made big eyes at the ring on my hand.

Oh shit. I gave the ring a tug, but the dang thing was stuck.

176

CHAPTER 21

GARRETT

I tugged her into the downstairs powder room and locked the door behind us. The locked door, the privacy, her in that ridiculously adorable dress—I forgot what it was I brought her in here for and kissed her. I'd been thinking of her sweet mouth, sexy hourglass curves, and everything wet and delicious that I didn't get a taste of since this morning. I'd been hard off and on for hours, work was impossible, and I still had to go back after lunch and finish the day. I couldn't concentrate for shit and I needed her. I wanted nothing more than to take her home, work her up to naked and wild, then slide into her sweet little body until she was screaming my name.

She moved to put her arms around me, but I grabbed her wrists and held them behind her back as I arched her over the pedestal sink and deepened the kiss, slipping my tongue in her mouth with a growl. If she got her hands on me, I'd lose it right here. She moaned and opened her mouth beneath mine, meeting my tongue with hers. Yeah, I held her wrists, but that didn't stop her from rubbing her body against mine and touching me every which way she could without the use of her hands.

Loosening my grip on her wrists, I slowed the kiss. I pulled back to glide my lips across hers, nipping at her full lower lip, then soothing it with my tongue. "Gosh, you're a good kisser, Garrett," she murmured against my mouth.

"You drive me crazy, Molly. I want you so bad." My chest heaved with the effort it took to pull myself away from her. But I did it, stepping back to lean against the wall across the room.

She adjusted her dress and rubbed a fingertip over her lips. "I want you too. Why can't we just leave? We could go to your cabin and bang the rest of the day away. It's so deserted up there, I won't have to worry about how loud I get without my hearing aid in."

A startled laugh burst out of me. "Good god, Molly, don't tempt me. We can't leave because we're here for Sabrina and Wyatt and we're not jerks, right?"

She laughed. "Right. What are you doing here anyway? This is a baby shower—I think it's against the law for guys to attend."

"Mom called me right after I saw you this morning. She invited me and my brothers. She said it would be a family thing. Dad will be here too, but all the kids are in school."

"Oh, okay. So, you're saying I get to eat eggplant parm and look at your sexy self the entire time? Sounds like foreplay to me."

"You're coming to my place tonight," I declared. She was better at sexy banter than I was. All I could seem to manage were caveman demands.

"Count on it, hotshot." Her grin shifted to the side as she winked at me.

My jaw dropped for a second before I pulled it together enough to respond. "Alright, then, let's get this shit out of the way. Birth control? Condoms? What are we doing?"

She grinned at me, and it was then that I knew I would never be able to match her. She was the best kind of trouble. "Yes and no and we can start with missionary, then I could get on top? Or my personal favorite, the lotus flower. I'm very bendy." Her eyes sparkled with amusement as she waited for my reaction.

"I—holy shit, Molly. Just . . . good lord, are you trying to kill me right now?" I huffed out a laugh. Why had I waited so long to pursue her?

Her laughter was full of naughty promise as she reached for my belt buckle to pull me close to her hot little body, tipping her head way back with her chin against my chest to look up at my face. "I knew what you meant, Garrett. Disease-free, on the pill, we can do what we want, when we want with no worries. Even right here . . ."

I gulped because we *would not* be doing it right here in my mother's powder room no matter how hard she had made my dick get. "Uh, I'm also disease-free, Lacy was the last and that was well over a year ago."

"Chris number four was my last and same. Also, I was teasing about right here. I can't do it with your mother in the house. That's grody." She released my belt and took a step back.

A laugh escaped along with a relieved puff of air. "Thank god. I would never be able to say no to you. And honestly, I'm so hard right now and you're so fucking hot in that dress. Combine that with the fact that we're alone in here, it makes me almost forget she's here. *Almost.*"

"Before we go back out, why did you bring me in here if you weren't gonna bend me over the sink and give me the goods?"

"I was going to ask about the ring and make sure you were okay. Lacy called. She also told me about what Jackie said to you."

She held her hand up between us. "This ring? Like a dumbass, I forgot to remove it after Sadie got it off Lacy's finger. Jackie called your mom. Basically, your mother thinks we've been secretly seeing each other for months, I'm pregnant, and hello—Great-Aunt Jade's ring on my finger which, ironically, is now stuck. Could this be any worse?"

"Not really." I sighed and pulled her into my chest for a hug. "I'll talk to her after the baby shower and clear everything up."

"I hate the thought of upsetting her . . ."

Then forget about this un-dating bullshit and let me tell her the real truth . . .

"She'll be okay. Don't worry." I bent to drop a kiss to her forehead. Maybe I should just keep procrastinating, not talk to my mother, and make her fall in love with me instead, thereby rendering the talk with my mother moot. "We'd better get out there. But I'm gonna need a minute to get control of myself. You'll have to go first. I'm still hard and it will never go away with you in here."

Her eyes drifted down my body as her hand reached for the doorknob. "See you out there, Garrett," she whispered, then walked out the door. *Mine.* She acted like she wanted to be, but the secrets cast a pall over our time together no matter how hard I tried to ignore them.

We were halfway through eggplant parmesan when a shocked scream pierced the quiet. "Fuck! Wyatt! Oh my god. This hurts!" Sabrina shoved her pink-bunting-covered chair back and clutched her stomach. Every head in the dining room whipped to her, for several reasons. Sabrina was the quietest, sweetest, most gentle and shy person any of us had ever met and she had just cursed loudly and doubled over in her chair. And as the person sitting next to her, I could see she was definitely in labor. Her stomach jerked around through her shirt and *holy crap that had to hurt.*

Wyatt, seated on her other side, didn't miss a beat. "I got you, darlin'." He kissed the top of her head, then lifted her face to his. "I promise, I won't leave your side, not once."

While nodding her head, she took a huge breath and grabbed his cheeks. "I know you'll stay with me. I know that. But—I didn't know it would hurt this bad, Wyatt." She let go of his face to grip the arms of her chair. She let out a loud moan before turning away from him to yell at the room, "Why didn't anyone tell me it would hurt this fucking baa-aa-ad?" She started to pant. I slid my chair back and stood up to push the table away from her so I could help Wyatt get her out to his truck. There was no way she could walk on her own; she could barely even sit. "I don't want to do this anymore. Let's go home, Wyatt. Can we just go home, please? I want to go home."

"You're going to be just fine, I promise you. We're going to the hospital right now. Garrett?" Wyatt looked at me.

"Yup, whatever you need, man," I answered. I mean, I was right there to see her stomach go crazy, slow down, then start moving again like my new niece was having a dance party in there. I was ready to do whatever I could to help.

"I'll get your truck pulled around for you," Barrett offered.

Sadie started digging through her purse. "No, take my minivan. It's lower to the ground, parked right there on the curb, and Wyatt can sit in the back with her. Becky Lee and Willa will fit too."

"Good thinking. Thank you, Sadie," my mother said. "I'll call when she's ready for visitors." My mother and Willa had been going with Sabrina to every doctor's appointment that Wyatt couldn't make because of his work schedule, and would be in the delivery room along with Wyatt and Sabrina.

"Sabrina," Sadie said as she tossed Barrett her keys. "If you change your mind and decide to take all the drugs they'll give you, don't feel guilty. I took everything, I pushed two out in one go, and I barely felt a thing. Also, if you don't want to take the drugs, don't feel bad about that either. You do you, no matter what anyone else has to say. Just get that baby out."

Sabrina nodded. "Okay, I got this. I can do this. I'm ready." Wyatt and I each took an arm to help her stand, slipping our arms around her waist and back once she was up.

Willa and my mother dashed out ahead of us with Barrett to the van.

Barrett pulled me aside after we got Sabrina settled with Wyatt in the back and Mom and Willa in the middle. "You drive them. Sabrina is seriously reminding me of when Lizzie was born—in the car on the side of the road. She's racing to the finish line and the hospital is a good half hour away. You got first aid certification in the Marines, yeah?"

"Yeah, I did."

"Wyatt is certified too. She'll be in better hands with y'all two than me. I'll be along later."

"Shit, man. I need—does Sadie have a first aid kit or anything in here?"

"Yeah, she has two wild little boys. It's extensive and under the passenger seat. And here." He thrust a gift bag into my hands. "I grabbed this on the way out. It's full of baby blankets. Just don't use the one on top—I knitted that myself. Took me a month."

"Got it. Later." I slapped his shoulder, took the keys, then we were off.

CHAPTER 22

MOLLY

"That was intense, and I swear to god right now, I am never doing that," I announced once Sabrina had left the room. The sight of her bent over and screaming would be singed on my retinas and haunting my dreams, probably for the rest of eternity. I'd seen people on TV shows have babies and it looked like a little bit of fancy breathing, a few screams and *boom,* baby time. Sabrina's stomach was moving around like right before that little alien dude popped out in the movie. I'd only known Sabrina for a few months, and she was as cute and pure as Snow White, so the F-bomb shooting out of her mouth was some serious shit.

"You mean, you're not really pregnant?" Everett teased, his eyes laughing at me over his glass of iced sweet tea.

Crap, I'd just outed one of the secrets myself by accident. "No. I'm sorry, y'all, but I'm not pregnant." I held my hand up. "I'm not engaged to Garrett either. We've only been, uh, hanging out, becoming friends again —I don't even know how to describe it—since Genie's the other night. Sadie and I got the ring back from Lacy at the Piggly Wiggly before we got here. Sadie slipped it on my finger for safe keeping and now it won't come off." That felt good. I was no longer drowning in secrets. Part of the truth was out, and I felt like I could finally see the surface through the lake of bullshit I'd been swimming in lately. I decided to keep the undating thing to myself for now; that was nobody's business but mine and Garrett's.

"You're fine, honey," Bill said with a chuckle in his voice. "I told Becky Lee that Jackie wasn't being honest with her. She's just stuck in wishful thinking is all. This was a big day for her already without Sabrina going into labor. You know how she gets about parties and babies." Becky Lee felt the same way about parties and babies as I felt about kitty cats and pie. In other words, we got squealy, lost all control, and our sense of reason went out the window.

"Yeah, I know how she gets. But I'm still worried about letting her down."

"I love you like one of my own, Molly. And Becky Lee does too. Quit that worrying and smile, girl! We're about to gain another family member. I'm about to be a grandpa times five today."

"Exactly what Dad said," Everett added. "You don't need to worry. We already know the truth. Plus, Garrett would not give Aunt Jade's ring to you, not after he already gave it to Lacy. I still can't believe he did that in the first place. We all told him not to do it."

"He was just lonely, Everett. And she's a sweet girl but they didn't suit each other." Bill agreed. "Not like he does with you, Molly." Holy crap, he thought I was well suited to Garrett. I was equal parts elated and scared to receive Bill's approval. Clara grabbed my hand and squeezed, which was our unspoken way to say, *"Woo hoo!"* It was also our unspoken way to say, *"Holy shit"* and *"What the fuck?"* so I wasn't one hundred percent sure how she felt, but her smile led me to conclude it was one of the good ones.

Barrett popped his head in the door. "I'm going to head to the Bandit Lake site and shut it down for the day. Sadie, I can drop you off at home when I'm done if you like. One of us can return your van tonight. Molly, Garrett is driving them to the hospital. He said he'll text you later."

"Okay, thanks."

184

Sadie got up to leave with him. "Thanks, Barrett. I'll come with you. Bye, y'all."

"I'm gonna take off too. I'm helping my mother at the farm stand today." Clara hugged my neck goodbye and smacked a kiss on my cheek. "It'll all be okay, promise," she whispered in my right ear before she took off.

Everett also stood up to leave. "I've got to get back to the shop and close it for the day. I'll catch y'all later at the hospital."

"I guess it's just you and me, kid." Bill laughed as he started stacking plates to clear the table.

"I'll help you. I'm not in the mood to work anymore and Landon has it covered at the inn." I grabbed an armful of glasses to carry to the kitchen.

"You know, Becky Lee was scared to give birth the first time too, Molly. Don't let fear hold you back if you want to be a mother someday. You can do anything you put your mind to. And if it's Garrett you're worried about, he'll make a great daddy if it comes to that."

"I know, you're right. It just looked so painful." I ignored the Garrett-as-the-dad part of his statement. It was better that way.

"They have better drugs nowadays than when the boys were born. Maybe it's like Sadie says and you don't have to feel much of it," he mused.

"I just wish . . ." I sat down hard, setting the glasses I carried on the table with a clatter.

His eyes softened as he sat across from me. "You're missing your daddy right now, aren't you?"

I inhaled a huge breath and marveled at how Bill Monroe had always managed to know how I felt.

"And you miss your momma too." He sighed as he remembered my mother. "She got so lost after he died. It broke her, and she never came out of it. Lane would have been a wonderful grandpa to your babies. He loved you and your brothers so much—with all his heart. To the moon and the stars and right back home again, remember? He always said you were his special little treasure, his reward after having all those wild brothers of yours. We'll never get over his loss, Molly. He was my best friend in the world. I just—I see you still hurting, and I don't like the thought of you being lost in grief like your momma. I know it's not the same as having him, not by any means, but I'm here for you, Becky Lee is here, and the boys are too. You and your brothers are family. You're honorary Monroes, and you always will be."

I blinked back tears. "I do miss him. Thinking about him hurts and I never let myself remember him because whenever I do, my heart breaks all over again. It's almost worse than the day he died, because the shock of it is gone and all that's left to feel is the absence."

"I know, honey. Like I always say, sometimes memories are the worst form of torture, even the good ones. And it's funny how stuff like this always stirs them up, isn't it? The little, random things that make you miss a person always come at you like a surprise. But the big life stuff, babies being born, holidays, weddings"—he looked at me pointedly—"or discovering you could possibly love someone and then letting yourself take that fall . . . those kinds of things will always make you wish the person you're missing was here to see it with you. You'll always have a taste of bitter with your sweet, Molly, but that doesn't mean you should stop living. Lane would want you to live the life he'd always dreamed for you—full of happiness and love."

"I know he would. And my mother does too, in her way," I whispered. "How do I stop being afraid?"

"I wish I knew what to tell you. Fake it until you make it, then maybe one day you'll be so happy you can look back and realize the fear is gone."

"Yeah . . ." I murmured.

"I'm gonna take these plates to the kitchen and get some of Becky Lee's lemonade. Would you like a glass?"

"I would love a glass, and I'll be right behind you with the rest of the dishes."

I found Becky Lee's covered cake plate in the buffet and set Sabrina's gorgeous cake inside, covering it with a smile on my face and allowing myself to dream of the day I'd have a cake like this of my own.

Fake it until you make it.

I'd spent my entire life faking one thing or another. Why couldn't I fake this? Could I pretend to be brave and date Garrett for real, no more un-dating or hiding from him how I felt? He deserved to be with someone who could show him how wonderful he was out in the open, the way falling in love should be.

Was I falling in love with him?

Was I brave enough to admit my feelings, even if it started as a secret I only told to myself?

I decided I could. I decided I deserved to be happy just like anyone else. But as for falling in love? It was too early to tell; I'd never let myself come close to it before.

Bill stepped out of the kitchen with a huge smile on his face. "Becky Lee just called. Sabrina had the baby in the hospital parking lot. They're getting them into a room right now. Let's go."

"Oh, uh, I don't know if I should. I only met Sabrina a few months ago. We're friends, but not the going-to-the-hospital-on-the-day-you-give-birth-in-a-parking-lot-for-a-visit kind of friends. At least, not yet." We'd get there eventually though, because Sabrina was good people. Maybe she would visit me in the hospital when I had Garrett's baby someday.

Imagining having a baby with Garrett felt scary, but I enjoyed thinking about it all the same. Hopefully, whenever I gave birth, I would be suffi-ciently loaded up on the good drugs in a nice comfy hospital bed with Garrett feeding me ice chips and at my beck and call. He seemed the type to be a beck-and-call father-to-be and I was one hundred percent sure I would be a pain-in-the-ass pregnant woman. Honestly, I was a handful with just a head cold.

Bill laughed. "I'll show you the baby through the window of the door . .
." He was trying to cajole me with a cute baby for some reason, and it
was almost working. I mean, if she'd had kittens, I'd be in the car
already. Cute things were irresistible to me. "Okay," he said, and it
sounded like confession time. "I have to be honest with you. I can't do
this stuff, this tricky kind of sneaky stuff. Becky Lee told me to bring
you with me so she can get you to drive Garrett home. She's matchmaking again."

I burst out laughing. "I'll go with you. I don't want you to get in trouble
with Becky Lee." Plus, Garrett and I had plans for later tonight that Bill
did not need to know about.

CHAPTER 23

GARRETT

*B*arrett had wanted me to drive based on my first aid knowledge, but who knew my driving skills would be what saved the day instead? Wyatt caught little Cora Louise the second I pulled into the emergency room parking lot at the hospital in Knoxville. The staff and Sabrina's dad, Dr. Roy Logan, were waiting for us outside the doors since Willa had called from the car to let them know we were coming. The drive here was thirty minutes of pure adrenaline and I couldn't wait to point out to my mother how useful my time racing at The Canyon back in high school had turned out to be—but now was not that time. She was in her grandma/momma bear zone and unlikely to even hear anything that wasn't about Sabrina and the baby, or possibly Wyatt.

Sabrina and Cora were swept away the second I stopped Sadie's van. Wyatt, Willa, and my mother followed, and I drove through the half-circle emergency area to find a parking spot.

Even though I had just become an uncle for the fifth time, Molly was on my mind instead of my new niece. Lacy was also on my mind. If I was honest with myself—which I rarely was—my whole entire miserable dating history was on my mind.

I preferred to do, not think. I liked things I could see, feel, and touch over wondering where I stood in any given situation—the intangible qualities of human interaction had always made me twitchy. This thing with Molly was driving me insane. I'd been home for almost four years, and in that time, I barely got her to interact with me and it had hurt. No, it more than hurt, because I never understood why. In high school, I got why she slipped away from me because she was troubled after her dad died. But as adults? I couldn't figure her out. And every time I'd seen her, it had killed me a little bit inside to the point I finally had to force myself to give up on her and move on with Lacy, who was sweet but ultimately not for me. Now that Molly was finally reciprocating my feelings, it was so heady, I could explode with it. The rapid forward progression of our—for lack of a better word—relationship, concerned me and thrilled me in equal parts.

There had never been a moment in my life when I didn't love Molly. As a kid, I'd always pictured myself growing up and marrying her someday. Obviously, not in the way a grown man would think of marriage and love. My current thoughts included a lot of sex that my younger self couldn't have even imagined back then.

Was my regard for her rooted in our shared past? Or was it growing out of our recent interactions? Hopefully it was both, but I was too in the middle of it to see straight. Or maybe beautiful little Cora Louise had given me baby fever—was that possible in a guy?

I locked up the van and hurried to the hospital's information desk. "Sabrina Monroe's room?"

"Hey, Garrett! Over here!" Willa waved me over from where she stood in front of the bank of elevators.

"Never mind," I told the receptionist and jogged over to Willa.

"They're both fine. Sabrina's doctor is with her. Come on."

We traversed the sterile, white floors of the hospital until we arrived in the waiting area where we took seats by my mother.

"You're up next, my sweetheart!" She held Willa's hand and smiled huge at her. "How are you feeling? Do you need a snack or a drink? Garrett, honey, run and get Willa a bottled water and whatever looks the healthiest out of that vending machine in the hallway. My purse is on the coffee table."

"Ma, I have money. What would you like, Willa?" I chuckled at her expression, her mouth was half open and her eyes were wide as she looked at me. Like she still wasn't quite used to my mother's constant affection.

"Uh, I'm not hungry. I'm fine. You can sit down, Garrett. But, thank you."

"You let me know." She nodded as a bemused smile crossed her face. My mother's goal in life was to make sure we were all happy, and now that two of my brothers were married, that goal extended to their wives. Willa would get used to it eventually.

"We're here! Where's my grandbaby?" The deep country twang of my father's voice drifted across the waiting room and my mother stood up to rush into his arms.

"We haven't seen them since they checked in. The doctors are with them now. But she's just beautiful, Bill—as precious as can be."

"Of course she is. Just like her momma. Molly's on her way. She stopped in the gift shop to get some flowers—said she felt weird coming up here with nothing to give."

"Oh, pish. When will that girl realize she's family?" My mother shot a pointed look in my direction. "You make her feel like family again, Garrett. See to it!"

"Yes, ma'am." I grinned.

"You're the only one of my boys who has ever sounded sassy when you say ma'am. You have always been a little stinker."

"Ma, come on." I shook my head as I sprawled in a chair across from a snickering Willa.

191

"No, I mean this, Garrett William, from the bottom of my heart. This is the truth. So, you listen to your momma right now. That poor girl has been lost ever since her daddy died and *you* have been lost since you came back home to Green Valley. It's about darn time you two found each other again. I've been doing my best to be subtle—" She glared at my father when he interrupted her with a chuckle. Her definition of subtle was clearly different from ours. Luckily, I had managed to keep a neutral expression on my face. I froze when I saw Molly lurking at the edge of the hall behind my mother. How much had she been able to hear? "I want what's best for y'all and I'll see to it that you get it," she finished.

"Hi." Molly's soft voice turned my mother's head.

She pulled out of my father's arms and hugged Molly against her chest. "Honey, I'm so glad you're here, and those flowers are stunning."

"Thanks. I'm not going in, I mean, I came to drop off these flowers because—"

"You're family, Molly. The end," Dad said in his *"and that's the final word"* voice.

She grinned and crossed the waiting room to sit by me. We'd both been on the receiving end of his *"dad"* voice many times before—but not since it had involved water balloons, painting the house with mud, tag in the living room or something else equally destructive or messy. We used to be a handful whenever we were together, always in trouble for something. "Hey, y'all." She greeted Willa and me with an amused grin crossing her gorgeous little pixie face.

Barrett joined us in the waiting room at the same time Doc Logan popped in to let us know Sabrina and Wyatt were ready for us to visit for a few minutes.

"You go first, Garrett," my mother bossed. "Then when you're done, Molly can drive you home." She turned to Molly to at least give the pretense that she was asking and not ordering us around. "You can give him a ride, can't you?" Sweet as pie and very satisfied with herself, my mother beamed at her.

"No problem, Becky Lee," Molly said as she and Dad exchanged amused looks.

"I won't be long," I told Molly. She passed me the flowers to take to Sabrina.

After stepping inside Sabrina's room, I saw my brother with one of the biggest smiles I'd ever seen on his face and in his arms was his new daughter—with the addition of this little one, they had four kids between the two of them.

"Hey, y'all. How are you feeling?"

"Perfect," Sabrina answered. She looked much better now, relaxed against her pillows and beaming with happiness.

"Say hi to Cora Louise Monroe." Wyatt beamed at me so hard I could swear his face was going to end up freezing that way if he didn't stop smiling. "Want to hold her?"

I nodded. "Hey, little angel." I took her in my arms, and immediately fell in love. Not just with little Cora, but with the possibilities my own future held. I wanted what Wyatt had, all of it. On some level I'd been seeking it out ever since I got home. Holding this adorable bundle in my arms confirmed it.

"I'll get out of your way now and let you rest. She's just beautiful." I passed her back to Wyatt. "It was very nice to meet you, Cora. Congratulations, you two."

"Who's next?" I asked when I got back in the waiting room.

"That would be me," Dad said and stood up. After an unsteady step forward, he took a deep breath. It was odd and shaky as it shuddered into his body. "Becky Lee?" The urgency in his voice startled me. He put a hand to his chest.

My mother hopped to her feet in alarm. "Bill? What's happening."

"What's wrong, Bill?" Doc Logan asked as he and Barrett also stood up to help.

He staggered to the doorway and left the waiting room. Barrett and Doc Logan followed closely behind, grabbing his elbows, then catching him before he could fall to the floor. "We need help!" Barrett shouted. But a nurse had seen Dad's unsteady walk out of the room, and she was already on her way.

"I'm okay . . . don't want to scare Molly and Willa . . ." He gasped through a grimace as his hands went to his chest.

Too late; she and Willa were already following behind him and saw his legs buckle while Barrett held him up.

"Mom?" I questioned as Barrett and Doc Logan helped him to a chair until a stretcher could arrive.

"I'm . . . fine . . . probably . . . just heartburn . . . from that eggplant stuff . . ." Dad insisted through his gasping breath, the stubborn old man.

We were in a different waiting room now, Mom, Barrett, Everett and Willa, Molly and me. It was white and sterile. There was not a smile to be seen in this part of the hospital.

Everett had arrived with Wyatt and Sabrina's kids, plus Ruby and Weston, her niece and nephew, and dropped them all with Doc Logan. Wyatt had been going back and forth from Sabrina's room to here with us.

The doctors were running tests.

We were still waiting for news.

None of us had been able to see him.

The uncomfortable silence, the absolute stillness in this room, was in direct contrast with the joy in the other one. It was jarring.

Like the difference between life and death.

We all sat staring at the floor, occasionally exchanging worried glances and nervous smiles of encouragement, as if we could somehow reassure each other he would be okay when we all knew nothing.

"Bill Monroe?" A doctor appeared in the swinging doorway at the rear of the waiting room, startling us all.

"Yes," my mother said. She stood up quickly, immediately followed by Barrett, who had become her shadow since the moment they'd taken Dad away.

"He is stable. Two of you can go in, if you'd like to follow me."

Mom stepped forward, followed by Barrett who looked around the room questioningly at us.

"You go with her," I answered his unasked question, as did Everett. I sensed he needed to do this, that taking care of our mother was helping him hold on to his control. With a nod, he followed them.

Molly took my hand without looking at me and squeezed. Her haunted expression gave me pause, but I could barely focus on my own state of mind right now. Silent comfort was all I had to offer as well. "He'll be okay," she declared. "He has to be. We were just cleaning up the party dishes not even an hour ago. He was making jokes and so happy about the baby . . ."

"Of course he will," Willa affirmed. "Dads like him always stay around." Her eyes widened in horror on Molly once she realized the implications of what she had said. "Oh, I—I can't believe I said that—"

Molly held up a hand and smiled softly at Willa. "It's okay, and you're right. Dads like Bill *do* always stay, but if they can't, they'll let you know they wish they could." Her eyes drifted over Everett, then settled on me. "No matter what happens, Bill loves you boys. He was just telling me how much earlier . . ." Her eyes shone with unshed tears under the fluorescent glow of the lights before she ducked her head. I let go of her hand and pulled her into my side.

We collectively rose to our feet when we saw Barrett and my mother coming our way. "Is he—" Everett started to ask.

"Your father is sitting up in bed and he wants to go home! I am beside myself. I just—he had a heart attack and he thinks he should go home to sleep it off!" Tears filled her eyes as she opened her purse and rummaged around until she found a small pack of tissues.

A relieved laugh escaped me on a huff. "That sounds like him."

"They ran tests—an EKG—and they took his blood. He had a mild heart attack called an SMI—silent myocardial infarction," Barrett explained. "He's going to have to make some changes when he gets out of here. And we're lucky he was here with all of us or he probably would have just gone to bed to sleep it off, the stubborn old goat."

"So, he's going to be okay," Everett confirmed.

Mom dabbed at her eyes with a tissue and answered. "Yes, he should be okay, but changes will have to be made, just like Barrett said. He won't be back to one hundred percent anytime soon, no matter what he thinks. Heart attacks are serious even if they are silent! Y'all can go tell him goodnight, then go home and get some sleep. I'm going to stay here with your stubborn daddy and make sure he stays in that darn bed."

"No way. I'm not leaving you here—" I started to argue but stopped at the look on Barrett's face.

"I've got you, Momma," he said. "We're grown men. Let us take care of you for a change. I'm staying with you." To the rest of us, he said, "Y'all go home. There's no sense in all of us being here. Garrett, you're in charge of keeping the company going for the time being. Everett, get Willa home and take care of your girl. I'll call you if anything changes." Barrett's default reaction to any sort of stressor was to control everything that surrounded it until it was gone. I was afraid of how he would react when he realized there was no way he could control this situation; our father's health was a variable that was too unpredictable at this point.

196

"You got it," Everett agreed. "Come on, sweetness, let's go say goodbye to Dad for the night, then we'll go home." They hugged my mother, then took off down the hall.

"Garrett, you'll need to go to the office tomorrow instead of the site. What about putting Chris in charge of the inn for now?"

"Good thinking. Will do."

"I'll call if anything changes. Say goodbye, go on home and take it easy for tonight. I've got this."

"Molly?" I held my hand out, she took it, tightly squeezing it with hers.

"I have my car and I already talked to Landon. I have the rest of the day off too. Whatever you need from me, I'm here. For all of you."

"I love you, my sweeties." My mother attempted to hug us both, but only succeeded in squishing Molly between the two of us, a moment of levity we all needed. "Say goodbye to your daddy. Y'all two take care of each other, promise me."

"We will," I answered.

"Promise it," she demanded.

"We promise, Becky Lee," Molly agreed, dropping a kiss to her cheek before tugging me down the hall to say goodnight to my father.

CHAPTER 24

MOLLY

*W*e were halfway back to Green Valley, each of us lost in our thoughts. I wasn't sure what I could possibly say to make him feel better. Mainly because after a shock like this, no words would be adequate. Not to mention the fact that this was one of the weirdest days in the history of ever. "Are you okay?" I broke the ice.

He blew out a breath. "I feel weird not being there with them, even though we saw for ourselves that he's pretty much fine now. Sitting up and smiling like nothing happened—"

"He's going to get through this. The doctor even said so when we got in the room. And you know the second your mother gets home, she's going to head straight to the pantry and throw away all his pork rinds and beer. No more biscuits and gravy on Sunday mornings for Mr. Bill Monroe. She's probably sitting in his hospital room right now ordering a treadmill and plotting ways to lower his cholesterol and force him to exercise. Your dad has no choice other than to recover—Becky Lee won't accept anything less. You know it, Garrett. And don't forget Barrett is there tonight too. I would not want to get on the wrong side of his bossy ass. He's going to back your mother up so hard your dad won't know what hit him."

He chuckled. "You're right. It was just—"

"It's scary to see your parent that way. I know."

"Yeah, you do know, and I'm so sorry, Molly."

"What for?"

"This has been your life for years and now I—I have gotten a little taste of it, and I feel like my heart is about to break—"

"It's—I wish I could say you'll get used to it, but that would be a lie. Parents are people too. They get sick. Sometimes they die, or just go away . . ."

"I thought I understood how you felt back then. I tried to imagine what it would be like to lose my mom or my dad so I could talk about it with you, to help you. But at the end of this, my father is going to be okay and my imagination didn't even come close to how terrible it felt to see him in that hospital bed. I'm so sorry, Molly, I—"

No. I couldn't listen to any more of this or I'd make it all about me instead of him and then I would have to jump out of the car and run away. "Do you want to go home? Should we stop for food? Are you hungry? No one really ate much lunch at the baby shower." I changed the subject immediately. It was so obvious he had to know what I was doing.

I didn't have to look at him to know he was smiling that knowing smile. The one that said he understood the game I was trying to play. This was why I was pretty sure he was perfect for me. But that didn't mean he wasn't infuriating at the same time. "I want to go home," he said, playing along with me. "Will you stay with me tonight? I don't feel like being alone. Stan's good company, but his lack of conversational skills sometimes leaves me feeling lonely."

"Aw, Stannasaures Rex! You know how I feel about that fluffy little chunk. Yes, I'll stay with you. Anything you need and I'm there."

"I—what changed, Molly?"

I spared a quick glance in his direction. "What do you mean?" I knew what he meant. I just needed time to think of a good answer.

"What changed between us? Why, after all this time are you—" I saw him drive his hand through his hair in frustration. I quickly looked back at the road. "Why after all these years are you letting me into your life again? I need to know we're on the same page here, or at least in the same book."

Wow, he was determined to take a deep dive into the bottomless, screwed-up pit of my psyche and push all my buttons today. I was trying so hard to be there for him; I couldn't let myself turn into a blubbering mess because that would be selfish. Luckily, I was good at digging holes to bury my feelings inside of. But it seemed like he had his own shovel for my dirt, and I needed to get rid of it so he would quit unearthing my secrets.

I took in a long breath before I answered. The truth was in there some-where, so I dug it out to answer him. "I guess when I saw you walking toward me at Genie's, I sort of remembered all the times you were there for me in the past, growing up and stuff. And how after all these years of me being a bonehead, you were *still* showing up for me. You never gave up on me even when I was lost in my head. And honestly, Garrett, I still get lost. I get caught up in my feelings sometimes and—"

"I know you do, Molly. I do it too. Why do you think I still can't sleep?" He reached out and squeezed my thigh, leaving his hand there as I drove us home.

The dirt went flying as I shared more truth. "Uh, if I'm being honest, there was also that first kiss that I only eighty percent remember. That kind of shook me up a little bit too. Oh, and your beard. You look super-hot with a beard. And in the continued spirit of honesty, I will add that as long as we're un-dating each other, you have to keep it. I'm afraid it's a requirement. No shaving allowed."

He chuckled as he cocked his head to the side. "I'll keep the beard. I'm sick of shaving anyway. And yeah, that kiss shook me up too. I can't get you out of my mind."

"I don't want you to get me out of your mind. I like being on your mind. I'd also like to think it gets pretty dirty in there."

"When it comes to you, it's been getting downright filthy." He responded in that growly voice that tickled me in the best places.

I shot him my grin/giggle combo; it was my second-best flirt move. "Filthy is my favorite. I have a good imagination."

"Is that a warning or a promise?"

"Feel free to take it as both," I answered.

His big hand squeezed my thigh again, this time up my dress and I shivered. "I should have taken a shot with you years ago." The growl was back, ripe with promise.

"You know, I think maybe it's good this is happening now," I mused. "Maybe we had to drift apart so we could drift back together. Sort of like those crazy-big icebergs that smash against each other, then apart, then end up making one big-ass iceberg together. I dunno . . . that was a lame analogy. I mean, if we got together a few years ago, or even back in high school, I would have driven you away real quick. I was a total pain in the ass back then."

"Just back then?" he teased.

"Ha ha ha. I admit, I can be a handful, okay?"

"Don't worry, I like having my hands full of you. And I can be too quiet sometimes. I get stuck in my head and forget how to communicate. I don't do that with you."

I peeked at him from the corner of my eye. "I don't think we could ever have been one of those couples who fell in love as kids and got married at age eighteen. I would have driven you crazy and wrecked it all. Probably during junior year of high school. And you should know that I still might wreck it. You have to watch out for me, Garrett. I'm nothing but a high-maintenance pain in the ass," I twirled my ponytail and flipped it over my shoulder. I couldn't stop flirting with him even when I tried. See? *Trouble.*

I busted him rolling his eyes during a quick glance over at his face. "You're not high maintenance, Molly, you were just with the wrong guys before. But thinking back to high school? Yeah, you, Clara, and Sadie were pretty wild together back then, with poor Leo always trying to keep y'all from getting caught."

I nodded my head. "The whole boyfriend-girlfriend thing wouldn't have worked for us in high school. Clara and I set the record for most cuts in one school year—that wouldn't have meshed well with your goody-goody student council thing. Like, we spent more time drinking under the bleachers than we did in actual school, Garrett."

"Yeah, I know. Everybody knew about y'all." He put his hand on the back of my seat and leaned in. "But, did you know Leo called me a few times to pick you two up when you were drunk behind the library and couldn't make it to the school bus to go home?"

"Shut up!" I gasped. Because, no, in fact, I did not know that. In a lot of ways, Clara, Sadie, and I were lucky to be alive. We were also lucky we'd had a friend like Leo. Garrett too, apparently.

"I'd have to borrow Barrett's car to do it."

"Shut up even more!" I gasped.

"Barrett made me take his chore schedule for a week every time too."

"Dang, Garrett, I'm sorry—I owe you a beer or maybe a handy or something."

He burst out laughing. "See? Only you could make me laugh the same day my father had a heart attack. Maybe I needed a little of your wild in my life, Molly."

"And maybe I needed a little of your steady."

"Or, like you said, we could have driven each other crazy."

"At least now we both know what else is out there, which is not much. I mean, we'll never wonder if we could do better with anyone else."

"I don't think I could do better than you."

"I agree, I'm a great catch. Just don't ask any of the Chrises in town about me and my wacky ways."

"Okay, avoid all the Chrises. Anything else I should take note of?" he asked.

I shook my head and flopped a hand against his chest with a laugh. "Uh, well, you already know my feelings about your cat, your beard, and pie. How do you feel about bubble baths? For or against?"

"For."

"Good, that would have been a deal breaker. As my official non-boyfriend, I expect us to have an un-date in your big tub. I haven't forgotten about it. Let's stop at Daisy's for dinner," I said as I swung into the parking lot.

"Looks like Everett and Willa are here too. There's Willa's van." I pulled into the spot next to her van. "Maybe we can join them?" he asked.

"Sounds good to me," I agreed. But they were leaving with takeout as we were almost to the door.

"Hey, y'all. Going home?" Garrett asked.

"Yeah, man. Willa needed to meet her daily meat quota." He smacked a kiss on her cheek as he teased her.

She beamed up at him. "I swear, y'all, this baby is going to come out and demand a T-bone. I can't seem to get enough."

"And I'm here to make sure you get it. I'll go out and hunt down a cow if I have to." He winked at her, thereby proving that all Monroe-brother winks were devastating to the entire female population at large. Well, three out of four, anyway. I had never witnessed Barrett wink at anyone —yet. Sadie had better step up her non-game. She was after Barrett the same way I had been after Garrett—through willful denial and an unwill-ingness to admit her feelings. I was still halfway in that space and was not in a place to judge her. Plus, that kind of approach oddly seemed to work on the Monroe brothers, so she was on the right track even if she refused to drive the car.

"Well, goodnight, you two. Let's get takeout too, Garrett," I said without thinking.

"So, the two of you really are a thing now?" Everett's raised-eyebrow question caught me off guard and I cringed inwardly as his eyes teasingly bounced between me and his brother. It reminded me that I needed to put my guard back up. Why are secrets so difficult to keep?

Maybe because I shouldn't keep this a secret?

I shoved that thought out of my brain. I wasn't fond of introspection when I knew I was wrong. *Ugh!* It was better this way. When I eventually screwed this up, the less people who knew about it, the better it would be for both of us.

"We're just hanging out. Like we used to," Garrett replied, coming in for the save like a boss.

"Well, goodnight, *you two*." Willa echoed my earlier words with a sly grin. I sighed; I was getting too comfortable with Garrett. It was so easy to be with him. And I had always been comfortable around his family— that had never stopped. Which made this whole un-dating thing super hard. I felt weird. Ever since I talked with Bill earlier today, my heart hurt. Could it be sympathy heart attack pain? I thought sympathy pains were something husbands told their wives they had so they could pretend to relate to labor pain.

I followed mindlessly behind Garrett inside of Daisy's where he insisted on paying. He even ordered for me because I was stuck in a daze as I stood next to him contemplating my aching heart. When he laid a hand on my shoulder and asked if I was okay, it only made it worse. "We need pie," I blurted out, making the waitress taking our order laugh.

"There you are, Molly. How're you doing tonight?" she asked.

"Huh? Oh, I'm fine, thank you."

"I guess you didn't hear me, like usual." She tapped her ear and mimed turning up a dial. She was new-ish, had a soft voice and was prone to mumbling. I had given up on ever hearing her and she never bothered to listen when I explained. So c'est la vie, or whatever. There were plenty of other awesome servers here, so I usually sat in one of their sections.

Garrett bristled next to me, but I put my hand on his arm so he wouldn't say anything. I was used to this kind of thing, less so in town, but it still happened occasionally. I sighed. "I'm okay, it's just been a long day. You know how it is," I addressed her.

"I sure do. Two slices? What kind of pie?" This was why I preferred the Donner Bakery for my pie needs. Offering the entire pie was their default. Jeez.

"Surprise me."

"You got it." She turned away and headed off behind the counter to put our order in.

"I don't like that. What she did was not okay. Why didn't you let me say anything?" He bent to speak softly in my ear.

"She didn't mean anything bad by it. And I'm just way over explaining myself. Unless someone is a total dick, I don't bother. I'm not alive to be a lesson for people to learn. I've got my own shit going on and I'm not a damn teacher."

"It goes against my nature to let shit like that slide. But since you want me to, I will," he grumbled before pulling me in for a hug and kissing my forehead.

I shouldn't let him hug me in public, let alone kiss my forehead. Forehead kisses sucked out my mental powers, they were dangerous, and people might get the wrong—*right?*—idea. But my heart had started doing that swirly pain thing again and hugging him felt necessary.

So, I allowed it.

I also hugged him back and touched the top of his left butt cheek with my fingertips. It was firm, like I knew it would be.

And maybe I also inhaled real deep so I could get a hit of his manly, clean-soap smell. He smelled like an entire forest had been shoved into a bar of soap, or maybe like he put on a leather jacket and rolled through a meadow after taking a bath. Basically, I wanted to rip his shirt off and lick him right now and it was hard to fight that instinct. The whole protective vibe he had going on was a turn-on. Who knew, right? None of my Chrises had ever felt moved to defend me.

The server brought us our order. I didn't bother remembering her name since she couldn't be bothered to listen to my explanation for my hearing, and I was okay if that made me a jerk. "Thank you," I said.

"Let's get out of here." He took the bag and my hand, and we were off. Anticipation sparked through my body as I followed him out to my car, along with those pesky heart swirls pinging around my chest like a broken pinball machine.

CHAPTER 25

MOLLY

J turned off the highway onto the now-familiar nightmare forest road that led to Garrett's place. But this time felt different—like a million years had passed between us since the last time I had been here.

I smiled at him and took his hand, jerking him to sit upright so I could hold it while I drove the rest of the way. We were both kind of driving now, but I didn't care. He laughed when I had to turn the wheel sharply to make the right turn before we got to his driveway and I dragged his hand along with mine. I had feels and they were growing, my heart was about to explode, and I was beginning to think it was because of him and not some dumb sympathy pain thing. I felt more for Garrett than I had for all the Chrises combined. Our infamous Genie's fake kiss felt like a lifetime ago and I still couldn't understand why.

Because you've known Garrett your entire life, stupid.

Holy shit.

I threw my VW into park and sat up straight. "We're here!" I announced with an insane brightness in my voice. I was suddenly unsure of how to act around him. Was I falling in love? Or was I about to drop dead of a sympathy heart attack?

I don't know these things!

I was a go-with-the-flow kind of girl and not one to dwell on stuff. Plus, every man I had ever dated found me annoying by the fifth or sixth date and had broken it off. Since I'd never really cared that deeply for any of them, I've never had to deal with feelings like this before.

"Want to eat on the deck?" he asked, wrenching me out of my thoughts.

"Sure, but I have to say hi to Stan first," I informed him, because obviously.

He tugged lightly on my ponytail with a grin, then turned to unlock the door. "Of course. I have to feed him too. I also want to call and check on my dad real quick." We stepped inside. Garrett headed straight for the kitchen and I headed off to find Stan, my one true love.

I clicked my tongue against the roof of my mouth, smiling when I saw his royal chubbiness waddle his fluffy patootie out from behind the couch. "Come here, my wittle chunk monster, and get your sugars." I knelt and gathered him up, kissing the top of his furry head.

There was nothing in this world better than kitty-cat cuddles. Except for maybe good dick, and every woman over the age of twenty-nine knows that good dick is a scarce and diminishing resource. Hence the rise of the cat lady, of which I would probably join the ranks of if I couldn't rein in my crazy long enough to land a husband. I took Stan to my favorite chair by the fireplace where I scratched his neck and listened to him purr. I could relate. I, too, purred whenever my neck got the right kind of attention.

But alas, the *pop* of the kitty-cat food can opening in the kitchen took Stan from my arms before I was ready to let him go, so I got up to console myself with the cheeseburgers Garrett had ordered from Daisy's —no onions, thank you very much. I had managed to notice that little request Garrett had made through the fog of my earlier brief mental breakdown. I was excited because saying no to onions meant saying yes to kissing and I was all for the kissing tonight.

I had to question whether I was having real feelings—the swirly heart stuff, the fog in my brain—or was it just low blood sugar? If I still felt this way after dinner, then I'd consider scheduling another freak-out or a lunch with Clara, which, come to think of it, would amount to the same thing. My talk with Bill had unlocked feelings that I could no longer deny. But the heart attack had cast a huge apprehensive pall over them. As always, I was one step forward and two more back.

"How's your dad? Did you get to talk to him?"

"I talked to Barrett. Dad's doing fine. He was asleep, so Mom and Barrett are having dinner in the cafeteria."

"Good. I hope Barrett and your mom can get some rest later too."

"Me too. I'm starving. Let's go outside. Flip the switch on the wall and I'll grab the food. Want a beer?"

"Sure, thanks." I flipped the switch, stepped outside and crossed the deck, which was the same as before, then went down the stairs into the yard, spinning in a circle to take in all that he had added. He had wound tiny fairy lights up the trunks of several trees and hung lanterns from their branches. It still looked enchanted out here, like Hansel and Gretel's magical forest, but I no longer had to fear the witch because I could see beyond his yard. He'd lit it up so it was magical instead of scary. My heart flipped over in my chest.

I squealed as his arms wrapped around my waist from behind and he buried his face in my neck. "Do you like it?" he whispered, then kissed my cheek.

"It's beautiful. I love it."

"Good. This is my favorite place to be and I want you to love it as much as I do." I leaned back into his arms and tilted my head back to look up at him. He was so tall, all he had to do was bow forward a bit and he could look at my face upside down. But that wasn't good enough. I pivoted in his arms and reached high to pull his face to mine.

I stood on tiptoes but couldn't reach his mouth to kiss him since, for some reason, he wouldn't bend over to let me. I really needed a kiss, dammit. These feelings needed to get out of my body and his mouth seemed like a good place to put them. "Why do I have to be so dang short?"

"So that I can do this." He finally bent, sweeping his arms around my bottom to lift me up so I could wrap my legs around his waist.

Cradling his face in my palms, I allowed my crazy heart to take control as I pressed my lips to his and kissed him like I never wanted to stop. Because for once in my life, I didn't want to run away from how I felt. I had the scary thought that I wanted to kiss him forever. Garrett didn't feel temporary. In this moment, he felt like everything I had been missing in my life.

It scared the crap out of me.

He carried me back up the stairs to the deck and set me down at the table. Smiling at me in the glittering light of the deck, his brown eyes twinkled. "This is the least romantic dinner ever." He laughed as he opened the Daisy's bag and passed me a burger.

"We don't need fancy food, Garrett. Just each other, right?"

"You're right. Molly, I don't know what I would have done without you at the hospital. Holding your hand helped me keep it together."

"Same. Your dad is like a second dad to me. I don't know what I'd do if something happened to him."

"It was a shock seeing him in that bed. I can't get it out of my head even though I know he'll be fine." He set his beer down and stared out at the yard. The sun had gone down and all we could see beyond the deck were the shadows cast by the moonlight and the shimmer of the lights he had strung in the trees. Their stark beauty was a contrast to the vivid light on the deck. Like we were in our own glowing little world surrounded by thousands of tiny fallen stars.

"Let me take care of you tonight, please?" I reached for his hand to link our fingers. Making him feel okay again had suddenly become the only thing I wanted to do.

He smiled. "This feels familiar, doesn't it?"

"I guess it does. But maybe this time we can get in that big tub of yours together instead of just me. What do you think?"

"I think you might be brilliant."

"Of course I am. Naked comfort is always the best kind. It's just like my great-aunt Belle always used to say—when all else fails, show your boobs."

"Do I even want to know what prompted her to give you this advice?" I counted his laughing voice as a point scored in my newly invented *Make Garrett Smile Tonight* game.

"I'll have you know it's solid advice. She's been married, like, eight times. Anyway, we'll see if it works on you after dinner. For science."

"Ah, I'll do anything for science. If you recall, I won the science fair twice in high school."

"I do remember. You were very impressive, hotshot. So, when would you like to take that bath?"

"Hmm. I've always heard the ideal time is thirty minutes after eating. We wouldn't want to drown."

"Brilliant," I teased. "But I have to warn you—I had big plans of getting behind you, *Pretty Woman*-in-the-bathtub-scene style, but I'm too short, so I'll have to straddle your lap instead."

"I am totally okay with that." His hand squeezed mine as he chuckled. "I'm so glad you're here, Molly," he quietly added.

"There's nowhere else I'd rather be." We finished our dinner, quietly enjoying each other's company.

He gave my hand a light tug and I stood up with him. "I'll go run that bath now," he offered.

"No, I'm taking care of you. Go inside and pet Stan." I gathered our trash and dashed inside, making a quick stop in the kitchen to throw it away. We'd already had the obligatory condom talk, so we were good to go. He made me feel like I was bursting with electricity. I tingled with anticipation but also felt languid and at peace, as if I could lie down with him and let the world just drift away into nothing. No more fears, no more of the noise that constantly filled my head with trepidation. All of it was gone, at least for now.

I kicked off my shoes near the couch and set my hearing aid on the coffee table before making my way into the bathroom. I pulled up the blinds nestled within the frame of the floor-to-ceiling windows surrounding the tub, filling the bathroom with the moon and the stars and the flickering lights from the trees outside.

After twisting the lever, I knelt to add a few drops of lavender bath oil beneath the flow of hot water, swishing it around with my hand, watching as it created a sweet-smelling sheen and blending it in to make something that was already wonderful even better as my starlit reflection faded into the water.

I stood and, with a reach behind my back, unzipped my dress to pull it over my head and hang over the towel rack. I turned to see him watching me with his hip against the doorframe.

"Come here," I murmured, reaching for his hand. He took it, allowing me to tug him into the room as he kicked the door shut behind himself. He reached out for me with his other hand, but I shook my head no. "I'm taking care of you, remember?"

A faint smile drifted across his face as his chest rose and fell with his quickened breath. "I remember," he said as he let his arm drop. I had to read his lips to understand his words. But I wanted to do more than read them. I needed to taste them, kiss them, feel them on my body. I wanted to disappear inside of him and give him everything he needed, like he had always done for me.

Lifting the hem of his shirt, I struggled to get it over his head. With a soft chuckle he bent forward allowing me to remove it.

Once I'd undressed him, I led him to the tub. He allowed it even though I got the feeling he would rather be the one to strip me bare. "Take that off and get in here with me," he demanded, gesturing to my undies.

"Not yet. Scoot to the middle." He obliged, bending his knees and shooting me a side-eyed look of amused patience as I grabbed the shampoo from the shower adjacent to the tub, then sat at the edge. "I'm taking care of you . . ." I murmured as I tipped his head back to wash his hair, using my palms and the cup from his counter to get it wet, running my fingers through and gently scratching his scalp in a massage before rinsing it. Goose bumps rose over his broad shoulders and down his arms as he shivered beneath my touch.

Turning my back to him, I unfastened my bra and set it on the counter as I reached for the soap in the shower. "Hold this." I passed him the soap, grinning as his eyes roved over my body, hot with perusal. He liked what he saw.

"You are fucking beautiful. *Get in here with me.*" It was another demand, one I couldn't wait to obey. I slid my panties down my legs, kicking them to the side as I stepped to the edge of the tub.

He held my waist as I stepped over the ledge to place a foot near his thigh and lowering myself to straddle his lap. I was thrilled when his hardness brushed against me beneath the water.

Just like when we crashed to the forest floor, I slid my center along the length of him before coming to rest on his thighs. "Soap. Gimme," I bossed.

He shook his head with a grin and handed it to me. God, he felt good beneath my fingers. I worked the soapy lather up the ridges of his abs, to his wide chest, hard and dusted with just the right amount of hair to make it interesting. I pressed my breasts against him, shivering as my nipples hardened. I was running my hands up and down his back, with my face buried in his neck when he started swirling his fingers between my legs. *Oh, yes.*

I pulled back to watch his face as he touched me. His eyes grew hooded as his tongue darted out to wet his lower lip before he bit it. "You're staring at my mouth. Do you want a kiss?" He grinned as he slid a finger inside me.

"I'm not wearing my hearing aid, Garrett." I gasped when he began to thrust it in and out, using his thumb to press on my clit as he moved. "I don't want to get it wet. I have to read your lips." I panted my answer through the mindless haze of pleasure he gave me with each movement of his fingers.

"Ah, of course . . ." He pressed his mouth to my neck, right behind my ear. I shivered in his arms as he slowly glided his lips down my neck, then along my collarbone, pressing soft kisses and swirling licks along the way.

"Garrett," I gasped, threading my fingers into his hair to clutch him closer.

He tilted his head back and bent his knees, lifting me higher as I sat on his thighs. I had to look down to see his face. "Go ahead and read my lips, Molly. I have a lot to say to you." His tongue darted out to lick my nipple into his mouth.

My head fell back, ponytail dipping into the water as my brain stopped working. Between the feel of his beard against my sensitized nipples as he sucked and placed biting kisses to one, then the other and back again, his capable fingers creating magic between my legs and the tip of his hard cock poised at my entrance, it was all I could do not to lose my mind.

"I've waited forever to be right here," he murmured against my skin.

"What did you say?" I moaned as he pulled me up, gaze blazing into mine. I could see it in his eyes—he was as hungry for me as I was for him.

"This is happening, Molly. You and me."

"God, yes, Garrett, yes. Come inside. Please . . ."

His hands at my waist with his eyes burning into mine like he finally had what he wanted and was never letting it go, he lowered me, slowly sliding my body down until I was stretched full of him.

Suddenly, I was not just physically naked with him—I was vulnerable, too. "You scare me sometimes," I accidentally confessed, overwhelmed with how it felt to finally have him inside of me. His body was mine and mine was his. In this moment we belonged to each other and I never wanted it to end.

"I know I do, baby. Give it time and it'll pass." Big palms gripped my hips, holding me up so he could move, taking me with smooth hard strokes, the water sloshing back and forth as he rocked up into me.

"Time, yes. Oh, god, please don't stop. Please." He didn't stop and, as though he was compelled to do as I ask, he went even harder. Until with a heave, he stood me up, my legs on either side of his. "What . . .?"

"I want to watch you come before I do," he said right before burying his face between my thighs, entering me with his tongue, then lapping up to suck my clit into his mouth.

"*Gaaaa . . .*" I tried to say his name, but lacked the ability to form words. "Oh god, oh god, I'm close," I finally managed to say.

"Get closer," he growled against my clit. My legs buckled as I let go and exploded into tiny bursts of light, just like the stars shining through the window.

With a glance to the side, I saw our reflection. His head was between my legs, hands digging into my bottom to hold me up as I trembled, hovering there above him.

Gently he helped me lower to my knees as he rose to his behind me, joining me in watching our silhouettes in the star-speckled glass. With one hand on my hip and an arm wrapped around my waist, he entered me from behind.

"Look at us." His voice was a harsh rasp in my ear as he cupped my breasts in his palms, then let one go to drift down my stomach and gently pinch my clit between his fingers. My hands gripped the edge of the tub, white-knuckled and trembling as he worked my body toward another release.

I opened my mouth in a silent moan as my knees slid further apart and his big body bowed forward, pressing his chest to my back until there was no separation between us. Until I couldn't tell where I ended and he began. He felt so broad as he surrounded me, filling me up over and over until I was mindless, boneless, and limp with pleasure in his strong arms.

"Do you see how we belong together?" he growled into my right ear, thrusting harder, moving faster. My hands slipped from the tub, but he held me firm, pulling me up with a hand beneath my chin as we watched each other fall apart in the glass.

Hours later I awoke to darkness, wrapped in Garrett's arms and pressed against his solid warmth. My heart was heavy as I tried to fit all that had just happened between us inside of it. I wanted to keep it there, hold it tight inside of me so it would keep my doubts at bay, but little by little the fear crept in, shoving away the feelings I had before.

My eyes burned as I slid out of the comfort of his arms to sit at his side. In sleep he was at peace, relaxed and beautiful. A faint hint of moonlight shone through his blinds casting him in a silvery glow. He looked other-worldly in this light, like something out of a dream. Chin to my knees, I watched him, startling when he started to speak in his sleep.

Squinting in the dark, I watched his mouth, leaning toward him as close as I dared so I could hear while at the same time trying not to wake him up. "My Molly. Love you . . ."

Gently, I got up, bending to tuck the covers around him.

CHAPTER 26

MOLLY

*A*fter one last glance down at his sleeping face, I decided I couldn't do it. I couldn't stay here. He shouldn't have to put up with my flip-flopping fears and most likely insurmountable pile of doubts for the rest of however long this un-dating thing lasted between us. He should be with someone as steady as he was. I was the opposite of steady. I was a lopsided teeter-totter stuck in a frickin' hurricane. He was a grown-up and I was—I didn't even know how to describe myself and that was part of the problem.

I should go before his feelings for me became real. Sleep confessions were not real—everyone knew that. Plus, I couldn't be the center of anyone's world, and I didn't deserve to have him be mine. Maybe I'd never let him in before because I'd known on some level, he would take everything I had until I was his and he was mine and the only thing left was a hopeless oblivion. If I never had him, I could never lose him. Now I was just lost.

Don't ever make someone your whole world. They will always leave you, Molly. My mother's words to me at my dad's funeral flittered through my mind. She was right, of course. I mean, just look at what happened to her. She checked so far out of her life that we barely knew her anymore. Hell, she'd forgotten who she was too.

I had to let Garrett go. It was the right thing to do. The best thing I could do for him.

I slipped my undies and dress on in the bathroom, then came back to take one last look at the best thing in the world that had ever happened to me. I'd been so stupid to let it get this far.

My hearing aid and purse were on the coffee table and I'd left my sandals by the couch. Of course that cute little floof, Stan, was asleep on them. Dammit! "Stan, you have to move. I've got to go. I'll visit you someday . . ." *Lie.* I could never come back here. This place contained all my top-five favorite things, plus the one very best thing I could not allow myself to have.

I slid my shoes from under him and put them on. "I'm sorry, Stan. It was nice knowing you." I grabbed a piece of paper from my purse and scribbled a fast note for Garrett. I dashed into the bedroom and stuffed it under my pillow before running back in here. I found my keys and spun around for one last look, then twisted the lock on his door so I wouldn't leave them alone in the murder woods in an unsecured house, got in my car and drove the heck out of there.

No crying.

I inhaled a sharp breath. The thought of going home was unbearable. My thoughts were horrid. I didn't want to be alone with them and there was no way pie could ever fix something like this. I hit the Bluetooth button on my steering wheel to call Clara. She was a night owl, and even if she wasn't, it was her stupid Tinder idea that had started this whole mess in the first place. She owed me.

"Yeah. I'm at Genie's, Molly. It's late, you were with Garrett and now you're calling me? I'll grab a booth with Sadie. Meet me here and you can tell me all about how you screwed everything up with him." Rude. Yeah, maybe I was screwing up, but that was because I *was* a screw-up. It's what I did.

"Real nice, Clara. And fine, I'll meet you at Genie's. Order me a Dr. Pepper and some fried pickles. Get some chicken wings and cheese fries too."

"Damn, girl, that's a whole lotta bad mood food." She laughed.

"I'll share it with y'all, Clara. Jeez. I'll be there in ten."

"Yup. I'll tell you all about why I'm at Genie's at this time of night, since you didn't ask."

"Holy crap. I'm sorry, I had a bad day and—"

"I know all about it. Sadie is here too. Hang up and drive." Dang, Clara had her cranky pants on tonight. *Sheesh, I really was an insensitive screw-up.*

Since it was a weeknight, Genie's parking lot wasn't too packed. It was a relief since that meant it wouldn't be quite as loud. Which was not saying much, since this was a bar.

I didn't hear her, but I did see Sadie jumping up and down, blond curls and boobs bouncing like crazy near a booth by the dance floor, and yes, she was attracting a lot of attention. "Hey, Molly! Over here!"

"Simmer down, Sadie, or your breasts will bring all the boys to our booth," I grumbled as I slid in next to Clara.

"What did you do?" Clara pulled back with narrowed eyes to study me. "Ohhhh, you experienced the legendary Monroe stamina, didn't you? Was it good? Wait, don't tell me. I do not want to know anymore. It's been three years for me. Three. Years. What did you do? Freak out over his magic penis and leave him in bed? Did he give you all the feels? Blow your mind? Make you fall in love with him?"

Sadie leaned over, hugged Clara into her side and dropped a kiss to her temple. "Hush your grouchy mouth, Clara." The words were harsh, but her tone was sweet. "What happened? Did he tell you he loves you? Is that it?" Strangely, Sadie was the more sympathetic Hill sister tonight. Odd, but I could go with it.

"Well, sort of. He said it in his sleep." I picked up the Dr. Pepper they'd ordered me and took a sip.

"Are you sure he was talking to you and not Scarlett Johansson or Wonder Woman or some other dream girl?" Clara questioned.

"Yeah, he meant me. He said my name . . ."

"Aww, honey." Sadie grabbed my hand and held it over the tabletop.

Clara snorted. I had noticed the shot glasses lining the table when I got here. Were they all hers? I got worried. Clara rarely ever drank, and whenever she did, it wasn't much. "God, the two of you are driving me crazy!" she burst out. "I mean, Sadie has been flitting around Barrett for months and he's finally become receptive to her wacky ways. But does she flit herself underneath that big, hot bod of his and let 'er rip? No, she does not. You pick fights with him, Sadie, and run away. You act like a looney bird and try to turn him off when we all know those Monroe boys love a challenge. Both of y'all are total wackadoos. If I had a man like either one of those after me? A good man who would *finally* treat me right? You would have to force me to keep my clothes on and my legs closed. I wouldn't be here with y'all two idiots. I would spend all my time bent over a firm surface getting laid. Regularly."

"Hey, y'all." Our heads whipped to the sound of the voice at the edge of our booth. It was deep and masculine, like sexy sandpaper sliding over a big piece of wood. His cheerful tone was an odd contrast to Clara's rage-fest.

"Hey . . ." we answered him in unison.

"Oh, it's Chris! Hey, Chris!" Sadie answered once the hot-guy haze lifted from the table and we saw him clearly. Tall, with sandy brown hair and blue eyes just like Becky Lee's. Sadie's eyebrows rose conspiratorially toward me and she tilted her head. "You know Molly already." He nodded to me and I smiled. Manners before misery, as my momma always used to say—obviously, that was before her own misery took over her life and she left town. "This is my sister, Clara." She introduced Clara and I was pleased to see his eyes light up. She was the reason he had come over here and I couldn't help but do an internal fist pump on her behalf. It shook me out of my sorrow for a minute and I was happy for her.

"Hello, Clara." He addressed her with a big, gorgeous smile.

"Clara, this is Chris Barrett, the Monroe boys' cousin from Knoxville. His dad is Becky Lee's brother. Becky Lee named Barrett after her maiden name," Sadie explained.

"Well, holy shit, Chris Barrett, it's nice to meet you. Let's go to the bar. Buy me a drink and get me away from these two psychopaths." She glared at each one of us in turn. "See this? I don't say no to potential. Opportunity knocks and Miss Clara Jean Hill opens the freakin' door, okay?" Sadie shook her head and let Clara out of the booth.

Chris chuckled and extended his hand. Clara took it and off they went to the bar. Hopefully this Barrett cousin was into complications and drama when it came to his female company.

"She got fired today," Sadie leaned across the table to tell me.

"Oh no!"

"Yeah, I guess in that company, if you don't screw the owner when he tells you to, you're out."

"Holy crap! Did she say what she's going to do?"

"Yeah, she's filing complaints against him and all kinds of legal stuff I already forgot about and moving back to Green Valley. She's buying a house in town and we're moving in together. She has loads of money, so she'll be okay. But still! She's beside herself. She worked so hard to get where she was, and that asshole just took it away in one fell swoop."

"Well, it will be nice to have her close for a change, but man, I feel bad for her."

"Don't take any of what she said personally. She's in a mood. So, what happened tonight? How's Bill? Last I heard from Barrett, he was asleep."

"That's what I heard too." My eyebrows rose.

"What?" She replaced her curious look with an innocent one and I couldn't help but laugh.

"You're in touch with Barrett?" I prodded.

She looked away and shrugged, twirling the straw in her glass before answering. "Yeah, we text about work and other stuff sometimes. But back to you. You didn't really leave Garrett in bed sleeping, did you?"

"I made a mistake, Sadie. I never should have let it get this far. I'm no good for him. Look at me! I ran away to go to a bar instead of talk to him like a grown-up. And I did it the same day his dad had a heart attack. Who does that?" I shrank back in my seat and ran my hands into my hair.

"Did you leave a note at least?"

"Yeah, I said there was an emergency at the inn."

"Okay, that's good! He'll never have to know you got scared. Just talk to him tomorrow morning. *Boom!* Problem solved. You're welcome."

"It's not that simple."

"It totally is that freaking simple. You got scared. You're human, it happens. You can tell him about it or not. It doesn't matter because you were smart enough to give yourself an out by leaving a note. You deserve to be happy, sweetie. We all do."

"He deserves better than me. I'm a total mess. Sadie, we had the most beautiful—*Ugh!*" I looked away. I never let anyone see me like this— never. My eyes were tingling and I was pretty sure I was about to cry.

She reached across the table and took my hands in hers. It freaked me out briefly, but I played along. "Molly, how long have we been friends?"

"I don't know, like, ten years? Twelve? Longer? I don't math, Sadie, you know that. I failed freshman algebra three times."

She chuckled. "A long damn time, okay? In all those years I've never seen you cry or get upset. Not once, and neither has Clara, except for the very first day we all hung out together." What was happening here?

224

Where was this contemplation coming from? Where was the real Sadie Hill?

I choked out a laugh. "Right, yeah. We were all hiding under the bleachers with Leo. It was a total sob soirée. Snot city." I smiled at the memory. Even though it was a bad one, it was one of my favorites.

"We were all crying that day because our lives as we knew them were gone forever. We were stuck back in school—a place that never changes —but we had changed so much. Your daddy had died, and your momma was a mess. Our father left town for who knows where and, well, you've met our mother. Leo's parents kicked him out for being gay. We found each other and lost our way together. To this day, none of us, except for Leo, do much reflection or—" She paused as she struggled for words. "None of us do a lot of thinking, Molly. We just wander through life and hope for the best. Do you want to stay that way, or do you want to make something of the rest of your life? And I don't mean your work at the inn. I mean your real life—love, babies, maybe even Garrett?"

"I can't have all that stuff!" The idea horrified me.

"Why not?"

"Because. I just can't! I have to go home. I'll call you tomorrow. Say bye to Clara for me." The strap of my purse almost pulled me off my feet when it got hung up on the table but I didn't let it stop me. I flung it around, spun in a circle and ran across the dance floor dodging boot-scooting boogiers all along the way, only to run into freaking Jackie at the edge of the floor, near the coat hooks at the front exit.

Getting right up in my face, she snarked, "Alone in a bar again, are you? Garrett dump you already, just like all the Chrises?" She smirked and slid out of her jacket, turning to hang it up.

"*Ugh!*" I poked her in the chest and stepped closer. "What is your problem with me? Say it to my face right now, Jackie. Is this really because Duane asked me to the dance one billion years ago? Really?"

"No! It started with that but then you stole my brother. You act like a crazy kid all over town and everyone thinks you're the cutest thing ever."

"That's it? That's your big beef? Ancient history and the fact that I'm a weirdo? I like stupid stuff, so what? I get excited easily about sparkly things and cats. Maybe I wear dumb dresses and look silly sometimes, but I don't go around town spreading rumors and hurting people like you do."

"You stole my brother. Leo barely talks to me and it's all your fault."

"Try being less of a malicious bitch and then have a talk with Leo. He's your brother, he will always love you! God, I don't have time for this. You're the one who needs to grow up. All I'm going to say is if you mess with me one more time, I'm going to have to kick your ass."

She burst out laughing which was not the reaction I was going for. I felt wretched, I needed an outlet for my bad mood and her laughing at me sucked. "Oh my god. Are you even five feet tall? You weigh what? One hundred pounds soaking wet, and you're going to kick my ass?"

"Okay, fine, no—" I felt like a cartoon character, almost as if a light bulb literally popped over my head. "You're right, I won't kick anyone's ass, obviously. I've been putting up with your stupid crap for years. I'm a pacifist at heart. But I wasn't the one here alone tonight. I met Clara and Sadie, and everyone noticed on account of Sadie activating her Wonder Twin boobs at the table. But it's about"—I flicked my wrist to check the time—"one in the morning and *you're* here alone. Are *you* looking for some company tonight, Jackie?" She blanched and I grinned the evil grin that I reserved only for my meanest occasions—so yeah, this was the first time I'd ever used it. "I'll bottom line it for you, so you'll be sure to absorb this information into your tiny, mean, little pea brain. You keep your big mouth shut about me for—I don't know, the rest of your life, and I'll keep mine shut about your nightly hookup activities, okay?" She looked away and huffed out an annoyed breath. "And, you might want to try the Wooden Plank. I've heard the men are less discriminating over there. Bye now."

I stomped out the door and the cool breeze smacked me in the face as I trudged through the gravel lot to my car.

Finally telling her off felt good.

But maybe she had a point about me. Maybe they all had a point tonight. I did need to grow up. Or at least stop being stuck in the same place, making the same decisions and screwing up every good thing in my life because I was afraid to let things change.

That burst of insight was exhausting. So, naturally, I went home to hide in my treehouse for the night.

CHAPTER 27

GARRETT

*S*he was gone. I woke up from one of the best nights of my life to an empty bed. Well, not entirely empty. Stan sat on Molly's pillow staring plaintively at me, and tucked beneath it with the corner sticking out was a piece of paper. After squinting at the words in the predawn moonlight filtering in through my window, I turned on the lamp to read it.

I had to go home. Landon needs me at the inn. Talk tomorrow. Xoxo

Obviously, the note was utter horseshit. She got spooked. I could hardly blame her; in some ways, this felt like it was going fast. But was it really that fast considering we'd known each other since we were babies?

I didn't know what to think. I had no real sense of clarity when it came to her, but one thought stuck out like a beacon in the dark—she would most likely smash my heart into a thousand little pieces, and I would smile at her the entire time she did it.

After throwing the covers back, I got up and stretched. I dressed quickly, grabbed my phone, and headed to the kitchen to feed Stan, then get out of here to find Molly.

It was still dark when I pulled into the parking lot of the inn. I didn't bother checking her house first because I was pretty sure she had gone to her treehouse. No matter what she said about it belonging to Abbie now, everyone knew it was her special spot and always would be.

Following the path around the front of the inn, I crossed through the rose garden to the treehouse only to stop at the bottom of the stairs. I didn't want to sneak up and startle her like last time. So, I stood there trying to decide what to do. I was about to pull out my phone and text her but her voice calling me from the window upstairs startled me instead. I headed up the stairs, trying to come up with something to say that would convince her to give us a chance.

"I know it's you, Garrett. I saw you from the window. I am an idiot," she called out from her perch on the upper bunk bed, legs dangling over the side in such a way that it blasted me right to the past. *"I'm an idiot, Garrett. Why can't I just be normal?"* She had said such things off and on for as long as I could remember, usually while she was hiding out exactly where she was right now.

"No, you're not. You know you're—" I stopped mid-sentence as I was enveloped by another memory. "Do you remember what I used to say to you? Normal is boring—remember that? You're not boring, Molly. You're the most fun person I've ever met. You didn't believe me then. Will you believe it now?" She looked away with a small shake of her head. "Okay, do you remember how after you would finally come down from that bed, we'd pinky swear to be best friends forever?"

"How did you ever put up with me? I didn't act like a friend when I left you in bed," she insisted as she hopped down to land in front of me, dressed in a short Catwoman nightie with matching knee-socks. I took in the sight of her mussed-up bed head, irresistible curves, and pretty eyes, and a huge smile split my face as she held out her pinky.

I linked it with mine before hauling her into my arms, hugging her close to my chest while she sagged against me and wrapped her arms around my waist. "In the moment you decided to leave, we weren't friends. We

230

were something else—somewhere way beyond friends—and it scared you."

"How can you be so understanding? Why do you get me, when I don't even get myself? It's not fair how that's possible," she griped.

"I don't know." I winked at her. "Years of practice?"

Her shoulders sagged in defeat. "I've had years of practice too, and yet I still confuse myself. I feel terrible. What we did was beautiful." Her eyes shone into mine. "You made me feel special, like I could let go of everything and just be with you, like it was supposed to happen. Then I woke up in the dark. And everything I—"

I tipped her face up to mine with a fingertip beneath her chin. "Next time wake me up."

"What?" she breathed, like it was a revolutionary idea to just simply talk to me.

"Promise me, Molly. The next time you get scared or freaked out or worried, you won't leave. You'll wake me up. Or just tell me about it so we can talk it through, and I can make it better."

"I think I can do that. I can promise to try," she agreed with a sheepish smile.

"You used to tell me your fears. All of them, remember? We used to talk about everything. Until, um, until your dad died."

"Yeah, but it was easier back then when all I was afraid of were imaginary things, like aliens and monsters or the dentist. Once I had real fears, it got harder to talk about them." Her hands drove into her hair as she spun away from me.

"Are you still afraid of everyone finding out about us? Is that part of what it is?"

"Yeah, it is. Also, I don't trust myself not to—I don't know—drive you away like I've driven away every other man who's come into my life. My brothers are the only ones to ever stick around and they're blood related and we're all cut from the same drama-filled cloth. Plus, Jordan needs a free babysitter for Abbie sometimes—"

"Your brothers love you. Come lie down with me. It's so early the sun isn't even up. Let's go to sleep and wake up together like we were meant to." I toed my shoes off, took off my shirt, and kicked my jeans aside before sliding beneath the covers of the full-size bottom bunk. I patted the bed next to me. It was small, but I wanted her close, so that was fine with me. I also needed a couple more hours of sleep and the circles beneath her eyes told me that she did too. She crawled in next to me and I pulled her into my body. "No matter how hard I snore, wake me up if the thought of leaving crosses your mind. Promise me."

She laughed softly. "You don't snore. And I promise to talk to you. Can you forgive me for leaving, Garrett?"

"Of course I can. And we can un-date until you're ready to date-date."

"It sounds so silly, but I need it, Garrett. I need it to be just us, at least for a little while."

"I know you do, and I get it. Get some sleep, cutie." She was afraid of losing my mother, my family, of driving me away. But what she didn't know—and what I had no idea how to make her see—is that she would never lose me. I'd been hers ever since we were kids and I always would be.

She fell asleep first. I watched her smile, whispered goodnight to her and pressed a kiss to her cheek after her eyelids fluttered shut and did not open.

CHAPTER 28

MOLLY

*M*aybe sometimes couples were just meant to be. Like puzzle pieces snapping together or two pieces of a broken heart finally knitting itself whole again. That thought lodged itself into my brain as I opened my eyes to look down and marvel at the way my short, curvy body had molded right into Garrett's tall, hard frame as if it were always meant to be at his side. I smiled and snuggled closer. A quick glance at one of the clocks on the bedside table told me it wasn't quite time to get up, so I let my eyes fall closed again to sleep for a few more minutes. Waking up was always the worst part of the day. I had been a "five more minutes" kind of girl since birth.

"I'm up, I'm up." My head fell off Garrett's arm to bounce on the pillow as he bolted upright in bed with a shout, bumping his head on the bottom of the bunk bed in the process. "Holy shit, that's loud," he yelled over the sound of my multiple alarms going off.

Blinking in the now-bright morning light, I sat up and blindly reached toward the bedside table. One by one, I shut them off. "I'm so sorry! I don't sleep with my hearing aid in and sometimes it takes a lot to get me to wake up. Are you okay?"

I peered into his eyes, which were a bit wild as he clutched his chest and looked around the treehouse as if he didn't know where he was. "I'm okay. I'm fine, it's fine, it just startled me is all."

"Your poor head." I got up to straddle his lap and tip his face down so I could kiss it better.

He inhaled deeply as he wrapped his arms around me. "I'll live. Good morning." With a hand in my hair, he gave a gentle tug back so he could kiss me. I let myself sink into the kiss and into his arms as he fell backward on the bed, taking me with him.

"Garrett . . ." I whispered. I pulled back, resting my chin on my hands so I could look at him. He smiled up at me and it was different than the Garrett smiles I was used to. We'd discovered an all-new language together last night, one only we could speak. And even though I'd run off and left him alone in his bed like a weenie, he was here with me now. He understood me, and he always had. Maybe I could never drive him away. Maybe, if I got lucky, he would never let me go.

"I like this," he said. I smiled as I gazed at his face, letting my palms press against the hard planes of his bare chest while I inhaled his warm, clean scent. His eyes crinkled at the corners as his smile softened into yet another secret for us to keep between us. I wanted to memorize everything about this moment so I could fill my dreams with it and keep it safe forever.

"I like it too. I'm glad you found me." His grin grew wicked as he shifted his hips upward—morning wood. My thighs were spread over his, so I pressed back against the hard length of him, with my eyebrows raised in question.

"Yes," was all he said as his hands drifted down my sides. I slid down his body as he grabbed the hem of my nightie and held it, pulling it over my head as I moved lower, leaving me in only my panties and socks and him in his boxer briefs. My nipples hardened into stiff peaks, tickled by the crisp hair of his thighs on my descent.

"We've crossed every line but this one, Garrett," I declared as I let my tongue drift down the center of his abs. "Are you ready?"

I didn't expect an answer and I didn't get one. Unless you counted blazing eyes and sudden rapt attention an answer—which I did. He lifted to his elbows as he watched me. At my urging he raised his hips so I could remove his boxer briefs, then let out a low groan as I took him into my mouth with a swirl of my tongue.

Looking up at him, I saw not only the Garrett I'd always known, but also the man I'd met for the first time last night. I saw the man who took my body and made it his own, who made me feel like the only thing on earth he wanted was me. More than anything, I wanted him to feel the exact same way.

I watched as he gripped the sheets hard in his fists. His head fell back between his shoulders and his cock grew impossibly harder in my mouth. I loved how it felt, I loved seeing the muscles in his neck tighten and release, then tighten again as I sucked harder. The clench of his jaw as he held in his moans spurred me on until I was the one moaning. I wanted to make him lose control, I wanted to taste every inch of him—he was that delicious.

"Molly," he groaned. "Enough. Get up here—I need to be inside you." Like a jackknife, he folded, slipped his hands under my arms to lift me, sliding himself out of my mouth with a pop before lowering me little by little until I was full of him. Eye to eye we moved together, rocking slowly back and forth. His breathing slowed. His eyes burned into mine and I got lost in them.

On my knees, I started to move, sliding up and down on his cock, pressing kisses to his lips every time I took him back inside. His arms held me close, fingers drifting up and down my spine, featherlight and gentle as I moved over him.

This felt different than anything I'd ever experienced. This didn't feel like sex—it felt like love. The crazy kind of love that came out of nowhere and knocked you on your ass. The kind of love that changed everything you thought you knew about yourself. Sudden, head-over-heels, overwhelming love, the kind that got people married and turned them insane when they lost it. I hadn't been looking for it, yet here I was, drowning in it. Half of me wanted to sink all the way to the bottom and let him fill me up with it. The other half fought to reach the surface, screaming about how much it would hurt when I lost him.

"You feel so good," he whispered in my ear. His beard tickled my neck and I shivered in his arms.

So good—too good. It was too much and way too soon.

With his hands at my ass, he flipped me to my back and entered me with a determined, claiming thrust. He held my hands above my head and drove inside of me, hard, until I felt nothing else, saw nothing else but him. I wrapped my legs around his waist and held on, using his body as leverage to roll my hips and meet him thrust for thrust. Nothing would ever feel like this again. Not ever.

My heart had finally caught up to my brain and they were both chanting his name. Then I realized that it was me chanting his name for real and not my metaphorical body parts. I had no idea how loud I had been until I came, splintering into a thousand little pieces and shouting out my pleasure as if we were truly alone in the world.

"Oh god, Garrett," I moaned as he rose to his knees, hunched over beneath the top bunk to brace himself on one hand. He gripped my hip in his broad palm and surged wildly into me, out of control.

"Touch yourself," he ordered. "I want to see it." I slid my fingers down my body to circle my clit, relishing his enthusiastic reaction as he dipped his head to watch and went even harder, so hard he shook the bed frame into the wall. "You're so fucking beautiful," he groaned as we came together. He collapsed on top of my shuddering body, both of us spent. Before I could lose my breath from his weight, he rolled us to the side.

"I could wake up like this every day," I said before I had a chance to think about it. Throwing an arm behind me, I fumbled over the bedside table until I found my hearing aid.

"Me too. I've never—"

"What? Tell me."

"I never—nothing has ever come close to how I feel when I'm with you, Molly," he confessed.

"Same. I wish we could stay here all day . . ." I sat up in alarm, clutching the sheet to my chest. "How are you going to go to work with no one seeing you? Where did you park?" I could swear a hurt expression crossed his face before he hid it with a reassuring smile.

"I parked on the street, not in the parking lot. If I leave now, I can get home before anyone notices I was even here." He scooted to the foot of the bed and bent over, gathering his clothes.

I didn't stop him as he headed into the bathroom to get dressed, and even though it felt wrong, I let him kiss me goodbye and leave with a promise to see him later.

I wanted to find my way out of this secret so we could be in the open. But the tide of fear and doubt I was stuck in drowned out every other facet of my life. It was constantly ebbing and flowing, pushing me back every time I took a step forward. In the end I would never make any progress unless I stepped out of the sand.

Would I ever be able to trust my feelings? Or was I destined to end up alone, surrounded by adorable cats, subsisting on only pie, with nothing but my hand for entertainment?

Would I end up like Lacy? Desperate for good dick and willing to jam an engagement ring on my finger in order to get laid? With a bitter laugh, I glanced at my finger, still wearing Great-Aunt Jade's ring. Garrett had spoiled me. I was ruined. How do people go back to normal once they've experienced high-skill-level sex? And that didn't even get into the feelings that went along with it. Every time he touched me, my heart practically demanded to move into his chest and live with his.

Who was I trying to fool?

Yeah, Garrett had skills, but he was more than good sex. He was everything sweet and considerate I'd ever fantasized about and probably some stuff I didn't even know I wanted yet.

Throwing back the covers, I found my pajamas and robe and left the treehouse to go home and get ready for the day. With all the time I'd spent hiding out up here lately, I should stock the place with some clothes.

I squinted into the sunlight when I'd finally trudged up to my porch. Someone was sitting on my swing. "Molly! I'm sorry about last night." It was Clara. She stood up when I got there. "Forgive me?"

"Yes, I forgive you. Come in with me and we'll have coffee. After I shower."

After giving me a thorough up and down, she burst out laughing. "Oh my! I'll start the coffee while you clean the sex off. Good for you with the messed-up hair and puffy lips. Do I spy a hickey on your neck?"

"Stop it, or I'll start grilling you about how your evening ended up. Chris Barrett? Stamina? Feel like spilling about that?" She shook her head with a grin as I unlocked the door. "I didn't think so."

We split up when we got inside; her to the kitchen, me to the bathroom. We met at the table on the back porch with coffee and slices of emergency pie. I was shower fresh in a denim skirt and my Smoky Mountain Inn polo with my hickey all covered up beneath my buttoned-up collar.

"I really am sorry about last night. I feel terrible," she said.

"Clara, I know, and I'm sorry too. I've been too self-absorbed lately. I should have asked about you. You got fired! Do you want to talk about it?"

"No, I'm okay, I dumped it all on Sadie and Leo. I'm going to be just fine and—oh! Holy shit, Sadie hired Lacy as a real estate agent to find our house. They bonded over their divorces and lack of sex. It's insanity, I tell you."

"Lacy is a real estate agent?"

"She works for her daddy. He has offices all over Knoxville. Are you going to be okay with that?"

"I guess that's cool. Good for them. I hope she finds y'all an awesome house."

The glimmer of Great-Aunt Jade's ring in the sunlight reminded me of who had the upper hand with Garrett now. I should take it off, but I liked how I felt whenever I saw it on my finger—I was such an idiot. No one in their right mind would believe it was stuck anymore.

"We're meeting later to look at a few houses. But, Molly, we'll be in the same town again. Manis, pedis, and lunch once a week. Promise me." Her smile was infectious and I couldn't help but smile back.

"I promise. I can't wait."

"Now that's settled, we can get down to the real business. You flipped out last night." I nodded sheepishly. "Totally understandable because deep down you know you're going to end up marrying Garrett. In your heart, you know he's the one," she declared as she gestured to the ring. "And by the way, we need to smudge that thing with some sage to cast out the bad vibes. Wearing it right after Lacy is super weird and probably ten different kinds of bad luck."

My mouth was open to take a bite of pie but now it was just hanging open with shock.

Married.

Me?

Ridiculous.

Yeah, I still had the ring on. It was a fantasy I liked thinking about. But it could never happen for real.

"Shut up," I said, immediately shoving the idea of marriage out of my mind. The thought of me as a wife was ludicrous. Who would ever be able to tolerate my nonsense?

"She's right, you know." Our heads swiveled to the side as we heard Cam approach. "Also, I smelled coffee and I'm here to bum some. Ah, hello, beautiful Clara." He grinned at her once he'd made it closer to the table. Cam often bummed coffee from me. I sometimes had the feeling he'd bum Clara off me too, if given half a chance.

"It's in the kitchen," Clara informed him. But instead of heading into the house, he winked at her and sat down. He stole my cup and took a sip with a smirk.

I rolled my eyes. "You're lucky you always bring me dinner, turd."

Clara shook her head. "I'm glad I only have sisters."

They were interesting and any other day I might have indulged in some teasing, but not today. "He's not going to propose anytime soon. No. You're crazy. No way. No. It's too fast." I stared at the pie on my fork, pretty sure my eyes grew crossed as I got lost in denial.

Cam gave me a look—the rude big-brother look that told me he thought I was being a dumbass. "It's not too fast. You've known him your entire life. It was always bound to happen. Look at Mom and Dad. They were childhood sweethearts, married right out of high school. It happens. It can work, too."

"Yeah, and, Molly, I didn't say it would be *soon*. I said someday. But Cam has a valid point," Clara agreed. "You should have seen yourself when you walked up here. All dreamy eyed and floaty, like out of a freakin' romance movie. I was surprised you didn't throw your arms out and spin in a happy circle or start singing. And he's the same way about you. I saw him sneaking out to Everett's Bronco, all determined to keep your secret and do whatever you want. Y'all are adorable. I'm happy for you. Aren't you happy?"

"Uh . . ." Talking about my feelings was not my favorite thing to do.

"He's gone for you, Molls. Always has been. It was always just a matter of timing. You're already wearing a ring anyway. You might as well get ready for it," Cam added as he sipped my coffee and smirked at me.

"When did you get so observant, Cam?" Clara flung her hand out, smacking him on the arm.

"I grew up, same as you did, Clara. Maybe *you* should be more observant."

She let out a *hmph* as she looked him up and down. Objectively, I could admit my brother was good looking. All of them were. Maybe I should do some of my own matchmaking, once I get my life settled. Which, in reality, would probably be never, so I guess they didn't have to worry.

"I'm not listening to this. I'm going to work." I let my fork clatter to the plate and stood up to leave. "You can have my pie, Cam," I offered.

"Think about this while you're working, Molly, so you don't end up shocked later," Clara shouted to my retreating back. "Who did you compare all the Chrises to after y'all broke up? To each other or to Garrett?"

"Oh yeah, and Leo said you compared Garrett to Dad the other day. Think about that too," Cam added.

Clara gasped. "She did?"

"Hell yeah, she did," Cam said. I turned around to see him take a bite of my pie. Whatever.

"I feel it in the air, Molly. Get ready for the happy ever after! This time it's coming for you no matter how fast you try to run from it."

"Whatever, y'all!" I huffed.

"Hey, at least you had a good dad to compare guys to! Mine is a piece of crap," Clara said with a laugh.

"Have dinner with me, Clara. I'll give you something to compare guys to. I'll even wear my best suit. I know how to treat a lady." And he did. Cam could be very sweet when he had a mind to. Clara sat up straight in her seat, surprised.

241

"Maybe you sense your own happy ever after coming, weirdo!" I shouted, gratified when Cam raised his eyebrows and gave Clara a flirty up and down.

"Maybe I'll take you up on that, Cam. See? This is me saying yes to opportunity, Molly. Try it!"

They laughed together as I flipped them off over my shoulder. Both of them were crazy. I started speed-walking to the inn. I needed to get lost in my work and stop thinking. Thinking got me into trouble. Thinking made me do crazy stuff like run off in a pantsless panic to buy pie or run off in the middle of the night to a bar. No more thinking allowed. No more running. I couldn't hurt Garrett again, so shutting my brain off was the only option.

CHAPTER 29

GARRETT

*T*ime passed while I spent every day cooped up in my father's office instead of working at the inn. Even though he had been training me to take over, the sheer amount of work he did on a daily basis was unreal. It was much more complicated than running jobsites and supervising labor. I was now in charge of all aspects of Monroe & Sons and it took every bit of my time. I couldn't afford to mess this up; too many people depended on me for that.

My father would be here soon to meet me for lunch so I could get him up to speed on what he'd missed since my mother was finally going to allow him to talk about the company. However, I doubted that my mother would let him start working again anytime soon, if at all. I had the feeling his retirement would come sooner than either of us had expected.

I missed seeing Molly every day at the inn. It had become a physical thing, a dull ache that sat in the middle of my chest and never went away. The uncertainty of our un-dating combined with not knowing when I could see her again was no longer exciting, it was no longer anticipatory. It was making me miserable. I couldn't wait to just *be* with her. We snuck in a few overnights at the inn or my cabin and we spoke every night before bed and texted throughout the day, but it wasn't enough. My heart grew desperate as it broke into pieces. I needed more.

"Hey, Dad is on his way." Barrett poked his head into what would probably be my office very soon. Barrett's office was next to this one. Essie, my father's long-time secretary, had retired a couple months ago, and my mother had been handling her duties until we could hire a new one.

"Okay, thanks." I sat back in Dad's chair to take in the room. I'd been coming in here my whole life and the thought of it becoming mine was bittersweet. A goal I'd had for my entire life was close to being accomplished, but a massive life change went along with it, and not for just myself.

"You okay? This last week has been insane." Barrett stepped inside and took the seat across from the desk.

"I will be once everything settles down."

"*If* it settles down, you mean. It can get pretty crazy here sometimes."

Our heads turned at the tap on the open door. "Hello, boys! Your daddy is waiting for you in the dining room, Garrett. It's time for your lunch meeting."

"Later, Barrett." I stood up to head to the dining room, kissing Mom's cheek as I walked past her.

Dad sat in his usual spot at the head of the table. "Come on, grab some tea and sit down. We have a lot to talk about," he said with a smile.

They'd picked up takeout from Daisy's, but not what Dad usually ordered. No cheeseburgers, no fries, no pie. I saw green salad topped with chicken and veggies and a container of soup. "Mom made you order that?" I asked in what I hoped was a neutral tone.

"Nope." He grinned. "I've got a list of stuff I can eat and I'm sticking to it. I have four boys, five grandbabies, and the most beautiful wife in the world. I'm not ready to leave y'all behind." He looked great, back to his normal happy self.

"And you're okay with that? We were worried you'd fight the changes."

"I might be stubborn, but I'm no fool. I have a lot to live for. And that leads to what I have to talk to you about, Garrett."

"Okay." I sank back into my chair as fear I hadn't even realized I had been holding on to left my body. We were here and almost back to normal, so maybe everything would be okay after all.

"I'm cutting back on work. Stress played a big role in what happened. I love this company, so much that it didn't feel like a job. But I can admit I'm a bit of a perfectionist. I took everything on myself and it was a bad choice that I paid the price for. I don't want that for either one of us, so until I fully retire, we'll run the company together, you and me. We'll come up with new ways to run the business so that after I retire, it will never fall one hundred percent on you. We're going to learn how to delegate. Balance is the key, all the stuff your momma always talked about over the years—taking weekends off, evenings off, leaving the work at the office—it's all important, and she was right. I don't want what happened to me to happen to you. So," he said as he shoved a Daisy's bag my way, "here's your salad. Let's eat and discuss how this is gonna work. Family first, son."

"Family first," I repeated with a grin. "I love you, Dad."

"I love you too, and I'm glad I'm still around to show you how much. Don't take a minute of your life for granted, not ever, Garrett."

Molly flashed through my mind as did the fact that she didn't have this. The relationship I had with my parents was my guide to how I wanted to be, the blueprint for the life I had always wanted to live for as long as I could remember. Her parents were great, loving people but their tragedy —her dad's battle with cancer and her mom's all-encompassing grief— colored most of her childhood and her entire adult life, leaving her without the touchstone I had taken for granted.

"I won't."

"Good, because I want you to think about moving into the house. Your momma wants to live in the Bandit Lake house. She said she wants to downsize, but really I think she wants to keep me away from the office."

My jaw dropped. "What?" I breathed.

"You don't have to sell your cabin. Keep it for getaways and such. Maybe with Molly? How's that going?"

"Uh . . . fine, I think." None of what was between Molly and me had ever really been a secret, no matter how much she wanted it to be. "You're sure you want me to move in here?"

"Yeah, it's going to be yours one day anyway. Might as well get used to it now. And there's plenty of room for kids, as you know. I'm sure Stan will like it too." He grinned at me. "I wouldn't mind a few more grandbabies. And now that I'll be working less, I'll have plenty of time to spoil them rotten."

"Grandbabies," I repeated as an image of Molly, rounded with my baby inside of her invaded my thoughts. The phrase *"meant to be"* ran through my mind and just like that I wanted this house immediately. I saw us here together so clearly; I wanted us to make this place our own. I wanted to plant her inside and fill it with kids. Could I make her see what I saw? Would she ever understand that life changes could be exciting instead of something to fear?

"Is the inn still on schedule with Chris in charge?" he asked, wrenching me out of my meandering thoughts about Molly.

"Yes, they'll wrap it up by the end of the week. Landon and Leo are planning a party to celebrate."

"Good. Seems like you did just fine when I was gone. I'm proud of you."

"Thanks. I think I did all right. But I'm glad you aren't retiring just yet. I never realized exactly how much went in to running this place."

"By the time I officially retire, you'll have it down to a science. So, I was thinking I'd like a bit of time in my office to get up to speed. Maybe you should go check on the inn and see for yourself how it's going."

I laughed. "Or check on Molly? Did Mom tell you to send me out there?"

"Maybe." He chuckled. "But it's a good thing. Maybe you should go check on your girl and forget my clumsy attempt to do your mother's dirty work."

"Solid plan. I'll take you up on it."

He tossed me a set of keys. "I know you never wanted one before, but since you're stepping up, you should have a company truck. Don't you think?"

"Yeah, I think you're right." Breakdowns were getting old. Plus, I couldn't drive a wife and kids around in a beat-up old truck.

Molly

With a disgruntled shove, I closed the drawer on my desk and scooted back in my chair. I was miserable. Missing Garrett was a large part of it, but I refused to think too hard about why. I was in an odd pattern of denying half of my feelings so I wouldn't destroy the other half. Going on like this might make me go crazy. Obviously, I had fallen for him, but even more obvious was the fact that it terrified me.

Everything ends.

Bill's heart attack proved how fragile life could be. But that shouldn't stop me from living my life. I needed someone to shake some sense into me or teach me how to lose the irrational fear that everything would come crashing down if I let myself. Maybe my brain and my heart were not in alignment, just like Jordan said.

My phone buzzed in my pocket and I almost fell out of my chair. It had to be Garrett. He'd been texting me every day after lunch since our first un-date.

Can we meet at your place?

I texted back a quick, "yes."

"I'm taking a break, Landon!" I shouted and dashed for the front door of the inn.

"Okay, transfer the calls to my cell phone. I'm about to head into the rose garden," he shouted back from somewhere near the front door

"Done! Thanks!" I shouted as I passed him on the porch.

I did my best not to make a fool of myself by running full out across the grounds to my house. I managed to keep it to a brisk power walk, and I was only slightly out of breath when I reached my front door. I unlocked it and stepped inside, intending to take a quick peek at myself in the mirror by the door before he got here. But I got stuck there instead, I didn't know myself anymore. The face that stared back at me looked different—a mixture of happy and hopeful that was foreign to me.

"Molly! Are you in there?"

I flung the door open. My breath quickened and my heart skipped a beat at the sight of him standing there. This was the feeling I wanted to hold on to, the one that kept me going no matter what else popped into my head to make me doubt it. My past and the future were all mixed up in Garrett now. And I couldn't seem to sort it out.

"Guess what?" His smile was bright white and gorgeous as he rushed forward to sweep me in his arms. He turned me in an excited circle and buried his face in my neck.

"Your dad is finally back to work with you?" I guessed.

He pulled back, still smiling. "Yes, but that's not all."

He looked so happy. The joy in his eyes was glorious and I wanted to be part of it. "Look at you! Tell me everything."

He told me he would run the business with Bill. He told me about his company truck and that he would be moving into the house in town. He told me so many wonderful things that he wanted me to be part of. But each bit of news was like a brick being added to form an insurmountable pile. Engagement, wedding, marriage. Moving into the house in town, babies, being Garrett's wife someday. I didn't want any of it to feel like a weight on my shoulders, I wanted those bricks to build us a home.

I needed more time. But I *would not* run away. I would stay right here and talk this out with him.

His hands drifted up my body to cradle my face. "I have to tell you something. I want you to know that I'm falling in love with you, Molly. I think on some level I've been falling for years. Please don't freak out over this. Not telling you was beginning to feel like a lie, and I don't want to ever keep anything from you—"

"Oh! Garrett, I—I feel like I—I, I . . ." *LOVE YOU!*

He placed a gentle finger to my lips. "Shh, you don't have to say anything right now. I just couldn't keep it inside anymore. I had to let you know how I felt."

I nodded as I looked up at him. *Why couldn't I say it?*

Why was I stuck like this? What I felt for him was more than I had ever felt for anyone. I had been wandering around in an all-encompassing life daze for so long that the clarity of his words shining down on me was blinding. But I couldn't see my way through the swirling mass of emotion to reach it.

I love you too was locked inside my heart, refusing to come out. The words were pounding, beating, dying for me to say them. But I just stood there, wide-eyed and tongue-tied as he cradled my face in his big hands. He smiled, sweet and soft and everything I ever wanted. "Molly, baby. It's okay. I told you I could wait. Hush." He placed a gentle kiss on my lips.

"Okay . . ." I breathed. I had become overwhelmed by so many things; I couldn't pick one to focus on.

"But I did want to talk to you about something else," he said. "This secret we're keeping. The un-dating. I want you to go with me to the party tomorrow as my date. Can we do that? Will you be my date tomorrow night, Molly?" His smile shifted to the side as he waited for an answer.

"Are you sure we're ready for that? Your dad isn't one hundred percent yet and everyone will be there—"

"Isn't it time we think about the toll this is beginning to take? I get that we're not exactly lying, but erasing the truth from my daily interactions is hard. You are the biggest part of my life, and no matter what I say to the contrary, everyone seems to already know what's happening."

"Okay. I get that, I do. I really do. Can I, um—" Disappointment flashed across his face before he hid it. Quite suddenly I remembered him offering to go with me to the sixth-grade dance as my date. At the time, I had thought nothing of it. We were just two friends going to a dance together. The look on his face just now was the same as the one he'd tried to hide when I'd danced with someone else. I don't even remember who it was; all I could ever remember when I looked back was the sadness in his eyes. Sadness I put there and would probably keep putting there if I didn't wake up.

He took a step back, letting me go.

Don't let me go.

"You know what? It's too soon. I can see that now. We can meet there. No one needs to know anything yet. I promised I could wait for you to be ready, and I pushed you. I need to get back to the office. I'll see you tomorrow." He spun on his heel and left.

It was unlike any goodbye we'd ever had, and I hated it. The tables had turned—this time he was the one to run.

It hurt.

I died a bit inside when I realized I was finally feeling what I had made him feel so many times before.

CHAPTER 30

GARRETT

I'd blown it. I pushed too hard and ruined everything. I'd felt the pieces of my life start clicking into place, and instead of waiting for her to fit in on her own time, I tried to force it to happen. Maybe I was an idiot for leaving like I did, but the look on her face was killing me. It was a mixture of pity and fear that no man ever wanted to see.

I had rushed her; I knew it now. When we reconnected, time had ceased to matter. I'd been too busy falling in love with her to notice how much of it had passed. Or too little, as the case may be.

I got into my new truck and drove. I had to get away from her.

The sun started to set and I realized I'd been driving for hours. With a turn of the wheel, I headed for Barrett's house. Wyatt and Everett were both too happy with their wives to understand how I felt and I didn't want to be around either of them.

We could watch something historical and violent on Netflix. Maybe a war documentary or one of the *Captain America* movies. I could order a pizza and Barrett almost always had beer in the fridge.

It was okay. I swiped beneath my eyes with my wrist.

251

Shit.

Everything would be fine.

Probably.

I'd see her tomorrow and we'd be back to normal.

Maybe.

I pulled into Barrett's driveway and knocked on the door. He had a big house in town— four bedrooms, three bathrooms, huge yard—bought back when he and his ex-wife had planned on filling the place up with kids. Back before she cheated on him, then moved to Knoxville with her boyfriend. Now his daughter was in Knoxville too, and he missed her every day.

"Hey, man." His head drew back as he studied my face. "Catching a cold? Your eyes are all red."

"Uh, yeah. I must be." I swiped at my eyes again with the back of my hand.

"What's up?"

"Uh, wanna hang out? We could order pizza—"

He stepped aside with a knowing smile. "It's your lucky night because pizza is already on the way. Go sit down and I'll grab us some beers."

"Seems like we're in similar moods."

"We might just be. Hit play. I'll be right back." I headed toward Barrett's living room while trying to force Molly out of my mind.

Impossible.

I was keeping it together. Right until I saw what Barrett was watching. *Avengers: Age of Ultron.* He was right at the part where goddamn Captain America was standing in the doorway of Hawkeye's house on that fucking farm in the middle of nowhere. Cap knew he'd never have anything close to what he saw right there in that living room. No family.

No home of his own with kids and a wife or a fucking dog to run around and play fetch with.

Stan could use a mother, damn it.

I was motherfucking Captain America right now. I was all alone because I screwed everything up.

Shit. I pressed my palms to my eyes as my emotions started to leak out.

The bottom of a cold bottle pressed into my temple and I opened my eyes. "Bro, you okay?"

"Yeah, it's, uh, the movie. This part always gets me. Fucking Captain America . . ." My eyes burned; more tears pricked at the back, but I managed to hold them at bay.

"Maybe you have something in your eye?" Barrett suggested gently as tears started to spill over in earnest.

Shit. "Uh yeah, I had the windows down when I was driving over here, maybe some pollen or dirt or something blew in . . ." I sniffled. Barrett knew I didn't have something in my eye. He even knew that my tears had jack shit to do with Captain America. Maybe he already knew it was all about Molly. My heart felt like it had been through a meat grinder. It fucking hurt.

"Here. Give it a minute. Take a deep breath." It sounded like he was telling me to shake off a basketball to the face or a fall off a bike like when we were kids, totally cool, like everything was normal. He passed me a box of tissues, then sat down next to me on the couch.

He flicked the movie off and switched it to ESPN. One deep, shuddering breath later and I felt like I could breathe again, sort of. "Thanks." I took the tissue box and grabbed a handful to wipe my runny nose.

What the hell was wrong with me?

"You know how she is, man. Whatever happened tonight, you just have to ride it out. You know that, right? That girl is yours and everyone knows it. *She* even knows it. You've been talking about her like she's some kind of princess since you were toddlers. And she's always looked at you like you were her big hero. Always. We all saw it." He was right. Of course. Part of my heart had always been hers. No wonder I had lost my shit— there were women and then there was *Molly*. I let my head drop forward, digging my hands into the back of my neck as I inhaled a huge breath.

"Yeah, okay. You're right," I managed to choke out.

He patted my back, then left his hand there. "She'll come around. Ride it out, Garrett. You're okay for now. You can crash in one of my many empty bedrooms tonight, yeah?"

Of course he'd figured me out. That's what made him a great big brother. I nodded. "Yeah, thanks. Ride it out. Yeah, I can do that," I agreed and wiped my eyes with another handful of tissue.

"It's all you can do, really. Pushing too hard always ends up pushing them away. You gotta keep that in mind . . ." he mumbled, more to himself than to me.

"I won't do any more pushing if it ends up like this. Fuck, man, this sucks."

"Shit, I know it."

"Don't tell anyone about this, okay?"

"To the grave, Garrett."

"Thanks." We ate pizza, finished off a six-pack of beer and mindlessly watched ESPN despite the fact that neither one of us were sports fans until bedtime. Not one more word was spoken about Molly, but I felt much better.

CHAPTER 31

MOLLY

The sun was almost up but I was off the clock. We'd checked the last of the guests out yesterday afternoon and we were free until Monday. Landon wanted the party to go off without a hitch and he decided we could all use a weekend off.

Being alone in this melancholy mood was stupid, so I'd gotten dressed and wandered over to the inn to check out the brand-new kitchen. I moved one of the new barstools to the exact spot the old one had sat in and looked around the gleaming new space while thinking of my dad. He'd always wanted to remodel it just like this. I was worried my melancholy would head into maudlin, so I had hopes that one of my brothers would be here soon.

"Yo." I spun in my stool to see Jordan and Cam standing in the new half door that led out to the parking lot. They were working the same shift at the mill this week and were still dressed in their work clothes. They were probably here in search of food. Leo had done a huge grocery shop while Garrett's crew was finishing up yesterday. The shiny new fridge was fully stocked.

"Landon and Leo are upstairs with Abbie," I informed Jordan.

"Not anymore. Last night they drove her to spend the night with Ev and Willa, plus all of Wyatt's kids, except for the baby. I think even Sadie's boys are there."

"Whoa. I didn't know that. That's a whole bunch of kids."

"They wanted the practice. And Everett is like a big kid anyway. They want a huge family, so—" He shrugged.

"That's insane. I mean, yeah, he is a big kid, and Willa is awesome, but it's still insane." I marveled while suddenly picturing a bigger, even more well-lit, less murder-woodsy version of Garrett's cabin filled to the brim with kids of our own—and Stan. My sigh was both dramatic and tragic. I let my head drop to my arm on the counter.

"Right? One is a handful, let alone five. But I'm not saying no to a day off." Jordan uncapped a beer using the edge of the counter.

"Don't let Leo catch you doin' that on his new counter," Cam said before grabbing his own beer and pointedly taking the magnetic bottle opener off the fridge to open his own bottle. "You want a beer, Molls? I sense you may need one based on your not-so-subtle head flop on the counter."

"No, since it's morning." I shook my head.

"Not for us," Jordan replied. "We worked all night. Tell us what to do, Molly. If someone is the cause of that hurt look on your face, just tell us who to maim."

"She's seeing Garrett and I'm not going after him, man," Cam said. "He's family. Tell us how to help you, Molls."

I lifted my head because, huh? These two would usually rather knock heads together than talk about stuff. "What?"

"Tell us what the problem is." Cam sat next to me and ruffled my hair.

"Who even are you right now, Cam? And how do you even know about—"

"You are the worst at sneaking around," Jordan said as he leaned against the counter right across from me to sip his beer and make fun of me.

"And Garrett doesn't even try. Yeah, he parks his truck behind the dumpster, but come the fuck on, y'all are terrible at this secret shit. Plus, I don't know if you're aware of this, but you're not exactly quiet, you know. I've heard things no brother should ever hear. I'm traumatized! I may never be the same, Molly. And as payback for the therapy I need yet sadly can't afford, we will give you shit for this for the rest of your life."

"What? Nooooooo . . ." I breathed as horror flowed into my system. Garrett made me feel good and I liked to express it. But crap, was I really that loud?

Cam laughed. "Yeah, I heard y'all banging in the treehouse at least—" He turned to Jordan. "What, like two times, right? Once was way more than enough, but like Jordan said, after the second time? Scarred for life."

"Yup, I don't take Abbie to play in there anymore." Jordan nudged my arm with a laugh.

"I don't want to hear this." I lifted a hand to remove my hearing aid. I knew it was immature, but they were my big brothers and used to my shit.

Cam grabbed my hand with a laugh. "No way, Molls. We had to hear you banging Garrett, so consider this your penance. What y'all are doing ain't the big secret you think it is. Everyone knows and nobody cares. We love y'all, and if banging my dude Garrett makes you happy? Then do it. Get married and bang your way into eternity together."

"Stop saying bang. Can a person cringe to death? Because I am literally about to die right now." I slapped Cam's arm. Then I slapped it again, and then one more time because ew, ew, ew.

"The banging is not the big secret." We all turned as Leo entered the room from the stairwell that led to the top floor apartment.

"It's Dad. It's Becky Lee and Bill. It's you, Molly," Landon said, he had followed behind him to join us.

I got up to leave. I was not interested in getting real with them right now, or ever. But I sat at the table in the bay window instead. Maybe I should listen to them. I couldn't hurt more than I already did. I might as well go down the complete spiral and hit bottom. Maybe I could climb out of it if I listened for a change.

Cam and Jordan exchanged a look. "You really should start having dinner with us on Fridays, Molly."

I sat in my chair, staring out the window and shaking my head.

"Grief needs to be seen, sweetheart. Not hidden away inside your heart. Have dinner with us on Fridays like we always beg you to. Please? It's time," Landon added.

"We didn't move on either, Molly, if that's what you think," Jordan added. "We didn't let go of Dad once and then it's finished. We let go of him every day. Over and over. Every time I look at Abbie, I see his eyes. It's uncanny and it kills me every time, but I'm not going to hide from my own kid. I can't do that, can I? You need to quit hiding out, Molls."

"We miss him too, and talking helps. You don't have to keep doing this alone," Jordan chimed in.

"What? Why are you telling me this now?" I demanded.

"Because you're finally sitting down to listen," Landon shot back. "You're sitting in a chair and not halfway out the door with some excuse. You're never still."

Leo sat in the chair next to mine and held my hand. "We got you, Molls. I promise you. We're never leaving. Ever."

"You can't say that! No one can say that and really mean it because you don't know!" I shouted, sick of hearing the same promise that was impossible to keep.

"Garrett wouldn't leave you." He kept at me.

"Stop it, Leo."

"He wouldn't let you lose Becky Lee and Bill either, and you damn well know it." I did. I knew it deep down, and I always had.

"So, what's wrong with me, then? How do I fix this mess I've created?"

"You've divided your life into before Dad died and after. Before Mom left and after," Cam said. "You need to realize it's just *your life* and live it with no qualifiers. Make all the bad shit become part of your life instead of what defines it. You don't have to be healed to be loved, Molly."

"What?" I breathed as icy cold realization filled my veins, freezing me in place.

"You think you have to be over Dad's death, over Mom leaving. You think you have to be okay and fine in order to move forward with your life with Garrett. But you don't," Jordan said as he sat across from me.

"Don't be logical with me, Jordan!" I shoved my chair back and stood up.

"What are you scared of the most, Molly?" Landon asked. I shook my head. How could he ask me something like that? Wasn't it obvious?

"Say it. Out loud. Get it out of you." Leo stood up and wrapped an arm around me. "Come on, let it go."

"I—I'm afraid of being alone, that y'all will go, die, leave, whatever. I don't want to lose anyone else!" My chest rose and fell rapidly as my eyes darted around the room.

"If you try to keep this thing with Garrett a secret, you'll lose him. You know it," Leo said.

"I know, but I can't—"

"You're living a self-fulfilling prophecy," Landon said. "You're controlling when someone leaves by pushing them away."

"Oh my god." Tears filled my eyes when I realized he was absolutely right about me. "I do that. I always do that. He wanted us to go to the party together tonight. He wanted to stop keeping secrets, but I put him off. I probably ruined everything. I don't know what to do anymore."

"Listen to me. You clung to Clara and me, Molly," Leo said as he pulled me into his arms. "We stuck together, the three of us. Sadie, too. We were best friends back then and through the years, but we weren't the best with this." He waved a hand around the room. "We didn't just stick together; we were stuck in place together. Can you see that? Never moving on, never moving forward—" Tears filled his eyes. "I'd still be stuck, if it weren't for Landon. You need your brothers. You need Garrett. You need to let people in again—and not just the people who will tell you what you want to hear."

"What do I do, Leo?" I looked up at him. He swiped beneath my eyes with his thumbs.

"Come to Friday dinners with us, for a start," Cam said with a soft smile. "Sometimes we talk about Mom and Dad and get all—" He waved a hand around, lost for words.

"Dramatic and sad," Landon filled in, making Cam laugh.

"Yeah, that," he agreed. "But other times we just hang out with pizza and beer."

"You need us, Molly," Jordan added.

"And we need you," Landon finished. He pulled me from Leo's arms and kissed the top of my head.

"Okay, I'll stop hiding out on Fridays. I promise," I mumbled into his chest.

"*Oh!* I know exactly what you should do!" Leo shouted. "I mean about the Garrett situation. Let the secret out at the party! Let him know you're choosing to be with him out in the open. Let everyone know it. Then he'll believe you mean what you say."

"Can I just do that? Will that work?"

"He's got it so bad for you, Molls. It'll work," Jordan was reassuring as he grinned at me.

"Guys are easy, and clearly, y'all get along. I don't see the problem with just showing up and planting one right on him," Cam added.

"Should I just do that? In front of everyone? No, I can't do that," I scoffed.

"Do it. Let him know he matters to you. I double-dog dare you," Jordan came in with the surprise dare. I glared at him, the sneaky thing. He had just cut right to the chase.

"How?"

Leo framed my face with his hands and smiled. "Wear a pretty dress, let your hair down, wear high heels so you can reach to kiss him, honesty, truth, and let the secret go. That oughta do it."

"Sounds like a solid plan to me," Landon agreed.

"Of course it is!" Leo declared. "I'm never wrong about these things."

CHAPTER 32

GARRETT

I stood dressed in my best suit with my back against the side of my truck. The inn was lit up brighter than daylight. The kitchen completion party was in full swing, but I couldn't bring myself to go inside. Not with the way I had left things with Molly. She deserved better than to have me pressure her the way I had. I was better than that, dammit.

She had gone through something I had yet to understand and it hurt her in ways I could not begin to comprehend. Landon's words flashed through my mind. He had told me to forgive her if she couldn't let her feelings out. There was nothing to forgive, I had agreed to indefinite un-dating. It wasn't her fault I had wanted to change the deal.

Bypassing the side kitchen door, I went around to the front of the inn. Balloons and streamers and twinkle lights decorated the path to the main entrance and all along the porch. Landon and Leo had outdone themselves. Party guests were lingering in small groups, eating, drinking, and chatting. I saw several Monroe & Sons employees who I greeted as I passed. But inside the huge formal banquet room of the inn was who I was looking for.

Surrounded by our families, Molly stood in the corner, next to Leo and Clara. She was stunning in a silky red dress that flowed almost to her feet, with a neckline and side slit that should be illegal. She was gorgeous.

I had to get her to notice me without drawing attention to the fact that I *needed* her. Maybe I could get to her through Leo or Clara. I waved, and Leo caught my eye and elbowed Molly's arm with a sideways grin. Clara also grinned and leaned back against the wall as if to watch.

Molly caught my eye, and with a tremulous smile, headed my way, her high heels clicking over the gleaming wood floor. I looked toward the exit, thinking of leaving so she would follow, but she shook her head and I froze in place.

I backed up.

She continued walking.

I kept backing up.

I was still trying valiantly to keep this secret between the two of us. My eyes darted around the room at the grinning faces of our families and friends, but she didn't stop coming at me until she had my back against the wall. At my raised-eyebrow look of alarm, she smiled.

"Are you okay?" I mouthed.

"I love you, Garrett Monroe," she declared, and it was loud. Heads that weren't already facing us immediately turned in our direction, because of course. This was Green Valley and everyone else's business was always way more interesting. "I love you with all my heart and I want to be with you and only you. I want to marry you someday and carry your babies. I don't care if I turn into a roly-poly ball and have to eat weird-ass pickle food or a whole entire freakin' cow. I love you and I choose you and—"

She turned to the room to shout, "I love him." Her hand flew back into my chest, I took it to kiss her palm with a grin. "I've never *not* loved him for my whole entire life! We've been secretly dating ever since he kissed me at Genie's and that's the truth. He only kept it a secret because I asked him to. Because I was scared to mess up and lose him and scared to lose y'all. I'm still scared, but mostly—" She spun back to face me. "I —I hurt you and I messed everything up anyway, Garrett. Please forgive me. Please—" Tears flowed down her cheeks and her shoulders trembled as she stood there in front of me, beautiful as could be and radiant with her heart on display, wide open for everyone to see.

"Enough. Molly, baby, hush," I said, putting my finger to her lips. I had to let her know my heart felt the same way. "I love you too. I've always loved you, and I'll go right on loving you for the rest of my life." She covered her face as her shoulders shook with sobs and excited chatter filled the room.

We needed out of here, so I swept her into my arms. "Always, cutie," I said into her ear as I carried her out of the banquet room, through the side door and out to the rose garden.

"We heard!" Jordan hollered as I passed him. He was kicking a ball around on the lawn with Cam, Abbie, Melissa, and Sadie's boys. "I'm happy for y'all. Kids! Everyone, inside!" he yelled.

"Yup, it's gonna get loud up in that treehouse, right, Molls?" Cam hooted as he helped Jordan usher the kids inside the inn.

"Oh, god! Go to my house, Garrett," she murmured into my chest, where she was still hiding her face.

"You got it, baby." I changed course and jogged towards the back of the property to her little carriage house.

We made it to the porch, and I set her down. "Frick!" she shrieked through her tears. "It's locked and my keys are at the inn in my stupid cute purse that goes with this dress. *Ugh*!" She spun around. "Kick that door in. You know, like in a movie. Kick it, Garrett. You can fix it later. I'll even pay you."

I burst out laughing, then caught a glance at her chest, heaving up and down.

Her in that sexy red dress.

A semi-public declaration of love.

My dream come true.

Who gave a damn about a broken door?

I kicked it in.

"After you, cutie." I swept my arm out for her to precede me. I followed her in and propped the door up enough so it would sort of close. "I love you, Molly."

"I love you too." She rushed toward me, sliding her hands up my chest to grip the lapels of my suit jacket. "This is precious to me, Garrett. Too precious to destroy. This is everything I've always wanted and I'm sorry it took me so long to see what you saw."

I took her hands in mine, kissing each one before placing them back on my chest. "Believe this, please. It's always been you for me, Molly. Even when I couldn't have you, it's been you. For fucking always, okay?"

"Okay, Garrett. I believe you."

"Be sure. Right now, be sure. Because there's no going back after tonight. I won't allow it."

"I don't want to go back. I only want you. I've wanted you for as long as I can remember knowing what love was. I was just too scared." Her breath hitched on another sob.

"Take a breath, baby. I'm here now and everything will be okay." I let my hands drift down her cheeks, resting them against her neck. "You and me, Molly. This is where we start and it's never going to end."

"I don't want it to end." Those words were a promise. They filled a hole inside me, one that I hadn't known was there until she came back into my life, bringing smiles and laughter and fun right along with her.

"Good." I drew her closer, tipping her face up to mine with my thumbs beneath her chin. "I'm going to kiss you now. Then I'm going to take you to bed. And after this, I'm never going to be without you ever again.

I can't sleep without you. I can't *be* without you. You belong with me, and you always have."

"Yes, Garrett. Yes, to everything. All of it, please . . ." The tears were back, shimmering in her eyes like bursts of starlight. She was mine and I would never let her go. Never again.

"This is forever, Molly."

"Forever . . ." she repeated as her eyes drifted closed. I took her mouth, then bent to sweep her into my arms again to carry her to bed.

CHAPTER 33

MOLLY

Two Months Later

Garrett hadn't moved into the giant Monroe house in town yet. He said he wasn't ready for that level of housecleaning commitment and home maintenance. But really, I think he knew I was still baby-stepping my way through all the changes I'd been making lately and didn't want to add another one. Which gave me one more reason to love him.

Currently, I was sitting in my favorite chair next to Garrett's fireplace with Stan in my arms waiting for him to come home from work. I felt a little bit wifey, and I liked it. "Maybe I'll be your mommy for real someday, Stan." I snuggled the chunkalicious fur monster close and kissed his fluffy head as he purred and butted his face against my chin. "Would you like that? I betcha you would. Uncle Leo taught me how to make homemade cat treats, yes he sure did." I looked up with a start to see Garrett standing in the doorway watching me baby-talk his cat. I grinned at him. Nothing embarrassed me now that we were officially together. I was a loved-up mess and nothing could get me down.

"Hey, cutie. Making plans?" he teased.

My shoulders lifted in a shrug. "No, just getting the lay of the land from your murder cabin co-pilot is all. Stan likes me here, don't you, buddy?" Loud purring and a trilled meow were my only response. "See?"

"I know he does, and I love having you here." Well, that was a relief since I had been here every night for the last two months. Cam was eyeballing my house, I knew it. The second I moved in with Garrett, he'd be calling dibs and moving in there like a shot. "Come outside with me." He crossed the cabin and held his hand out once he reached the back door.

"'Kay. Is it hammock time?" I breathed. Hopefully we'd do some more practicing. On our last try, we'd almost managed to have a successful bang in it. But my response to Garrett had been overly enthusiastic as usual, and we'd ended up crashing to the ground instead, which, despite the dirty knees, was always worth it.

"Oh yeah." He grinned and held the door for me.

"I'll grab the wine," I offered.

"No, just you. Come on, baby."

"'Kay." I followed him. But he urged me to sit on the edge instead of helping me lie down with him. "What are you doing?" My jaw dropped as he sank to one knee in front of me. "Oh, Garrett."

Oh shit! Great-Aunt Jade's ring was still on my finger. He hadn't said anything about me wearing it, though I knew he noticed. I just couldn't bring myself to take it off. Also, the dang thing really was stuck.

"You and I were written in the stars, Molly." He held my left hand up with a sideways smirk as he dropped a kiss on my already beringed finger. I puffed out an embarrassed breath of air to blow an errant curl out of my eye.

My cheeks colored red. "Yeah, about the ring, I—"

His eyes met mine. "I love that you love this ring. Every time I see it on your hand, my heart smiles because I can remember you sitting on Aunt Jade's lap twirling it around and around her finger. We have a lifetime of memories together and I can't wait to fill the rest of our lives with more. But I can't make us official with a used ring. I'm sorry, cutie, it wouldn't be right."

I inhaled a deep breath as he tried to slip it off, and he laughed when it wouldn't budge over my knuckle. "It really is stuck," I murmured.

He bit his lip and bent his head, darting his tongue out to wet his lower lip as he slid my finger with the stubborn ring on it into his mouth. "Oh god . . ." I shivered as his eyebrows rose and he winked at me. "We can explore more of this later," I insisted as his tongue swirled around the base of my finger.

He released my finger with a *pop,* then slid the ring off. "More of what?" He chuckled.

"More of you sucking on me. I don't even care where," I answered.

His hot eyes held mine and burned with promises. "Anything you want." He slid Aunt Jade's ring onto my other hand, then reached into his pocket. "You know I love you?"

My smile was involuntary. Garrett brought smiles out of me simply by existing. "Yes. Do you know how much I love you too?"

He nodded as a soft smile drifted across his face.

I brushed a hand down his cheek. "To the moon and the stars and right back home again, Garrett. Forever. Big love—the biggest." I clutched at my chest when I said the words because I felt them so deeply. Loving Garrett had become part of who I was again. I felt whole and at peace and complete with him back in my life.

"I want you to be my wife, Molly Hazel Cooper. I want to take care of you and love you and make you happy every day."

"Every day," I repeated. Tears filled my eyes at the gratitude I felt for this moment, for the pure and simple joy. I let out a sob and clasped my hand to my mouth.

He took my hand and kissed it. "Will you marry me?"

"Yes, I will marry you." After slipping a perfect round diamond ring on my finger, he scooted into the hammock, wrapping me in his strong arms to hold me close.

Garrett had shaken up everything I thought I was and showed me things I never knew I wanted. My heart was full, about to burst with a love that had taken a lifetime to build. And now, one tiny, accidental spark blazed hotter than anything I'd ever known was possible.

EPILOGUE

GARRETT

The sky had long since turned dark as our wedding day rolled on into the wee hours of the night. Twinkle lights, lanterns, and white flowers of all kinds decorated the grounds of the inn as our families and friends celebrated with us. The best day of my life was coming to an end, but the future that was finally mine was just beginning.

I was dizzy. Leo was a good dancer but his go-to move aside from the two-step seemed to be a spinout. Letting him lead had been a huge mistake. "Get a new move, man," I complained with a laugh as I lost my balance and stepped on his foot. He released my hand and we walked to the edge of the wooden dance floor together to sit with a smiling Landon and watch Molly dance with my father.

Her beaded white dress swirled in a circle around the wooden dance floor covering the ground in front of the treehouse as he twirled her around. Every time the lights caught her, she sparkled just like the stars. The new Mrs. Monroe squealed with delight as he dipped her over his knee and her brown curls swept over the floor as he pulled her back up.

"Is it your turn with Molly now? You were a pretty crappy dance partner, Garrett. All you could focus on was her." Leo laughed and waved a hand in front of my face.

"Sorry about that." I grinned and tore my eyes from Molly to pay attention to him.

"We wouldn't have it any other way. She deserves the best and now she's got it." Landon sipped his champagne and grinned at me.

"Go get your girl," Leo said with a laugh. "It's been, what? Ten minutes since you last danced with her?"

I stood up and stopped at the edge of the floor. Molly caught my eye and smiled. It was the same gorgeous grin that had graced my life for as long as I could remember—but now it was mine to have forever.

Earlier tonight, I had vowed to keep that smile on her face, and I intended to do whatever it took to make sure I saw it every day, just like she did for me. A while back, I realized I had forgotten how to be happy without her in my life, but now that she was mine, my smile was back for good. She lit up my heart and I would never let her get away again.

"I'm happy for y'all." Barrett, glass of champagne in hand, slapped me on the shoulder with a grin. "I told you she'd come around."

"You were right about everything. Maybe you should ask Sadie to dance," I suggested when I saw her checking him out from across the dance floor where she sat at a table with Everett, the rest of the Hill girls, and Ruby and Weston.

He eyed me and handed me his glass with a determined smile. "I think I will."

"Everything is back on track with the family." My mother took Barrett's drink from my hand and sipped it gracefully as her gaze drifted over to Molly and Dad. Her smiling eyes landed on mine over the rim of the glass. "Send your daddy over here. Go dance with your wife, sweetheart."

"You got it, Ma." I kissed her cheek, then darted off to reclaim my wife.

Dad placed her hand in mine with a smile. "I'm happy for you, son."

"Not as happy as I am." I squeezed her hand and led her to the edge of the dance floor.

"Having a good night, Mr. Monroe?" She giggled as she reached high to wrap her arms around my neck.

"The best." I grinned down at her. "And you, Mrs. Monroe?"

"Dreams do come true," she murmured, her eyes suddenly wet with unshed tears.

I bent low to place a kiss on her gorgeous Cupid's bow lips. "I love you, my Molly Monroe. To the moon and the stars and right back home again."

ABOUT THE AUTHOR

Nora Everly is a life long reader, writer, and happily ever after junkie. She is a wife and stay-at-home mom to two tiny humans and one fat cat. She lives in Oregon with her family and her overactive imagination.

Newsletter: https://www.noraeverly.com/newsletter-1
Website: https://www.noraeverly.com/
Facebook: https://www.facebook.com/authornoraeverly
Goodreads: https://www.goodreads.com/author/show/19302304.Nora_Everly
Twitter: https://twitter.com/NoraEverly
Instagram: https://www.instagram.com/nora.everly/

Find Smartypants Romance online:
Website: www.smartypantsromance.com
Facebook: www.facebook.com/smartypantsromance/
Goodreads: www.goodreads.com/smartypantsromance
Twitter: @smartypantsrom
Instagram: @smartypantsromance

Want more from Nora Everly? Check out her self-published Sweetbriar Hearts series starting with *In My Heart*, available now!

Growing up, Luke and Lily were everything to each other.
He was her rock. She was his reason to live.
Ending up together was inevitable—until it wasn't.

Years later, Lily wants one thing. To spend a quiet summer with her kids settling into their new life in her old hometown.
But her long lost first love, nosy family, and an inept, yet scary stalker won't leave her in peace.

Luke also wants one thing. He wants Lily back.
He's out of the army, recovered from his injuries and wants to reclaim his life.

But Lily isn't ready to trust and Luke won't open up.
Will their second chance at first love be over before it begins?

ALSO BY NORA EVERLY

Sweetbriar Hearts Series:

In My Heart

Heart Words

Holiday Hearts (short story)

From the Heart

Heart to Heart (coming soon!)

Smartypants Romance:

Crime and Periodicals

Carpentry and Cocktails

Hotshot and Hospitality

Star Crossed Lovers (with Piper Sheldon):

Midnight Clear

If the Fates Allow (December 16, 2021 Preorder available!)

ALSO BY SMARTYPANTS ROMANCE

Green Valley Chronicles

The Love at First Sight Series

Baking Me Crazy by Karla Sorensen (#1)

Batter of Wits by Karla Sorensen (#2)

Steal My Magnolia by Karla Sorensen(#3)

Fighting For Love Series

Stud Muffin by Jiffy Kate (#1)

Beef Cake by Jiffy Kate (#2)

Eye Candy by Jiffy Kate (#3)

The Donner Bakery Series

No Whisk, No Reward by Ellie Kay (#1)

The Green Valley Library Series

Love in Due Time by L.B. Dunbar (#1)

Crime and Periodicals by Nora Everly (#2)

Prose Before Bros by Cathy Yardley (#3)

Shelf Awareness by Katie Ashley (#4)

Carpentry and Cocktails by Nora Everly (#5)

Love in Deed by L.B. Dunbar (#6)

Dewey Belong Together by Ann Whynot (#7)

Hotshot and Hospitality by Nora Everly (#8)

Love in a Pickle by L.B. Dunbar (#9)

Scorned Women's Society Series

My Bare Lady by Piper Sheldon (#1)

The Treble with Men by Piper Sheldon (#2)

The One That I Want by Piper Sheldon (#3)

Hopelessly Devoted to You by Piper Sheldon (#3.5)

Park Ranger Series

Happy Trail by Daisy Prescott (#1)

Stranger Ranger by Daisy Prescott (#2)

The Leffersbee Series

Been There Done That by Hope Ellis (#1)

Before and After You by Hope Ellis (#2)

The Higher Learning Series

Upsy Daisy by Chelsie Edwards (#1)

Green Valley Heroes Series

Forrest for the Trees by Kilby Blades

Seduction in the City

Cipher Security Series

Code of Conduct by April White (#1)

Code of Honor by April White (#2)

Code of Ethics by April White (#3)

Cipher Office Series

Weight Expectations by M.E. Carter (#1)

CPSIA information can be obtained
at www.ICGtesting.com
Printed in the USA
BVHW071409210921
617189BV00004B/157